Noah's Raven

Noah's Raven

A CHILCOTIN SAGA

BRUCE FRASER

THREE OCEAN PRESS

Library and Archives Canada Cataloguing in Publication

Fraser, Bruce, 1937-, author
    Noah's raven / Bruce Fraser.
Sequel to: The jade frog.

ISBN 978-1-988915-02-9 (softcover)
ISBN 978-1-988915-01-2 (e-book)

    I. Title.
PS8611.R366N63 2017   C813'.6   C2017-905861-4

Editor: Kyle Hawke
Copy Editors: Kyle Hawke and Sherry McGarvie
Additional edits: Sho Wiley
Proofreader: Carol Hamshaw
Cover and Book Designer: Iryna Spica / SpicaBookDesign
Cover Image: *Raven Looking Down Smoke Hole* © 2017 Glen Rabena
Author photo: David Hay

Map originally appeared in *Chiwid* by Sage Birchwater, published by New Star Books. Used by permission.

Three Ocean Press
8168 Riel Place
Vancouver, BC, V5S 4B3
778.321.0636
info@threeoceanpress.com
www.threeoceanpress.com

First publication, September 2017

For my children,
James, Lauchlan and Rebecca

Acknowledgements

Many people made this novel possible, some of whom have no idea that they had inspired me. They just lived their noble lives and a bit of them found their way into the pages of my story. I've lived in the Cariboo Chilcotin for over sixty years — ranching it, surveying it and practicing law there — and the greatest gift I've received is the embrace of the land and its people. This saga is my way of honouring them.

Then, there are those who should know their impact on these pages. My brother David was a fount of enthusiasm and a sounding board. My editor, Kyle Hawke, was tireless and patient. Copyeditor Sherry McGarvie offered welcome advice and ironic asides. All the others who are too many to list here know their efforts were valued.

A novelist is not complete without an audience and this book is my attempt to let my constant readers know that I value their time and support.

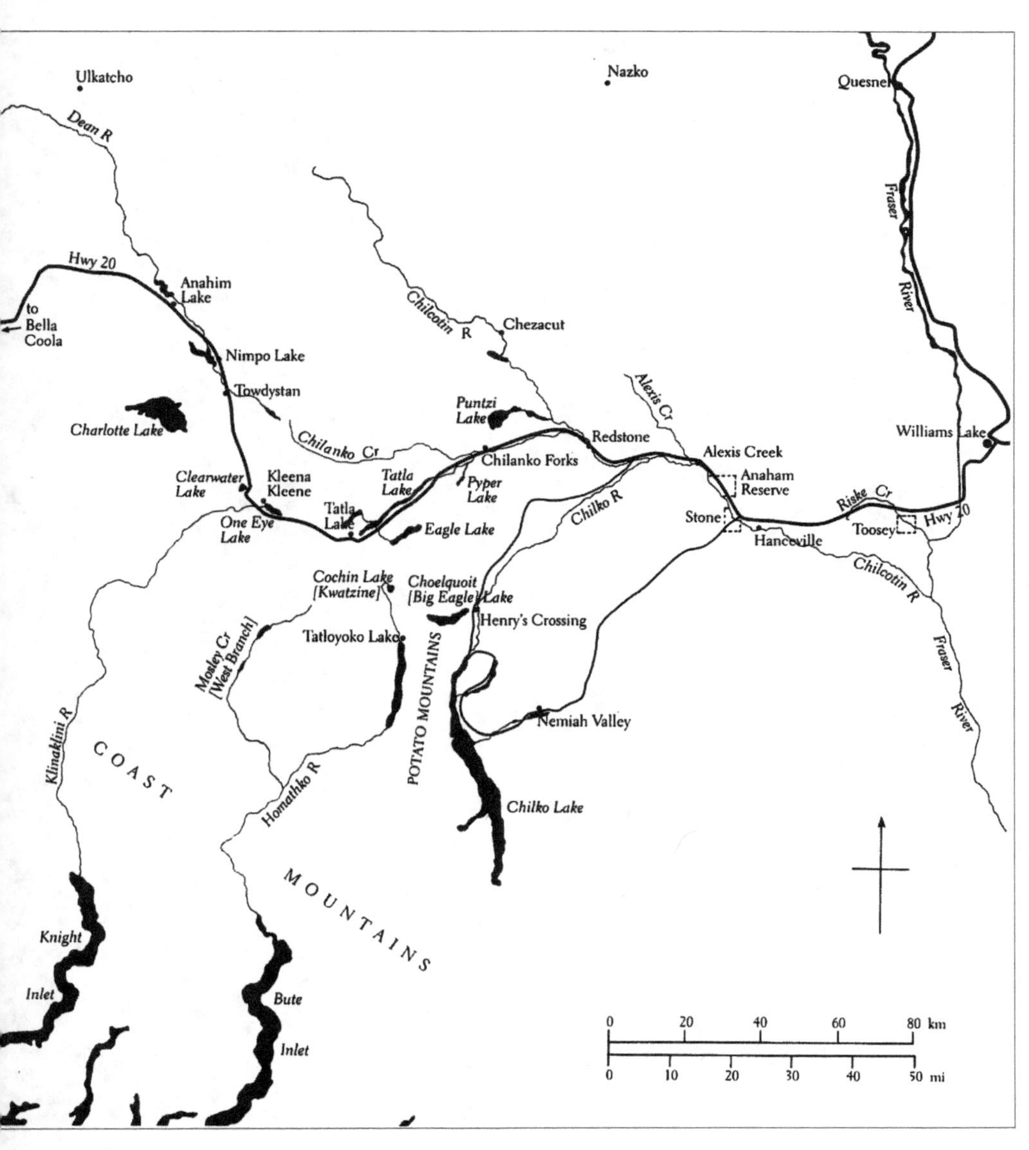

Ulkatcho
Nazko
Quesnel
Dean R
Fraser River
Hwy 20
Anahim Lake
Chilcotin R
Chezacut
to Bella Coola
Nimpo Lake
Towdystan
Alexis Cr
Charlotte Lake
Puntzi Lake
Chilanko Cr
Redstone
Alexis Creek
Williams Lake
Chilanko Forks
Clearwater Lake
Kleena Kleene
Tatla Lake
Pyper Lake
Anaham Reserve
One Eye Lake
Tatla Lake
Eagle Lake
Chilko R
Riske Cr
Hwy 20
Stone
Toosey
Hanceville
Cochin Lake [Kwatzine]
Choelquoit [Big Eagle] Lake
Chilcotin R
Henry's Crossing
Mosley Cr [West Branch]
Tatloyoko Lake
POTATO MOUNTAINS
Klinaklini R
Homathko R
Nemiah Valley
COAST
Fraser River
Chilko Lake
MOUNTAINS
Knight
Inlet
Bute
Inlet
0   20   40   60   80 km
0   10   20   30   40   50 mi

My paintings are but an attempt to portray the Chilcotin in all its splendour as seen and felt through the senses of a Tŝilhqot'in artist. My art is an expression of the values of my people who, since the coming of the white men, have not experienced freedom.

One of the hardest truths of human existence is that freedom doesn't come cheap. It's the most expensive commodity ever. The blacks in America and South Africa know that. The Tŝilhqot'in know it too.

It took one hundred and fifty years of resistance and the strength of our ancestors and elders before the Supreme Court of Canada finally recognized that we have, and always have had, what the lawyers call 'Aboriginal title'. Now, if there is a proposal for the development on our lands, we have a say and we get a benefit. With that judgment, we also won our freedom, our dignity and respect. All of that is reflected in the land — 1,900 square kilometres in the heart of our territory including Potato Mountain and the Brittany Triangle.

The question is: now that we Tŝilhqot'in have some freedom, what are we going to do with it?

— excerpt from a speech given by Noah Hanlon on receiving the Order of BC for his art, as recorded in the Williams Lake Tribune, *July 20th, 2014*

Potato Mountain

Noah rose before the sun, trying not to disturb Justine. She heard him go, but said nothing. It was something he had to do for her and she was grateful. He saddled up Rocinante in a temper, ready to challenge the fates that were threatening his wife. It felt right to take the quiet old grey mare which Justine had named and raised. He rode out of the Bar 5 Ranch, his twelve-year-old border collie Angus keeping pace alongside. The dog lagged behind as Noah, lost in his thoughts about Justine, urged the horse into a canter.

Non-indigenous people call Justine and me old-timers. First Nation people call us elders. I prefer the latter — it seems more respectful.

Elders have a long time to think about life and death and what lies inbetween.

He realized he'd forgotten both his surroundings and Angus, so he slowed. There were hours yet to go and he would need to pace himself, not just for the dog's sake. Knowing the land as well as he knew himself, it was easy to fall into the lines of it, to forget about his journey. Looking around and realizing where he was, he reined in Rocinante and waited for Angus to catch up.

I was brought up out here on the shores of Tatlayoko Lake. I could simply travel down that path...

But he knew he couldn't. Not today. Not even if there was time for the brief detour to the meadow where, in the beginning, he had watched Justine ride by without being able to reach out to touch her or speak her name. His confrontation with Bordy over Justine that night long ago had ended with the report of a rifle rising above their shouts, with Bordy lying dead, killed by the spirit of the Chilcotin. The circle of elders on Potato Mountain had understood that. His love for Belle, his adoptive mother, called him to revisit that old life in his thoughts, to pay his respects, but that was a separate journey for another day.

Today, he had an urgent mission. He was travelling now as *deyen*, if also as Justine's husband. He may have thought of himself as white back then, but he knows who he always has been. He was and is Wawant'x, even if he still carried the name the priest had given him.

Angus caught up with him, panting.

"Sorry, boy," Noah smiled. "We'll take it easy from here on out."

He rode on slowly, old Angus taking his time following, as if to hold him to his word.

I'm going on eighty years old, born before World War II. Then, all Canadians poured all their energy into fighting for liberty and freedom. All Canadians sacrificed for the greater good. There were the dead and wounded in the armed forces overseas, there was the rationing and the hardship at home. After the war came the glorious flourishing of wealth for many and the wonders of innovation in social structures and infrastructures for most, which brought us leisure and a new social order.

The irony was that while Canadians were fighting for freedom in Europe, their government continued taking freedom away from

2

the First Nations. Our children were taken away and put in residential schools. Yes, Canada also interned the Japanese-Canadians during the war, but didn't take their children away from them.

He started the steep climb up the mountain. In some ways, he was lucky to have grown up as white. In so many others, he was saved by finding his Indigenous heritage.

For Natives, there was no money for education, for job creation, for training, for infrastructure. The government wanted them off the land and shoved them onto postage-stamp-sized reserves. If it hadn't been for young — now old — lawyers like Tom Berger arguing for fifty years before the courts, we would probably still be limited to those reserves. Well, most of us still are.

He stopped again to give Rocinante a breather. Angus stopped as well, panting. Noah motioned the dog to a nearby stream.

"Water, Angus."

The dog trotted off to get a drink as Noah slowly scanned the landscape. The eastern sun was striking the mountains across the lake. It would be best to get some distance in before the midday heat.

"Angus!" Noah called. "Time to ride."

He rode on at a slower pace. However urgent the destination, the journey always matters.

This was the land where he'd been rescued and which had rescued him from a life as an outlaw. After he'd found his mother, she'd prepared him for a greater role among the Stoney, the people of the mountainous West Chilcotin. Ta Chi and Antoine, who had been *deyen* before him, over fifty years ago, had named him Wawant'x.

He was appointed *deyen* of clan Raven by Antoine.

He fell in love with Justine Paul.

I found my Aboriginal heritage when I met my birth mother. And again when I married Justine.

Justine had brought colour to his life, colour that went into the paintings she inspired him to create. It was her insistence that he paint the transformation story of the Tŝilhqot'in people. All the acclaim that followed, all the praise, was nothing compared to the stories of his people making their way through the world.

His greatest creation, though, was shared with Justine. Their love reflected in each of the four children they had together, but he had only fully recognized its magnitude when he saw Justine embrace Mary as her own child. Mary, the daughter created the one night he had strayed. Mary, who soon after finding out Noah was her father, had to deal with the murder of her mother. Justine had held and comforted Mary while he was trapped in the complexity of the moment and his own shame.

Riding on, he thought of what life would be like without Justine. There would be no colour, no laughter, no sharing.

Overcome for a moment by his dark thoughts, he paused and remembered who he was, remembered where he was going and why. He was going to Potato Mountain to ask Ta Chi to intercede with the Creator, to save Justine's life.

Ta Chi, as she had borne me into this life, bore me into the Indigenous ways of survival on the Chilcotin plateau, saving me. I will invoke her spirit. I will implore her to save Justine.

Four hours later, after pushing Rocinante up the steep climb, he was at Ta Chi's gravesite on Potato Mountain. Angus whimpered and, after padding a circle in the grass, settled down to rest in the shade a short distance away. He knew this time, this place, was not for him.

Noah stood silent, letting the dust and the air and his mind settle. The ride was long and he felt it in his bones, but had to leave that behind him. Once he felt clear, he took a carved hardwood dowel and a mixture of tobacco, sage and cedar from a pouch on his belt. He closed his eyes and breathed deep, then knelt. Dowel turning on wood, the friction created heat that fired the mix. Smoke began to rise. He carefully pulled an eagle feather from the inside of his vest.

"My mother who gave me life, then saved my life, I honour you. I light this smudge and, with this feather, cleanse myself with the smoke."

He brushed the smoke towards himself. He let his focus shift to the land, to Ta Chi's spirit and to the woman he loved.

Mother, for Justine.

Last June, on returning to the ranch from a ride with their grandson, Justine had complained to Noah of a sore hip. He had treated her with a liniment recipe given to him by Ta Chi, which seemed to relieve her symptoms, though they returned by morning. Over the next few weeks, each night Noah applied the balm and each day the pain came back. Although Justine had told Noah, "I think Ta Chi's remedy is helping," there was the time he was returning to the house from his studio and saw her taking extra-strength Tylenol through the kitchen window. When he came into the kitchen, she'd quickly hidden the bottle.

Help her, Mother.

He had sat down at the table afraid of the conversation he knew had to come next. As a nurse, Justine had often reminded him that those in the medical profession make the worst patients, that they were often the last to seek care. But, as always, she had been waiting for him.

"It's time I saw someone about my hip," she'd said in her professional voice. "I'll make an appointment with Dr. James."

He'd realized then that she'd been holding back, wanting to let him as *deyen* cure her, her faith in him ever stronger than his own. He'd taken off his battered hat, the one he wore when painting, and ran his fingers through his thinning hair, smiling at her wisdom and her concern for him, even through her own pain.

Help her, Mother.

Dr. James had been kind and efficient, but could only prescribe pain relief and refer Justine to a physiotherapist. After two treatments, the therapist had sent her back to Dr. James. He'd taken X-rays, probed her hip joint and scheduled her for a hip replacement. The earliest available date for surgery was a year away and, in the meantime, he'd given her a stronger prescription.

Some days were better than others. She had always taken an interest in the ranch and there hadn't been a day gone by she didn't ride her horse, but now the pain mostly confined her to the house. She'd done a bit of cooking and sewing and some reading. They'd played cribbage and she was still quite competitive.

Noah had worried, but without showing it. She had waited for treatment to be strong for him and the least he could do was return the favour. He'd encouraged her by telling her that all this would be behind her after the operation.

By late August, the pain was getting worse. They'd returned to the doctor and seen his locum, a woman a year out of medical school. She'd looked at the X-rays and arranged for Justine to take a CT scan on an expedited basis, then return in a week's time. They'd flown to Vancouver for the scan. A few days later, the locum had called and told Justine that she'd made an appointment for her with Dr. Jill Heather, an oncologist in Kamloops, to review the results of the scan.

Help her, Mother. Help her.

Elizabeth, their daughter, had gone with them to Kamloops. That was when Dr. Heather had told them that Justine had cancer. The oncologist had been tight-lipped about the prognosis until Justine pressed her, reminding her that she was a nurse.

"I think you should take chemotherapy for the next three months on a weekly basis," the oncologist had said matter-of-factly. "This may check the advance of the cancer and give you a few more years."

They'd all fallen silent at that, until Elizabeth spoke up.

"And it may not?"

"There's the possibility that if it doesn't," the oncologist had breathed in deeply, "then it could be a few months."

Help her, Mother. Help her.

They'd returned to the ranch the next day. That night, Noah, visibly upset about Justine's diagnosis, had spoken to her in bed.

"Dear," he'd said haltingly, "I am going to Potato Mountain tomorrow morning. To Ta Chi's gravesite. To speak to her and to the Creator for your recovery. Modern medicine is fine, but you mean too much to me to place all our faith in it alone."

Justine had smiled in the dark at her husband. She knew her only chance to be by his side, to watch their grandchildren grow for even a few years more, was to allow her doctor to confront her cancer and perhaps to control it. As Tŝilhqot'in, she also knew otherwise.

"Thank you, Noah," she smiled warmly. "Say hello to Ta Chi for me."

Hear me, Mother, and think of Justine, my wife.

Noah continued the smudge ceremony while he spoke and, after he cleansed himself, wafted the smoke over Ta Chi's grave.

Grant her a few more years with me free of pain. For I love her and need her by my side.

He waited for some answer while thinking of the times that he and Justine had visited this sacred place. The sparrows had always been Ta Chi's answer. Sure enough, they chirped in the bush nearby and Noah was comforted. His anger subsided.

He stood and bowed his head. Having done all he could do for Justine, he mounted Rocinante and turned toward home. Angus rose from his circle of grass and heeled. It was then that he saw Big Momma moving towards the twin lakes. He reined in Rocinante and watched her at a distance foraging for berries. She caught his scent and raised up on her hind legs looking in his direction. He marvelled at the magnificent grizzly. Big Momma was a legend amongst the Tŝilhqot'in and a talisman to Justine. She would be pleased he had made a sighting.

Before he could descend the mountain, Noah heard — then saw — a helicopter in the sky. Angus barked once before taking a cue from his master and falling silent. He looked back and saw Big Momma running from the threat towards the shelter of the trees.

The helicopter flew directly over Ta Chi's grave, its shadow passing over him. Noah and Angus watched its path until it settled about a mile away, near Echo Lake. Noah felt the rising wind and saw a storm gathering in the east.

Gathering in the East

Nothing was better than a harvest moon in Atlanta, Fred thought. And the one this Labor Day weekend was special. The graduation ceremony at Georgia State hadn't gone on too long. Some blogger named Procter was the guest speaker and her only message was that it was up to each graduate to find their own way in the changing landscape of journalism. Even the dean was succinct in his remarks, likely knowing that the new crop of journalists in the crowd would hold him accountable for every unnecessary word. There had certainly been a flurry of press about the strike which had delayed the ceremony, enough that the school and the union settled things just before the new term.

The dance, however, was a circus. Harriet finally let loose, going from studious and serious to wild woman seemingly overnight — dancing with abandon and making out with Fred every time they chanced across an alcove. Since Fred was driving, he wasn't drinking but even so, he couldn't keep track of her. Still, losing sight of her at times gave him the chance to say a farewell here and there.

He was talking to Dirk Campbell, the class valedictorian, when out of the corner of his eye, he saw her bee-lining towards him across the dance floor. She reached around Dirk, kissing Fred over his shoulder.

"Whoa!" laughed Dirk.

"I need this man to take me home right now," Harriet offered, her upper New York accent softened by a Southern drawl.

"You two go! Have fun," Dirk grinned. "Hey, Fred, you come see me in Wyoming when I get back from assignment."

Dirk handed him a business card for the Campbell Guest Ranch. Dirk had been his roommate in first year and had extended an open invitation to his family's ranch, but there had never been time. Since then, Fred had gotten a few freelance pieces published in the *Herald*, with a good prospect of a job offer. Dirk, go-getter that he is, was already signed up as a stringer for Reuters and had a posting in Greece. Fred would miss his confidant and sounding board.

"I'll see you in Greece," Fred called back, but Harriet was already leading him out of the hall before he could finish the sentence.

In the parking lot, Harriet danced around as Fred fumbled with the keys to his beat-up old Subaru Forester, wondering exactly how drunk she was.

"You know what 'take me home' could mean, right?" he asked.

Harriet suddenly stopped, touched her nose and stood on one leg.

"I'm not drunk," she smiled.

"What? But..." Fred was at a loss.

"It's all about appearances, my dear," she enunciated in a faux-British accent. "I knew exactly what I was making everyone think. Including you."

He thought back to his fourth-year Political Science seminar. It wasn't Fred's favourite subject, but was a necessity for a journalist. Harriet had been citing Machiavelli's *Prince* and

10

discussing the nature of absolute power when he'd first noticed her. Quiet in an intense way most of the time, she'd sat at the front of the class and her questions had always seemed to overwhelm the professor. Whenever called upon, she always had a sharp response, quoting everything from rabbinical rulings on murder to Gore Vidal speaking on the decline of the American Empire. Unusually, the prof would rarely ask her any follow-up questions.

In contrast, Fred couldn't understand how a constitution of checks and balances could possibly work where the two choices, Democrats and Republicans, *Tweedledee* and *Tweedledum*, as he liked to call them, could deadlock.

Harriet, however, knew. Fred found himself admiring her mind and, quite soon, her body as well. She wasn't the archetypal Southern belle, with her eastern Mediterranean olive complexion and a stylish bob.

She'd disappear after class and he'd never see her at any student functions.

He'd cornered her by the door one day.

"Hi, Harriet. I'm Fred Scully. I liked what you said on Adam Smith. His scepticism about unregulated business. If you've got some time later on today, I'd like to talk about it some more."

It was lame for a pick-up line, if said with some sincerity.

"My dad calls me 'Happy'," she'd laughed, her tone entirely different than when she spoke to the professor. "My mom's back from London tonight, so no. But we could study together next week."

She'd touched his arm, flared her eyes enigmatically and left.

She had the same look now, as she tousled his neatly-trimmed light brown hair and stared into his inquisitive blue eyes.

"You know, Happy," he grinned, "if you didn't want me to feel like I was the only one not drinking, you could have told me you weren't."

"Oh, please," she quipped. "You're like a St. Bernard. You loved having the drunk date bouncing around the ballroom. And now you love the idea of a sober companion for the drive and everything else before we leave for Dad's. Now get my door, driver."

Her dad seemed like some kind of ne'er-do-well, if a fun one, from what little she'd said of him. She spent her weekends with him and this time, if a day later than usual, Fred would be joining her. Fred wasn't really sure he was ready for the meet-the-parent stage, as their relationship so far had been mostly Thursday evening study sessions after PoliSci, with a bit of fumbling around here and there before she refocused their attention on their books and the next day's class. She spent weekdays at her mother's place in Atlanta, though her mother always seemed to be off somewhere else. She'd then disappeared for the summer, explaining only that she would be helping her dad. Seeing her again, he'd hopefully asked her away to the beach for the post-graduation weekend and she'd countered with a long weekend at her father's house somewhere in the country. Only after he'd accepted, after they'd gotten to the dance, did she throw in a night at her mother's beforehand.

Fred opened the passenger door for Harriet. She threw herself onto the seat and pulled off her spiked heels, tossing them into the back seat.

"Hey, the floor's dirty," Fred warned.

"Ugh," she spat. "I was born barefoot. Plus, Mom's house isn't that far."

Fred climbed in the driver's side.

"But Mom is," she grinned.

"Right. New York," Fred laughed. "You had me fooled tonight. You really didn't drink?"

"Well, I had one or two, but I wanted to wait for you so we could open a bottle at Mom's."

"You are *sweet*, Harriet Applebaum."

"Don't you tell a soul, Frederick Scully! Now, Frederica, go!"

He started the car and headed out of the lot. He kind of regretted showing her the articles he'd had published in the *Atlanta Herald*. Small-time stuff, but at least it was actually news, not a profile of some feisty shop owner. His byline had been 'Frederick Scully', which he thought made him sound more like a serious journalist than someone the bar staff knew by name. From then on, he was 'Frederick' whenever Harriet wanted to dress him down. His car consequently became 'Frederick's car', then simply 'Frederica'.

His anticipation made the road go by like another Political Science class, except this time it wasn't a study session waiting at the end.

Fred didn't have time to admire the tastefully decorated townhouse before Harriet poured him a tequila shot. Wine and beer were also on offer and he did his utmost to keep up with her.

She put music on and moved the coffee table so they could dance. Her tastes were traditional, it seemed. She told him she was going to start with Lady Gaga, but it was a duet with Tony Bennett, one where Gaga only spoke here and there.

> *You met someone and now you know how it feels*
> *Goody goody!*

Laughing, they were soon jiving around the living room in stocking feet.

By the end of the night, bottles lined the coffee table and they were dancing slow to Michael Bublé.

> *I'll be seeing you*
> *In all the old familiar places*

Dancing led to cuddling and kissing on the couch, until finally he suggested it was late and maybe he should tuck her into bed.

"I love you, Freddy," she whispered. "You make me laugh."

She'd never called him 'Freddy' before. Or the other thing.

Copper Beech

On Saturday of the Labor Day weekend, Fred woke early.
He was wide awake. He should have been horribly hung over, but wasn't. Maybe he was still drunk. He didn't care.

He lay in bed, watching Harriet stretched out on her side, facing the far window. He didn't want to move in case he woke her, so just lay back and listened to her breathing mingle with the ticking of the clock. *Ticking?* he thought. *She* is *an old-fashioned girl.* Eventually, he started scanning the room. Notes were pinned all over the walls and lying on every flat surface — compulsive lists by the looks of them, though most were too far away to read. He looked to his side and, sure enough, there was a pen and notepad on the nightstand. He picked them up and began to doodle. He realized he'd written "Harriet Scully" in the middle of a pattern of webs and spirals.

"That's rather old-fashioned, too," he thought aloud.

"What is?"

He dove for cover.

"You're awake!"

"I like lying in the morning light. And listening to you trying not to wake me," she muttered without moving. "What're you doing?"

He crumpled the page, tossing it down beside the bed. "Nothing."

He could hear her laughing, muffled as it was.

"Kiss me and go take a shower," she teased. "I might join you. Or I might just lie here some more."

He kissed her and got up to go to the bathroom.

"Love you," she said dreamily.

"Love you too," he replied, reflexively.

It felt right, he thought.

"If I'm not up when you're done," she called out, "you can make me breakfast."

At ten, their bags were packed into her mother's Cadillac convertible and so were they. Acting as the GPS navigator, Harriet barked commands to turn with little notice, just to keep him on his toes.

She had never said much about her father. Fred thought she was somehow ashamed. He had imagined her father's place was some kind of shack somewhere in the country and that her dad was probably an alcoholic. As the turn-offs got more remote and the signs of civilization further away, he found himself thinking it might not be bad, living low-key for a while and breathing fresh air for a change.

After he announced they were running low on gas, Harriet's directions became a maze of turns which, sure enough, led them to a rural gas station.

"You'd better have good directions when we get back on the road because I'm utterly lost now," Fred joked.

"Don't worry about it," she assured him. "I'll drive from here on."

She was a take-charge woman and Fred loved her for that, among other things.

The station was full-serve and an attendant came out. Now he *knew* he was in the country.

"Fill 'er up!" Harriet shouted to the young man. Then, to Fred, "Let's hit the store."

"Yes, Miss N," said the attendant, as he set to filling her tank.

Fred followed Harriet. He didn't ask about the 'Miss N' but noticed Harriet hadn't corrected the attendant.

While Harriet used the washroom, he picked up some chips — he had no idea how much of a drive there was left, but they could always use them on the ride home. Seeing the *Atlanta Herald* on a newsstand, he tossed a copy on the counter with the snacks. The last thing he needed was to see that some keener from his class already had a major story published, but he'd been reading the morning paper for four years now and needed his weekend fix. Whatever that blogger woman thought, Fred still found value in holding the paper in his hands — maybe he was somewhat traditional too. He paid for the gas as well and headed back to the car.

When Harriet came out, she was sporting a new pair of sunglasses.

"For driving," she explained.

As she drove, he pulled out the paper.

"Where'd you get that?" she asked.

"At the gas station," he replied. "Check this out. Big-type headline today."

He fluffed out the paper in front of him and began to read.

"*Northrop to Declare Candidacy on Monday*," he announced.

"Imagine that," Harriet replied, keeping her eyes on the road.

"'Sources,'" he read on, "'close to Billy Joe Northrop III speculate that the billionaire is planning to declare his candidacy for the Republican presidential nomination at a press conference this Monday.'"

"Well, if the papers say it, it has to be true, right?"

There was a mocking tone in Harriet's voice and Fred couldn't quite place the reason for it, so he skipped ahead.

"'His grandfather was the founder of Northrop Oil. The younger Northrop increased the family fortune through astute takeovers and buyouts.'"

"Mm-hm," Harriet murmured.

Fred took that as a cue to stop reading.

"They've got a chart with his holdings. Hey, apparently he runs something called the Northrop Green Trust."

"You didn't know that?"

"Whoa. It runs a sanctuary for migratory birds at Lonesome Lake. That's in the Chilcotin. I've never seen a reference to the Chilcotin in the *Herald* before. My dad grew up there. He and Grampa talk about it a lot. Seems like it was a good place to be a kid."

"Canada," she paused to laugh, "is a great incubator for migrating birds, snowbirds and comedians. We love 'em coming down, so long as they leave their socialist ideas behind."

Harriet wasn't joking. That was the voice that she used to shut the professor down back in PoliSci. Suddenly, Fred understood why the prof never asked her follow-up questions.

"You ever been to Canada?" he ventured.

"Yeah."

She kept her eyes on the road.

Fred took the hint and fell quiet, leafing randomly through the newspaper, hoping something else would grab his attention. Nothing did. Finally, he pulled out his phone and Googled the Northrop Green Trust.

When Harriet next glanced over, he was staring at her, his jaw slightly open.

"So now you know who I am," she said, turning her attention back to the road.

"So your dad's going to run for president?"

"The idea was that you were going to find everything out once we were at Dad's. Since you're a reporter…"

"I've only ever covered petty crime stuff."

"Even so," she continued, "you're a reporter. Dad made me promise I wouldn't tell you anything until he met you."

"Not even that you're on the board of a multi-million-dollar trust?"

"Well, I'm on a sabbatical to finish school," she sniffed. "Never get their facts right."

It wasn't a shack.

Billy Joe's house was a mansion. It had many rooms and, if the start of his day with Harriet's revelation about her father was any measure, just as many secrets. Fred and Harriet were given separate rooms, of course.

Copper Beech was named after the two-century-old copper beech trees lining the drive. It was a Southern estate on the scale of Tara from *Gone with the Wind*. Billy Joe's wealth wasn't just bluster and marketing, it echoed in every ornate detail in each huge high-ceilinged room.

Fred was sheepish and clearly out of his element through lunch on the terrace, even though Billy Joe hadn't arrived yet and it was just him and Harriet — if you didn't count the serving staff. Harriet seemed content to let him stew and didn't offer anything in the way of explanation. Instead, lunch was eaten in silence, looking out at the vast grounds.

"We could go for a swim after," Harriet finally suggested.

"Shouldn't we wait an hour?" Fred countered, no other excuses coming to mind.

"In an hour then," Harriet sighed.

They finished lunch in silence.

After lunch, Fred asked if he could explore the house on his own before they went swimming.

"Fine," Harriet said. "But don't rearrange anything."

He raised his eyebrows.

"Dad's very particular." she explained with a grin.

He left, holding in a scream, feeling like a pet being given a quick romp before being put back in the cage. It wasn't long, though, before he got lost in fascination. He wondered which was actually the living room, deciding the others must be a drawing room, a sitting room, a parlour and the like. Beneath the expansive staircase, he found the washrooms, clearly a later addition meant for large gatherings — the men's room had urinals and paper towel dispensers, not the stuff of homes. On one side of the staircase, a doorway opened on a lavish ballroom. On the other, he found a well-stocked library. He spent a little time there and noticed a set of the complete works of his favourite author, Joseph Conrad. He found himself taking mental notes.

It was the tradition, like Jack Burden in *All the King's Men* — young men who made themselves at home in the halls of power and brought down presidents and kings. He questioned a couple of the staff, trying not to seem like he was prying, and found himself feeling his role. Of course, he wasn't after a story here, he was a guest, but that was no reason to forget he was a journalist.

He was smiling by the time he met Harriet. She was already in the pool, lounging on a huge inflatable swan.

"I'm sorry," he apologized. "I needed some time."

"Well, I figured," Harriet smiled, glad he'd come around.

"You'll laugh."

"What?"

"I thought that… well, you'd said he lived in the sticks…" He hemmed and hawed a bit. "You never talked about your dad and I figured he was probably a down-and-out alcoholic."

"What?!?" she laughed.

"I was all set to live rough for a weekend and tough it out. All this," Fred raised his arms in an expansive gesture, "just threw me."

She splashed him with her hand.

"Get in the pool, you idiot," she laughed, "There's a spare swimsuit in the changing room."

He returned in a pair of trunks and dove in, as close to her as possible, tipping her inflatable.

"You barbarian!" she yelled as his head emerged from the water.

"It's a pool, woman," he laughed. "People get wet."

A Sense of Anticipation

G one was Fred's idea of furthering his relationship with Harriet on the long weekend.

He was to spend Sunday in the house of many rooms at a seminar in real politics which mocked his four years of Journalism and Political Science at Georgia State. It was in one of those rooms that Fred would learn a secret that would change his and Harriet's life.

Breakfast was served by a butler.

"This afternoon," Harriet announced, "we're having a rally for our campaign chairmen from each state in preparation for Dad's announcement." She squeezed his hand as if she was giving him a special treat. "I'll introduce you to him at dinner tonight."

Fred attended the afternoon rally on the lawn in front of the mansion. There must have been a hundred people there, a real cross-section of America, yet despite their sexual, racial and even cultural diversity, they all looked the same. Dressed in jackets, open-necked shirts and slacks, the men with their hair cropped close and the women meticulously groomed, they had a sort of forced good nature and smile. Fred took a seat at the back of the crowd where he could observe the proceedings. He was taking a reporter's point of view, being a guest rather than a participant.

Harriet acted as hostess. She knew all the participants, called them by their first names and got them seated in a semicircle of comfortable lawnchairs facing the mansion. Fred realized that her university friends had never seen Harriet in this setting.

Once quieted, there was a sense of anticipation in the crowd. Finally, Billy Joe opened the front door and walked slowly towards them. He was dressed in a white linen suit with a sky blue shirt and a red tie. His mane of white hair glistened in the sun. He reminded Fred of Colonel Sanders without the beard. Billy Joe stopped twenty feet in front of his audience and paused just long enough to draw attention to himself and allow the crowd to settle. It was clear to a reporter's eye that this was all choreographed. Speaking in a low voice, making his disciples strain to catch his words, he opened his arms and offered a winning smile.

"Welcome, you all, to Copper Beach. This is a historic moment in our nation's history."

His voice, like Harriet's, had that undertone of Southern drawl combined with a Yankee twang which offended no one ever since the senior Bush had perfected it.

"You folks in the forefront of the Northrop team are the first to know," he ratcheted up his voice, "that on Monday, I will be announcing to the people of this great nation of ours that I am officially placing my name on the ballot to be the Republican nominee."

The cheering rose with each word and his voice got stronger.

"For the leader of the free world, for the head of state of the greatest country the world has ever known. For," he shouted, "*the Presidency of the United States of America!*"

There was a roar of acceptance as the crowd rose to their feet. Even Fred was caught up in the moment, rising with them.

It was during the shouting and applause that Fred saw a man approach from the riverside, a man who in size and stature resembled Hulk Hogan. Dressed in a tailored grey suit and white shirt, he was bald and had no discernible neck, so his head and torso moved as one. Despite his enormous hands, he had small feet and a nimble, almost mincing gait. With all eyes glued on Billy Joe, Fred was the only one who noticed this man take a carefully-positioned chair on the side, in line with the front seats. As he sat, the man sensed Fred's gaze and locked his ice-cold grey eyes on him. Fred felt as if Lucifer himself had him in his sights.

The spell was broken when Northrop raised his hands to stop the applause. He pointed to this presence. When the spotlight focused on the grey man, he stood, a smile creasing his face, which in an instant turned him from Lucifer to Gabriel.

"For those who haven't met the best political strategist in the world," Billy Joe grinned, "let me introduce Bullivant Sullivan O'Connor. Bull's taking a leave of absence from his business to give his full attention to our campaign. Many heads of state in the English-speaking world owe their election to his genius. He'll turn our vision of the White House into a reality."

Again the crowd rose, shouting its welcome for this Houdini who Fred sardonically realized had written his own introduction.

Bull didn't presume to intrude on Northrop's space. He stood hesitantly, almost reluctantly. He spoke from where he stood. The eager audience were anxious to listen, ready to be mesmerized by the words of a political magician.

Bull's reputation as a political strategist was well-established. Books had been written about his accomplishments. One of Fred's classmates had given a presentation about the man. Fred was looking forward to seeing him in action even though his first impression was negative, formed from an innate aversion to pomposity.

"Looking about me today," Bull spoke in humble tones, as incongruous as that was, considering the bulk and menace of the man, "seeing all you bright people from every state in the union, prepared to change the history of our great republic, I'm reminded of what the first true Republican said at Gettysburg: 'Government is for the people, of the people, by the people.' You need no reminding that today our government is *not* for the people, it is for the rich. We are going to change all that when we announce tomorrow on Labor Day."

The audience rose as one, cheering. The irony of this audience thinking they weren't the rich wasn't lost on Fred. Bull nodded his head with a smile and they settled again.

"We have assembled here," Bull continued, "an outstanding core group of campaign chairmen, and women, ready to help us sweep the preliminaries and caucuses, get the nomination and rally the people behind Billy Joe Northrop III as he marches to the White House. We have in Billy Joe a candidate with the highest achievements, brand recognition and qualifications: an oilman and a philanthropist with green credentials."

There was little applause for Bull's mention of green.

"I know," he nodded, "you all think that the tree-huggers are a nuisance and that they're blocking our nation's wealth and industrial might, but they're also voters. We must throw a few concessions their way to get the presidency."

They applauded while Fred gagged at Bull's cynicism-soaked pandering.

"One of our campaign messages will be that Billy Joe is for love of country, love of capitalism and love of nature. Hell, that's what the Northrop brand is all about. The three Cs: Country, Capital, Cleanliness."

He made a sweeping motion with one arm, inviting his audience to look at nature. It wasn't lost on Fred, who grew up on an organic vegetable farm, that nature wasn't to be found in the manicured, toxically fertilized, weed-and-bug-proofed lawn. The crowd applauded anyway.

At this point, Northrop, thinking that Bull had finished, stood and addressed them.

"Thank you, Bull. I appreciate all that you've done and what you're going to do on the road to the White House and the presidency." Then, squinting into the hot sun, he called out to his daughter. "Happy, honey, would you mind getting these folks some lemonade? They look awfully thirsty."

Harriet leapt into action, as if she'd been waiting for the cue. Of course, that action consisted of a few simple hand gestures to the domestic staff, which responded with frantic movement. Bull was caught off-guard by the interruption and Fred noticed a scowl creep over his face. It was apparent to him that Billy Joe had gone off-script. Bull caught himself and the smile returned.

"I'll talk more this evening about how to package our message," he said.

The odd person out in this love-in, Fred had nothing in common with the political operatives billeted in the old slave quarters and Harriet was too preoccupied to pay attention to him.

That evening, Fred attended the reception in the ballroom where Bull was going to talk about how to package Billy Joe Northrop for the nation. Fred was conflicted. As a reporter, he was privy to the inside story on the build-up to Billy Joe's announcement. As Harriet's lover, he couldn't write it up or he'd be taking advantage of her hospitality.

He wandered into the book-lined quiet of the library. He took Joseph Conrad's *The Secret Agent* down from the shelves, intrigued by the word 'secret'. Perusing it, he noted it was the 1924 Doubleday, Page & Company edition and took extra care turning each page. He sat in a wingback chair facing the window and read. He was quietly engrossed in the novel when the door to the library opened and shut quickly. Two male voices began arguing loudly. They didn't notice Fred, hidden from view by the chair.

"What the hell is going on?" Billy Joe's voice took on a commanding tone. "All of a sudden you start acting annoyed in there."

"You're damn right I'm annoyed," Bull shot back, equally strong and authoritative.

"What's got into your craw?"

"Billy Joe, a year ago we made a bargain, you and I. You wanted to be president and you wanted me as your political strategist."

"And you said yes."

"With two conditions. One, my corporation and backers get a 50% stake in Northrop's gas play in the Chilcotin. Two, you give me full control of your campaign strategy. For that, I'd see that you would become the Republican nominee and arrange for a Super PAC to back your candidacy. That was the deal."

"I know. You don't have to tell me." Billy Joe sounded exasperated.

Lord, Fred thought, sinking deeper into the depths of the chair, *I shouldn't be listening to this*. His reporter's instincts kicked in. He slowly, almost unconsciously, removed the ballpoint pen he carried out of habit from his jacket pocket. Conrad's book was resting on his lap. *1924 edition*, he thought. He bit his lip, flipped back to the title page and started taking notes.

> *Chilcotin gas play, 50% interest. Political action committee. Tax dodge?*

"The first thing you gotta remember is to follow my directions and don't fuck me up. So when I'm trying to win over the attention of our core campaign staff, you gotta act presidential. Don't interrupt me by sending your daughter out for lemonade."

"Okay, Bull," Billy Joe grunted, "let's go back into that room. You fire up those people with your speech."

26

"Thank you kindly, Billy Joe." Bull's voice managed to convey sincerity and danger at the same time. "Just so's we understand each other. Now, before we go back in, there's a few things we gotta tidy up. You should know I paid a visit last week to that land that your Green Trust is thinking of funding."

"You went to the Chilcotin?"

"I'm not taking 'the richest natural gas finds in British Columbia' on faith."

"Harriet's not going to stand still while we drill parkland."

"I don't give a damn what your daughter thinks. It's good for Northrop Oil. And what's good for Northrop is good for America. Besides, the trust is only part of the cover. There are numbered subsidiaries buying the land."

"What about Canadian permits and the Indians?"

"I'm talking with the governments there. They're keen on natural gas development. As for the Indians, I bought me one. Some guy called Twoshoes."

"Okay. Let's just get our team ready for my announcement on Monday."

"Just so's you're clear, this is just between us now. I want to keep the deal under wraps."

"Why's that?"

"Northrop's publicly traded. We have to skirt federal law on campaign donations here. Don't you sweat about it. I have an in with a Super PAC and I may have to become aggressive with the Natives — you shouldn't have your name involved. Now, there's an agreement about the transfer of drilling rights to my corporations which you gotta sign."

There was some rustling of papers in the silence that followed. Fred hardly breathed as he pictured Billy Joe reading the papers thrust at him by Bull. He was hearing not only a betrayal of the system and a secret takeover of a gas-rich territory, but also a professional shakedown of Billy Joe by Bull.

"There, it's signed. Let's go."

The door opened and Fred could hear the noise of the crowd from the ballroom.

"Here he is," Bull shouted, "the next president of the United States of America."

Bull and Billy Joe left the library arm in arm, closing the door behind them.

Fred looked over what he'd written. He couldn't leave it there. He winced, looking away as he ripped out the title page. He folded the page and slipped it into his pocket, setting the book down on the chair. He opened the library door a crack to see the ballroom full of supporters. He listened to Bull's speech on selling Billy Joe to the Republicans and then, after the nomination was secured, to the American public.

Bull towered over his audience.

"Our candidate is a successful entrepreneur, not a politician. He has never run for office, yet he is a public figure who's gained the attention of the American people through his philanthropy and celebrity. Under the old order, he would be disqualified for his lack of political experience, but in the new order, where success in business and creating jobs is admired, Billy Joe is a welcome change. We will run on a platform of creating jobs."

There was a cheer from the crowd.

"Our slogan is 'America for Americans'."

There was another cheer.

"We will put up tariffs and bring American corporations back to America where they will pay their share of taxes."

This brought thunderous applause.

Fred realized this was the speech that Bull had intended to give on the lawn in the afternoon and he beamed with satisfaction. Bull went on for some time, applause punctuating his speech to the converted.

In the mêlée after the speech, Fred mixed with the crowd of

enthusiasts. He saw Harriet talking to Bull and waited till they separated. He caught her before she was whisked away in a swirl of well-wishers.

"Harriet, I heard something disturbing you should know."

Distracted, she didn't hear him.

"I want you to meet my dad."

She pulled him by the arm to where Billy Joe was encircled by a group of admirers.

"Dad, I'd like you to meet my friend, Fred."

Billy Joe turned to face them and Fred saw, up close for the first time in his life, a man who would do anything for power. He exuded an energy that Fred imagined Lorenzo de' Medici of Florence would have had in abundance. Thinking back to the newspaper article, Fred realized the seeds of Billy Joe's ambition had been sown by his grandfather, the founder of Northrop Oil. They were then fertilized by his father's riches and husbanded by private schools and privilege.

Fred was a nobody to Billy Joe, except as a friend of his daughter. Still, despite Billy Joe's fixation on being the most powerful man in the world, Fred saw from the deference he showed Harriet that he had within him a love for his daughter which betrayed a semblance of humanity. Bull would probably describe that as a weakness.

"Glad to meet you, sir," Fred mumbled.

Billy Joe grabbed Fred's hand in his and held it in a vice-like grip. He placed another hand on Fred's shoulder, leaving Fred no option but to look at the man directly.

"Fred," Billy Joe shouted over the din of voices in the room, "you're a lucky man to be a friend of Harriet's. You treat her well and we'll get along."

Fred was locked into this handshake, unsure if it was friendly or a threat. Harriet watched them both, expecting the men in her life to bond.

"Thank you, sir. I will," Fred nodded, wincing.

Only then did Billy Joe let go.

"Stay with us a bit so I can get to know you."

Fred looked blankly at Harriet.

"Dad," Harriet chided, "you know I invited Fred for a few days."

With a quick smile and nod, Billy Joe turned to greet another member of his team.

Harriet was pressed by others in the room before Fred could say a word. Many of these had become her friends over the summer when she had crisscrossed the country to help build the Billy Joe Northrop-for-President team. The Florida campaign chair was tugging on her arm, urging her to speak to him and a few others about the timing of her father's announcement.

"I'll talk to you later," she called back over her shoulder to Fred as she was led away.

Fred had intended to go to his room, but suddenly remembered he'd left *The Secret Agent* on the chair. He had to go back to the library and put it back in its place. When he approached the room, the door opened and Bull was standing there, blocking the entryway. He wasn't smiling anymore.

"Fred, is it?" he growled. "Would you step in here a moment? I have something to show you."

30

The Next Step

Fred's hands were shaking, his face ashen, as he re-packed his bag in the taxi. The cabbie assured him it would only be twenty minutes to the nearest bus station and he could still catch a midnight bus to Atlanta.

"You've got something on your jacket," the cabbie offered, looking into the rear-view.

Fred checked. He went silent for a moment.

"Nosebleed," he muttered.

He took his jacket off, emptied the pockets and folded it into his bag. He gave up on being neat and just crammed the things he'd taken from his pockets into the bag as well. He stopped when he got to the last loose item, the title page of *The Secret Agent*, putting it into one of the zippered pockets instead.

He pulled out his phone and, willing his hands to stop shaking, texted Harriet as the cab drove away from Copper Beech.

Dad sick. Had to rush home. See you in Atlanta
when you're back.

He leaned back, closing his eyes and breathing in deep, trying
to figure out his next step.

He would have a half-hour wait for the bus to calm himself
and try to understand what had happened and how he was going
to deal with it. He needed someone to talk to and the only one
he could think of was Dirk, but his friend was on an airplane to
Greece. Then he remembered Dirk's offer.

*I'll find a hole there to hide in. Then I can think through this
dilemma. I've chanced on a reporter's dream, but I can't ignore
the risks. Not to Harriet or myself. Or our relationship.*

He emailed Dirk to ask if it was all right to stay at his folks'
ranch in Wyoming. Dirk's reply was an email introducing his
parents to Fred, with an aside to Fred that he was sorry he couldn't
be there to show him around.

Fred assured him he'd be fine on his own. Typing the words,
he almost believed it.

Running

On Labor Day, behind the locked door of his bachelor apartment in Atlanta, an icepack held to the side of his head, Fred watched on TV as Billy Joe threw his hat into the political ring, Bull and Harriet smiling in the background. The sight of Bull on the same stage as Harriet made him physically sick, as if Norman Bates was walking through his brain. Billy Joe gave the same speech he had given to his campaign team on his lawn, what Bull had laid out as their message.

"I am running to ensure we keep America for Americans," he announced, to thundering cheers.

Fred sat mesmerized through the speech, experiencing a flurry of emotions. Finally, there was the big pause, the sign that he was about to wrap things up.

"I am a winner," Billy Joe shouted. "I'm running to support the workers of America, to secure their jobs and to create new jobs. Vote for me as the Republican nominee and I guarantee that I'll beat the Democrats."

Fred arranged to meet Harriet for dinner the night after Billy Joe's announcement. She offered to cook.

He arrived at seven with a bottle of wine and some flowers. He tried to act as normally as a man in love would. This wasn't difficult as he loved Harriet and knew she loved him in return, but he had to convince her that it would be best if they gave each other some space.

"You left so suddenly from Dad's," she said, her hand stroking his face and concern in her eyes. "I hope your dad is okay."

"Yeah," he mumbled. "My dad has a tricky heart. Mum was worried and drove him to the emergency."

"Is everything okay?"

"He's fine now."

Unsure how to bring it up, Fred put off telling her his plan until after dinner. Even so, when they were relaxing on the sofa and drinking brandy, he still found himself stalling. Unexpectedly, Harriet gave him an opening.

"Are you worried about your dad?" she asked. "Is that why you're so quiet?"

"Honey," he ventured, "you know I've wanted to write a novel based on my family."

She nodded, looking adoringly at him.

"Well," he continued, "you're going to be completely caught up in your father's campaign for the next fourteen months."

"Yes. Isn't that exciting?"

Harriet clapped her hands. Fred nodded before going on.

"I thought it would be best for both of us..."

He paused. She didn't know where he was going with this but gave him an encouraging look.

"...if I went to a secluded place to write. You should concentrate your full attention on your dad's election."

Her back straightened, she leapt up and stood over him, assuming the in-class role he knew so well, that of inquisitor of professors.

"Are you really telling me you are going to dump me because my dad is running for president?"

"No, no," he protested, jumping off the sofa. "You now have a full-time job that will take you all over the country. It'll put a huge strain on our relationship. I love you with all my heart and I want to be able to say that after this campaign. And I can do something to honour *my* dad."

He reached out to her and held her hand. She softened a little.

"I know I'm going to be busy. Dad named me Assistant Campaign Manager. But I need you to be there for me," she pouted.

"I'll stay in touch."

"Where would you go?"

"Dirk's parents have a ranch in Wyoming. He's invited me to stay in one of their cabins. It would be ideal to write."

"I understand, dear. We both have to make sacrifices. What's the title of your novel?"

Fred hadn't thought that through. He uttered the first word that came into his head.

"*Secrets.*"

"Oh, very mysterious. I can hardly wait to read it."

They sat back on the sofa and hugged. He told her nothing about what he'd heard or of what happened afterwards. He didn't even want to think about that horror. He had misgivings about his flight, but he was in no shape to fight. He'd asked himself if this was the honourable thing to do to the woman he loved, rationalizing that it was with the belief it could save his life. And if he was out of the picture, what he knew wouldn't compromise her.

Still, he had to keep in touch with her.

He told her before he left that night that he would be out of cellphone range and only able to phone or email her from a small town near his cabin.

Back in his car, he opened his laptop and downloaded IP hiding software. While it loaded, he pulled a disposable phone out of its packaging. He ran his finger across the word 'untraceable' printed on the package. He wondered if having a phone reserved for calling Harriet made up for not telling her the truth.

Autumn Leaves

Elizabeth had arranged to spend the Labour Day weekend with her parents at the Bar 5 Ranch. She came down to the kitchen at seven to make coffee to bring her mother in bed. Instead, she found Justine up and dressed.

"Hey, I thought you would be sleeping in today. It's Labour Day."

"I got up to feed the horses."

"Isn't that Dad's job?"

"Yes, but he's ridden up Potato Mountain to talk to his mother."

"What about?"

"A cure for my cancer."

Elizabeth put her arm around her mother.

"Come. I'll make you some breakfast."

"I'm not too hungry, but I'll have a boiled egg and some buttered toast."

Justine watched from the table as Elizabeth bustled about the kitchen preparing her mother's meagre fare.

"Can I help?" Justine asked, ever mindful.

"No thank you, Mother."

"I'm worried about your boys, dear." Justine seemed concerned and a bit distracted. "I know you're doing your best, but shouldn't their fathers get more involved in their upbringing?"

They'd had this discussion many times before. Elizabeth wasn't ready to go over it again.

"Maybe one day they will," she replied with a shrug.

Elizabeth, now in her fifties, had had three husbands. Each one in turn had tried to dominate her. When she'd let it be known that marriage meant an equal partnership, they each faded away. She'd been left raising one child from each marriage, each carrying a different father's surname. Clint's father, Leonard Lalula, had lived common-law with her for five years. Justine had insisted they marry when Elizabeth got pregnant, same as she'd done with the fathers of her other children. Leonard couldn't adjust to life with a baby, leaving when Clint was six months old, which at least was more time than he'd devoted to any one job. Bruce Hawthorn, a machine operator, had left Elizabeth a year after Jeremy was born. He had no interest in his son. Her only daughter, Alice Henry, was now in her early teens. Alice's father, John, had stuck around longer than the others. He still lived in the area and had a job as a sawyer in the Larson mill. Alice listened to her mother and, so far, was the most sensible of her children. She also was caught up in hockey and had a mean wrist shot from the top of the circle.

Elizabeth could see that both her boys were hurt by their fathers' neglect. The boys made up for it by looking after each other and being close to Noah. Clint was more like a father to Jeremy than a brother, though they looked nothing alike. Where Clint was dark, short and wiry, Jeremy was six feet tall with a mop of sandy blond hair and light skin. When both boys were in their preteens, they had fallen in with the wrong crowd, becoming involved with alcohol, drugs and gangs. It was her boys' welfare that had steered her out of bookkeeping and into social work in her mid-forties.

Later that day, the two women strolled about the ranch as Justine examined the lives of her children and grandchildren with pride, tinged with a bit of criticism.

Noah came down from Potato Mountain in time for dinner, confident in Justine's recovery. He was also in time to spare Elizabeth more of Justine's grandmotherly concerns.

After dinner, Elizabeth spoke to Noah alone.

"Dad, why didn't you go to Antoine's cave to have the ravens foretell Mother's future?"

Noah was startled by his daughter's question. Every year since the death of his mentor, he had sought the counsel of the ravens as he fasted and meditated in Antoine's cave near Homathko Canyon. He looked at his daughter with compassion and put his clasped hands together in a sign of submission to his Creator.

"Ta Chi knows your mother and the spiritual cures," he said with emotion. "She will intercede on our behalf with the Creator. The ravens at Antoine's cave foretell the future of our nation."

In bed with Justine that night, Noah told her of his ride to Potato Mountain.

"Did Ta Chi give you hope, Noah?" Justine whispered.

"In a way, dear. I have done all that I can do to intercede with the Creator on your behalf. I'm at peace and we will see you through this illness." He held back the part he knew Justine would be excited about till the last. "Big Momma was there on Potato Mountain. She looked well and I watched her forage for food."

"Noah, why didn't you tell me right away? You know that the spirit of that beautiful bear means so much to me."

"I wanted to save it till just before you sleep. So you can dream about her."

He didn't tell her about the helicopter.

On the Tuesday after Labour Day, Noah drove Justine and Elizabeth to Kamloops for Justine's first chemo treatment. This would become their routine for the next three months.

In Kamloops, they overnighted at Joel's house in the old town. His wife Joan and their two children, Hugh and Rebecca, greeted everyone at the door. The children were always excited about their grandmother's visits, ready to hear her stories and play board games with her. This evening, they chose a game called Camel Up. Noah watched for a cue to step in, noticing the effort it took for Justine even to lean forward and roll the dice. Come her turn, Rebecca couldn't make up her mind, squealing and jumping up and down.

"I don't know what to do."

"Whatever you do," her older brother bragged, "you're going to lose."

"Now, Hugh," his grandmother cautioned, "I think Rebecca has as good a chance of winning as you do."

That's Justine, the peacemaker, Noah thought to himself.

They never tired of the weekly journey, watching the slow change of autumn colours in the aspens from green through shades of yellow, then orange to the final shedding of their leaves. The change between the high plateau forests of the Chilcotin to the sagebrush desert of the Thompson River Valley, the dog days of summer to the apple-crisp autumn days — all of this stirred Justine's imagination. There was also a sense of optimism that the chemo would give her many more autumns.

By mid-September, Justine found it difficult to climb the stairs to their bedroom. Elizabeth moved her onto the main floor, into the library. There, she could rest during the day and avoid the stairs.

Justine became interested in organizing boxes of photographs taken of the family over the years, spending weeks cataloguing them and putting them in albums. Elizabeth suggested she could scan and digitize the photographs, but Justine would have none of it.

"Elizabeth," she explained, "I want to touch the photos. I feel that they are speaking to me as I arrange them on the page. Each one is a story. I'm having fun. This is my autobiography and this book is my family. I'm not going to digitize them."

"Okay, Mum. Have it your own way."

Justine smiled at the phrase. It had been what she had told Elizabeth when she was young and she'd disapproved of her daughter's choices.

Noah stayed close to the ranch and ate every meal with Justine. Next to the large Scottish lodge that Belle Hanlon had built, Brent, the oldest of the Hanlon boys, lived with his wife Carol in the old ranch house. Carol prepared dinners in her own kitchen nightly, though the family would most likely gather at Noah and Justine's.

Noah couldn't bring himself to go to his studio and face a blank canvas, so he and Justine spent their weeks talking, playing cribbage, reading and travelling to Kamloops. Spending so much time together in a common cause gave them a different, even richer, perspective on life, akin to the wonder of children. Justine took an interest in the movement of birds during the migration cycle. Noah dusted off their ornithological books and they walked down to the lake every day to identify the travellers going south.

In October, Justine excitedly called out to Noah.

"Quick, let's go down to the lake."

"Why the hurry?"

"The Canada geese have heard the call of the south. I want to say goodbye."

"Yes. And I want to say good riddance."

"Oh, Noah. You'll miss them."

"In a pig's eye."

Nevertheless, they walked down to the lake and watched the flock rise, form a V and head south, honking a farewell chorus.

"I'll miss them," Justine sighed, "but we have the sparrows and the ravens. Like us, they will never leave the Chilcotin."

Crossing the Rubicon

Fred arrived at the Campbells' ranch in mid-September. He'd subletted his apartment, then gotten his affairs in order at his folks' place on the Savannah River, scraping together the money to start on his odyssey. It had taken him two weeks to drive across America, including a week pumping gas in Omaha to earn enough money for necessary clutch repairs to Frederica, who was burning a quart of oil at every fill-up.

When he pulled up, he was warmly greeted by Dirk's parents, Sue and Pat. Hearing he was short on cash and finding out he rode horses, they offered him a job as a wrangler through mid-October, the end of their season. The job included one of the guest cabins, though as a friend of Dirk's, he was welcome to stay anyway. He gratefully accepted and spent the first night laying on his bed, his bags unpacked, unable to move but finally able to sleep soundly.

In the weeks that followed, Fred became addicted to news reports on the lead-up to the primaries. The only station that came in over the rabbit ears, if intermittently, would switch to

CNN's feeds when its programming day ended and he found himself staying up later and later to get caught up. The news out of the Republican camp was electrifying. Billy Joe followed up his declaration speech by accusing illegal Mexican immigrants of stealing American jobs and raping American women, offering to build a high wall along the Mexican border as his solution.

"Mexicans are a fine people in their place," he assured. "That place is Mexico. By building a wall, we will stop the migrants — some of whom are rapists — and we will stop the traffic in drugs which are sapping the strength of America's young people."

Fred recognized that Bull's strategy with that speech was to inflame and to attract media attention. It succeeded wildly. The simpler Billy Joe's solutions to the complex issues facing the nation — like "America for Americans" and "I guarantee your security" — the more support he got in the polls.

One reason Fred watched coverage obsessively was that, amongst the shots of the press conferences before the debates, Harriet would be there, looking pert and brainy. She seemed to be taking Bull's place, while he was fading into the background. He considered asking Harriet if Bull was falling out of favour with her dad, but felt he would be using her if he didn't tell her why he was so interested in the man.

Harriet's position in the campaign offered a bit of balance to Billy Joe's outrageous statements, which were resonating with a large percentage of Republicans and attracting huge media attention. Another of Bull's strategies given loud voice by Billy Joe was to insult the other candidates, calling the women 'ugly' and the men 'stupid'. Well, not all the time — sometimes he used less provocative words.

Fred could see this strategy was also paying off with more airtime — free airtime at that — than any other presidential hopeful, Democrat or Republican. When Harriet did a short interview on CNN, Fred texted her from the ranch.

> Darling, you were super on TV! If your dad wins the primary,
> he'll owe it to you. Miss you. Love you.

She replied in a matter of minutes.

> Never worked so hard in my life. You were right. No time
> to make love but I can dream about you. Hope your novel is
> shaping up. Love.

Fred only missed the day's news offerings when he took groups of guests on overnight trail rides. The guests hailed from all over the world and each one had a story to tell. One of the more interesting ones was a Latin teacher at a prep school in London. Despite having vacationed at the ranch each fall for the last twenty-five years, she was still 'Miss Cousins' to the staff. She took an interest in American politics, comparing them to the British Parliamentary system.

At night around a campfire, the wind whispering through the trees, she told Fred about her winter vacations in Zermatt and her students, the sons of royalty and the super-rich. When the conversation turned to American politics, he told her he'd graduated from Georgia State University and was only working on the ranch before he started to look for a journalism job. He hastily added that he had published work in the *Herald*.

"Tell me, Fred — you're a reporter — what's going on in the Republican party? Specifically, Northrop."

"Well, Miss Cousins," he smiled, "his campaign's run by a man called Bull O'Connor. A large part of the US electorate is dissatisfied with the political class, so he's running Billy Joe as anti-establishment."

"I think you know me well enough by now to call me Nora."

"Nora, then," Fred smiled. Not even Pat and Sue called her by her first name.

"Your Mr. O'Connor was the political strategist who advised some successful campaigns in England two years ago. I always thought he was a bit dodgy."

It could have been the rum that she had insisted on spiking their coffee with that loosened his tongue. It was probably that he had been suppressing this story for over a month and it just had to come out. He found himself anxious to open up to this worldly older woman.

"O'Connor is dodgy. I know something about him that could bring down Billy Joe Northrop's run for the nomination."

She took a sip of her coffee and looked closely at this young man.

"You're a reporter," she said curtly, "why aren't you doing something about it?"

"Because," he chose his slurred words carefully, "exposing it could put my life in danger. I'm off the grid. In hiding."

She controlled her surprise by nodding.

"I see," she said. "That explains your hair. It's getting long for that cut. Have you checked out the facts of what you 'know'?"

He felt the challenge in her words, her enunciation. And he felt himself failing it.

"No."

Under a canopy of stars, she talked to him as an aunt to her nephew.

"It's not for me to say how you should run your life, Fred. But… if it were me — or for that matter, Julius Caesar, who crossed his Rubicon — I would go find the facts and prove your story. *Veni, vidi, vici*, Fred."

The next day, he took the ripped-out title page from *The Secret Agent* from his suitcase and read the notes he'd taken while Bull and Billy Joe were spilling their secrets. He highlighted the passages that stood out from his scribblings.

*Chilcotin gas play, 50% interest. Political action
committee. Tax dodge?
"I will be in charge of the whole operation."*
— O'Connor
natural gas, British Columbia

*"I want to keep the deal under wraps until we
prove up the reserves and you become president."*
— O'Connor
against campaign donation law

"may have to become aggressive with the Natives"
— O'Connor

"you shouldn't have your name involved"
— O'Connor to Billy Joe

Nora was the first person he'd told about being off-grid and why. Had Dirk been around, Fred would have told him the whole story and sought his advice. Maybe the Latin teacher was right — maybe he *should* investigate the biggest political story since Watergate. Even though it might hurt the woman he loved.

On the other hand, Caesar didn't fare so well after crossing the Rubicon.

A Southern Gentleman

The three most significant people in Fred's life were relaxing in Billy Joe's den of unread books after weeks of campaigning.

Bull was watching the Texas Longhorns play the Alabama Crimson Tide on the television awkwardly angled between two massive oak bookcases. On his lap, a whole roast chicken sat atop a bucketful of popcorn. He tore the chicken apart with his hands, stuffing pieces into his mouth, pausing only to take generous swallows from a tankard of beer. From time to time, he glanced at the gap in the matched set of Joseph Conrad's works of literature where *The Secret Agent* had been shelved and scowled.

Billy Joe sat in the wingback chair, reading a draft of a speech. Harriet read from her phone and responded to texts and tweets from her team of volunteers throughout the States.

"Harriet, honey," Billy Joe called out, "I'm going to that rally in Iowa tomorrow. What are my numbers?"

"The polls show you're extending your lead in Iowa."

Harriet's eyes strayed to Bull and his disgusting appetite. She grimaced. A reminder came up on her screen about a climate change conference in Atlanta the next year.

"Oh, Dad. The Atlanta conference next June — Green Trust is hosting a leading grasslands expert. I'm going to introduce him. A Dr. Joel Hanlon."

"Hell, Billy Joe, I met that guy in Williams Lake," Bull said with a tinge of irritation and a glare in Harriet's direction. "Now you leave all those little bitty details to me. You ain't got time to sweat over the Green Trust. You've got the Iowa primary to fight. You concentrate on beating those candy-ass contenders."

"Dad, I can handle the trust," Harriet's voice rose in a challenge to Bull.

This heated talk wasn't for the benefit of Billy Joe. It was a struggle between the two of them for his attention.

"Like I told you a while ago, everything's under control, Billy Joe," Bull asserted. "The Trust is buying up ranches in that country. Northrop Oil will use the land as a carbon offset for your oil sands project. Our lawyers are working on it. I'll be going up to the Chilcotin to sign the contracts."

Bull punctuated this with a loud belly belch. Harriet turned away, not bothering to hide her disgust.

"Bull, you're my political strategist. Get someone else to handle the Chilcotin. I want your input on the debate. We've only got two days. What do you think of the speech?"

"I've read it. Look, Billy Joe, I've told you, you can't read from the same script as those losers. You're in the lead by being different. Don't start getting nice all of a sudden. I changed your opening remarks. You gotta attack your opponents and their middle-of-the-road policies."

Bull handed a sheaf of papers to Billy Joe, red edits liberally sprinkled over them.

Billy Joe started shuffling through them. Billy Joe was exactly as he described himself, a gentleman, with only his ambition overriding his gentle manners. That ambition and the polls told him that he had a chance of becoming president and Bull, with his proven ability to win elections, was the man to make that happen. Yet, the closer he had gotten to Bull, the more concerned he was.

He came across an edit to the speech that worried him.

"Bull, don't forget I'm a Southern gentleman. I can't say that Prudence Wright is as ugly as her policy on illegal Mexicans."

Bull knew that Billy Joe had no such compunctions, but decided to humour him.

"Okay, what *would* a Southern gentleman say?"

"Ms. Wright is as *unattractive* as her policy on illegal Mexicans, some of whom have overstayed their welcome."

"Don't get too cute. Your core voters want blood."

"I know, but I have to reach out to the middle-of-the-roaders, the right-leaning liberals."

"You know, Billy Joe, there is such a thing in campaigns as timing. Now's the time to be controversial and win the rock-bottom right-wing Republicans. They vote in the primaries. To do that, you gotta talk tough and hit against the establishment. Once you got the nomination sewed up, then you can inch toward the middle to start sopping up some of those liberals. Then we got the whole Lincoln protectionist Republican political machine behind us and nothing can stop us."

"I like what I'm hearing, Bull, I really do," Billy Joe replied, confusion in his voice. "But I *am* the establishment."

Bull didn't waste a second thinking about that.

"The difference is that you aren't the political establishment." Bull paused to give his next utterance weight. "I was going to hold this in reserve, Billy Joe, but I'm going to tell you now, with Harriet in the room. I've had our pollsters conduct a nationwide poll on the question of whether you should campaign by yourself or with Harriet at your side on every stage and every stop on every news and talk show. It'll be like Harry Truman and his singing daughter, Margaret. What do you think the results of the poll are?"

Billy Joe looked down thoughtfully.

"People didn't know I had a daughter," he mused, "until I announced my candidacy. Her mother and I were only together for a few months. We even gave her her mother's name. Keep her out of the limelight and all."

Bull shook his head.

"The poll shows that she would be a huge asset to your campaign." He wiped the back of his hand across his greasy mouth and, his eyes on the game, asked, "What do you say, Harriet?"

Harriet was conflicted. She wanted to help her father, but wasn't happy taking orders from this grotesque man.

"I'd really like to help Dad."

"You'd have to hold off on going back to your Green Trust duties."

"I could arrange that until Dad is elected."

Her father smiled a big Georgia smile.

"Thank you, Happy. Come here. Give me a hug."

She got up, leaned over her dad and put her arm around his shoulders. He looked up at her.

"You're a comfort to me, darling. Hey, whatever happened to that young man you introduced me to?"

Bull's attention was at red alert, yet not a face muscle twitched. His eyes were glued to the TV while he stuffed handfuls of popcorn in his mouth.

"He's looking for a job," she ventured. "He's a really good journalist."

"I could use a good writer in my campaign. What do you say, Bull? We could use a new speechwriter."

"I dunno. What's he doing now?"

Bull looked searchingly at Harriet.

"He's in Wyoming. He's working on a novel."

"It wouldn't work." Bull dismissed the idea with a wave of his hand. "Novelists try too hard to create reality. Speechwriters create illusions. We'd be better off with a science fiction writer."

Billy Joe took little notice.

"Anyway, honey, get in touch. Fly him here for a weekend."

Bull jumped up, spilling popcorn on the floor. He raised his right hand with the index and little finger extended in a Longhorn salute.

"B-T-H-O Alabama!" he yelled. "Hot damn! My Longhorns beat the Crimson Tide."

Billy Joe and Harriet said nothing as Bull marched triumphantly toward the door. He paused at the threshold.

"By the way," he said to Harriet, "send that boyfriend of yours my best."

Bull went directly to his room and got on the phone. He was concerned Harriet would arrange to get Fred back to Atlanta, and that could prove embarrassing. Fred needed a little reminder of how dangerous it would be to return and how important it was that he keep his mouth shut.

"Dexter? It's me. ... I want you to find a Fred Scully. ... He'd have entered Wyoming from Georgia in late September. ... Older model Subaru Forester licence plate DUF 351. ... Don't let him know you're on to him. Phone me when you've found him. I'll give you further instructions."

Harriet, excited about her father's interest in Fred, went back to her room and emailed him.

Dearest Fred,

Guess what? I was talking with Dad and Mr. O'Connor in the
library and Dad suggested I invite you to Copper Beech for a
few days. He even suggested it would be a good idea, if you're
interested, for you to work as a speechwriter for him. Mr.
O'Connor was cool on the idea. I told them you were writing
a novel in a shack in Wyoming and probably couldn't pay
for the airplane ticket, but Dad said it would be a campaign
expense. What do you think? I'm missing you and want you
to come. It would be wonderful if we could work together.
Mr. O'Connor sends you his best.

Love,
Harriet.

A day later, the phone rang in Bull's office. Lying on the couch
half-asleep, Bull lifted the receiver and grunted.

"Mr. O'Connor," a voice came over the line. "I've found him!
He's working on a guest ranch near the Wind River under his
own name."

"Yeah?" Bull grunted again.

"I phoned the ranch. They close down on October fifteenth,
so he may be moving on."

"All right. This is what I what you to do. Arrange for him to
have an accident. And let him know why."

Wind River Canyon

T here was a week to go before the end of the season.

Fred hadn't opened his email since Harriet's last missive. Thinking about her tore him apart. He wanted to see her, yet Bull was lurking in the background and, unknown to her, had sent him a coded message.

Most of the guests were gone, Miss Cousins included, but two new guests, Jim and Jean Dexter, arrived in a rental Mercedes, decked out in new western gear.

"We can't get enough of fresh air and living rough," they told Sue when they checked in, babbling as one.

They quickly signed up for an overnight trail ride into the foothills and had to be talked into taking a day to settle in. They kept to themselves that first day and night. In the morning, though, they put on a show of enthusiasm and chatted up Sue. At breakfast, Sue introduced them to Fred, looking grateful to hand off the couple and get back to her own work. The Dexters, in turn, seemed happy to have someone new to talk to.

Fred took them to the corral to select their horses. He liked to gauge the guests' knowledge of horses by having them saddle and mount up under his watchful eye. Jean threw the saddle on her horse backwards and had no idea what a bit was. Both needed help just mounting up. It was obvious to Fred that if they'd ever ridden a horse, it had been on a merry-go-round. He suggested an easy ride through the meadows and lower valleys, but they wanted to test themselves against nature and insisted on a ride through the mountain passes. Fred was doubtful.

"Well, I don't know about that. You're novice riders and there are some tricky bits of riding on the narrow trail through Wind River Canyon."

"We came here for adventure," Jim beamed. "That's what we'd like to do. Isn't it, Jeannie?"

"Anything you say, Jim," she said without enthusiasm. He hadn't told her when she agreed to accompany him that she would have to ride a horse.

Sue watched the three of them leave the corral all saddled up and leading a packhorse.

"They'll be back before dark," she told Pat, shaking her head.

An hour into the ride, it was clear the couple wouldn't last the day. Fred led the packhorse slowly and pointed out the scenery as they walked their horses on the Wind River trail.

"This is one of the routes the pioneers took on their way to California," he shouted, trying to get them engaged in the experience.

He got no response.

Further on, he pointed out a grove of pines.

"There was an Indian massacre there."

Jim grunted.

"Can we stop for a bit and rest?" Jean asked.

"We're coming up to Pine Tree Ford. You can rest there for a while."

He had picked a gentle route, but they had to cross the river. Fred showed them how by riding his horse, the packhorse in tow, through the water up to the horses' bellies. He tethered the packhorse on the far shore then came back for his clients, who seemed to be having an argument. He took the reins of Jean's horse and told her to hang on to the pommel. She looked apprehensive.

"Can't we stay on this side of the river?" she asked plaintively.

"Now, Jeannie," Jim corrected her in a commanding voice, "you know we came out here at great expense to get to know the country. So you just ride across with this young man."

They started across. Halfway over, Jeannie panicked and fell off her horse, screaming and yelling.

"Help! I'm drowning! Help me! My leg! My leg!"

Fred jumped off his horse and went to her. Jim dismounted and waded into the river behind him. They'd almost reached Jeannie when a current swept the three of them into a deep pool. Fred grabbed the back of Jean's shirt and started to swim her to the far shore. Jim, in over his head, grabbed Fred to pull himself up.

"I can't swim!" he yelled, emerging from the water.

Fred pushed him back.

"Wait here," he shouted. "I'll be back for you."

Then, with powerful strokes, he got Jean safely to the bank of the river. There, she held on to the ground in a deathlike grip.

"Save me!" Jim yelled.

Fred turned to see Jim go under again. He swam back out and got him above the waterline, then started pulling him to shore. When the water was at chest level, Jim pushed Fred into the deeper and swifter water, trying to hold him under.

Fred decided that he couldn't hold back if they were all going to get through this. He dove further down, beyond Jim's reach. With his feet planted on the riverbed, he turned and rose out of the water, elbowing Jim in the face.

He dragged Jim's dazed body to the shore.

Jean was moaning on the riverbank, the untethered horses were wandering all over creation and Jim was lying on the bank like a beached whale. Fred had no time to wonder what Jim's motive was for trying to drown him or even if that was the man's intent. He caught the packhorse with the supplies, set up camp, lit a fire and got them settled down. Jean had injured her right leg in the fall. It was more of a twist than a break, but she couldn't possibly ride a horse. He gave Jean some pain relievers and some dry clothing. While she changed, he built a fire to heat up a billycan of soup and some tea.

Jean finally calmed down a bit when the food was ready. Jim sulked by the fire.

"I'm leaving you some soup and the tea I made," Fred said. "I'm going to get help. I'll be gone a couple of hours. In the meantime, you'll be fine here."

Jean looked panicked again.

"You're not going to leave us alone in this wilderness, are you? What about bears?" she grimaced.

"You'll be fine. There are no bears in this area. Jim's here. He'll protect you."

"That's what I'm afraid of," she said.

Fred mounted his horse. The last thing he heard as he headed out was the two of them quarrelling.

"I don't care what you got for this job, Dexter. It's not worth it," Jean shouted.

"Oh, shut up."

Fred came riding hard into the compound at four that afternoon. He reined up in front of the office where Sue was doing the books.

"We've had an accident. Jean fell off her horse and injured her leg about an hour out. We'll need a wagon to haul her in. I've left her with Jim and gave her something for the pain. I'll tell you the details later."

Sue phoned the local doctor while Fred harnessed the work horses to the buckboard. He, Sue and the doctor were off within the half-hour. It was early evening when they retrieved the couple and brought them back to the ranch to wait for an ambulance.

It wasn't till ten that night, over a bottle of Jack Daniels, that Fred was able to tell Sue and Pat what had happened on the trail. When he got to the end of his adventure with the couple, he poured himself another shot of bourbon with a shaking hand. Sue began ladling out some stew she had simmering at the back of the Aga cookstove.

"Go on," she said. "It's hard to believe that this happened."

"Why in tarnation," Pat asked, scratching his head, "would Jim have tried to drown you?"

"When we loaded Jean onto the ambulance, Jim went to his car to follow. Before he pulled away, I asked him that very question. His answer was chilling: 'I'm here to tell you to keep your mouth shut.'"

Sue stopped ladling stew onto Fred's plate. Holding the big spoon mid-air, she let the stew drip on to the kitchen table.

"Dirk didn't tell us that you were involved in crime," Pat said, horrified. He leaned in. "Is this *drugs*?"

"Oh, no. This is something far more complex. You're not involved and it's better you don't know. I'll leave first thing tomorrow. I appreciate you putting me up."

"You better eat this stew. You look as hungry as a she-bear waking in the spring."

Sue had always believed a full stomach could solve most problems.

At first light, Fred packed Frederica and got in. Pat came up to the open car window. He stuck out his hand — there were five hundred-dollar bills in it.

"Take the extra as a bonus. You've earned it and you'll need it. When all this is cleared up, let us know. Any help you need, we'll give it."

Crossings

Fred headed north to Canada.

He'd heard about British Columbia from his dad, Earl, and from his Grandpa Alex, a draft-dodging hippie who had lived in the seventies on North Rendezvous Island, off the central coast of BC. Earl had spent the formative years of his life fishing for red snappers and picking peas and potatoes from the garden, which was surrounded by a ten-foot fence to keep out deer. Earl had been homeschooled by Grandma until she'd run out of things to teach him. At about that time, the owners of the island decided they didn't want squatters on their land anymore and 'encouraged' them to move on.

The family had moved to the Chilcotin after Grandpa Alex heard of another American named Edwards who had homesteaded Lonesome Lake in the thirties. Grandpa thought he would try that too. Earl went to school in Tatla Lake for a couple of years, but the family returned to Georgia when the US opened a window of amnesty for draft-dodgers. The Scullys were poor, but they weren't *dirt* poor, and they made a deal for a bit of land on the Savannah River, growing organic vegetables for market.

Now Fred was in the same boat as Grandpa Alex when he'd fled to Canada to escape the draft, though the war Fred was avoiding was with mad Bull O'Connor. *I'm a journalist,* he reasoned with himself, *and I've got a degree to prove it. I'm not proud of running. I don't think I'm a coward, just a realist. Who'd believe a 25-year-old's story about what he heard in the library without proof? Or for that matter, what happened afterwards?*

He didn't think Harriet would, because she had faith in her dad. What had happened after he'd overheard the conversation was meant to frighten him into silence. So far, it was working. He was a nobody who had witnessed two of the most powerful men in the nation cook up an illegal scheme that breached the Federal Election Campaign Act and fiddled with PAC money. It would also affect a foreign country, more particularly the Chilcotin, a land and a people who had nurtured his family years ago.

It had taken him a month to overcome the shock of what had happened. Bull's reminder at the Wyoming ranch brought it all back. He'd had a relapse of anxiety, but was determined to follow the story to its end. What he *could* do was go to the Chilcotin and see for himself the land that had been home and sanctuary to his grandfather and father. His dad had told him about living in Tatla Lake as a young boy, working with a hay crew and feeding cattle for a local rancher, a Noah Hanlon. A plan, perhaps more of a hunch, slowly shaped in Fred's mind — he would find the Hanlons and somehow, through them, find the evidence he needed to write the story.

On leaving Georgia, he had told Harriet that he was going out to Wyoming to write a novel in a cabin and would send emails from time to time. He'd continue to let her believe he was still in Wyoming. Exposing Bull would harm Harriet's father's presidential run and, by extension, Harriet herself. He doubted their romance could survive.

With all this going through his mind, Fred replied to Harriet's email from a rundown motel in Eastern Oregon.

> You don't know how important it is to me to hear from you and to be invited to see you. My delay in replying is…

He paused and listened to his inner voice.

No big stories. Keep it simple and straightforward and reasonable.

> …because I was on a trail ride for research on my book and had no internet connection. I am now deep into the writing of my story and expect that it will take…

Tell her you want to rush back to her. No, don't burden her. And give yourself as much time as you can.

> …another eight months to finish. This is as important to me as you seeing your father elected president.

That's good. Let her know you respect her work.

> Since we are both dedicated to our respective goals, we must finish what we have started and look forward to the day that we can be united.

> You mentioned Bull O'Connor.

You can't tell her. But you have to tell her something. Let her know to watch out for Bull.

I have no respect for the man and you should be careful in dealing with him.

All my love,
Fred.

Fred reached the border from Washington state into British Columbia. It would be his first time in a foreign country and he was nervous. He hadn't had a haircut in two months, nor shaved in two weeks, and looked scruffy. His slim-fitting trousers and form-fitting shirts were in his suitcase and he was wearing Levi's broken in by all the riding at the ranch. With limited funds, he couldn't replace his contact lenses and was still getting used to wearing glasses again. Any thoughts of keeping a low profile were countered by Frederica blowing black smoke out of the exhaust pipe.

Dexter drove the rented Mercedes, his eyes shifting between the road and a screen showing Fred's location. His stomach growled but he kept his focus on the decreasing distance to the red dot on the screen.

Fred didn't have a passport, but had renewed his driver's licence in Wyoming and that was good enough to enter Canada by land. A friendly customs officer looked at his licence, then stared at him uncertainly. He stepped back, taking a long look at Frederica, then scanned Fred again.

"Would you mind taking off your glasses, sir?" the officer asked with a smile. "You don't have them on in your picture."

Fred took off his horn-rimmed glasses and squinted up at the officer's face.

"Yes, there's a likeness," the officer nodded. "Now, what is the purpose of your visit to Canada?"

"I'm going up to visit friends of my family," he told the officer. "I expect to be about a month in your fine country."

He was waved through. He was expecting a more thorough investigation and was relieved to be in a new country so relaxed at its borders, yet so similar to his own.

Driving through the border town of Creston, Frederica took exception to Canada and refused to start at a stoplight. Fred got help from a friendly local and pushed the car to a garage. *At least it didn't happen in the border line-up,* he consoled himself.

The mechanic there shook Fred's hand, introducing himself as Darren. He then lifted the hood, poked around the starter and checked the battery and generator. He stood back, looked at the car and shook his head. He lit up a roach and offered it to Fred, who declined.

Fred realized he wouldn't have been offered the joint back in September when he was a clean–cut, short–haired graduate student.

Darren took a drag and exhaled slowly.

"I got to tell you, man, this old lady needs a complete over-haul. Just to get her running will probably cost you more than she's worth."

"What are you talking about?"

"I'm saying about two grand."

"I've got five hundred," Fred offered. "American."

"Tell you what. I'll take her off your hands for $200 which is about what you would get for scrap."

"That's good of you, but could you maybe raise it a hundred?"

"Well, I have to make something for my trouble. What the hell, I'll give you $250."

Darren pulled the money out of his wallet. Fred looked away from him, scanning the car slowly. He gently kicked Frederica's front driver-side tire. It was almost bald. They had been together for five years. He had courted Harriet in this car. He wasn't happy to see her go but needed the money.

"Okay, I'll do it."

He dug into his pocket and handed over the key. He signed the paperwork that Darren produced.

"Thanks, man," Fred sighed. "Could you direct me to the bus station?"

It was 1:05 p.m. when Fred got to the station. The clerk told him he'd just missed the bus and the next one didn't leave till four. Fred bought a ticket to Williams Lake and thanked him. Having time to spare, he changed in the station washroom, tossing away his worn jeans. He decided to take a walk around the small town, careful to be back to the station at 3:45.

Dexter's eyes lit on the red dot now stopped in Creston. He figured he had some time, so had a bite to eat at a roadside café.

He drove into Creston at two-thirty, quickly spotting the Subaru at the garage. Fred wasn't around. A mechanic had the car's hood up and was tinkering with the engine. Dexter approached the mechanic.

"Hi. I was driving by and noticed the car. Is it for sale?"

"Nah. I'm working on it."

"Oh. Perhaps I can speak to the owner. Do you know where I could find him?"

Darren stopped working and took a good look at this plump, clean-shaven stranger in his suit, narrow-brimmed felt hat and shades. He put down the hood, went around to the driver's side and turned the key. The engine roared to life. He turned off the engine and went up to Dexter.

"I'm the owner," he announced. "Some guy sold it to me and took the one o'clock bus to Vancouver. I'm not interested in selling."

"Thanks. Thanks a lot," Dexter replied curtly, walking away.

Darren fished around in his pocket. He pulled the tracking device out, looked at it, then at Dexter walking towards the Mercedes. He put it back in his pocket. He watched the stranger drive away, back towards the border.

The bus rolled in at 3:55 p.m. and a few passengers got off. Fred watched impatiently as the driver took some parcels into the station.

"Sorry to bother you," another waiting passenger said. "If you're wondering about the driver, he's always back in about five minutes. Last chance for a washroom break."

Fred used the opportunity to freshen up. As he did, he wondered, *Why are Canadians so damn nice?*

When Fred returned, the door to the bus was open. He was about to mount the steps when he saw, between buildings, maybe two blocks down the street, the telltale billow of Frederica's exhaust pass through an intersection. He stepped back from the bus to try and see more, but the column of smoke disappeared behind the buildings. He couldn't believe it — Darren had conned him!

What the hell! Canadians aren't so nice after all.

He was cursing the mechanic in his mind as the Subaru screamed up in front of the bus. Darren hopped out.

"Hey, man!" he shouted, running up to Fred. "Glad I caught you. I fiddled around with your starter and it wasn't busted. It was just a short. You should be able to get a few more thousand miles from the old bitch."

Fred smiled at Darren over a beer and a shared joint back in the garage.

"Canada isn't so bad after all."

Darren nodded. He took the tracking device from his pocket and placed it on the car without a word.

"What's that?" Fred asked.

"Fred, you've got some friends who want to keep close tabs on you."

"What do you mean?"

"I found this tracker on the undercarriage of your car. A man came by the garage with 'private eye' written all over him. I told him you took the one o'clock bus to Vancouver. What do you want me to do with it?"

Fred looked over the device.

"I'll take that."

When he left the garage, Fred threw the device into the box of an old pick-up with a New Mexico licence plate parked next to his Subaru.

He drove north to the Chilcotin.

Remembrance

By Remembrance Day, there was a foot of snow on the ground in the high Chilcotin plateau.

Elizabeth drove from Williams Lake with the kids, planning to drop Clint and Jeremy off at Clint's father's in Tatla Lake. Leonard Lalula, a victim of the residential schools, had a sporadic and strained relationship with his son. When Elizabeth and the boys met Leonard, he greeted them in an orange shirt and a gentle but uncertain smile.

"Hello, Leonard," she smiled half-heartedly. "Here they are. Have you got anything planned for the weekend?"

"Not really. Thought we may do some hunting when we get back to my place. Besides, they probably got friends to see."

"Well, just keep an eye on them."

Elizabeth continued on with Alice to Tatlayoko Lake, arriving about eight, in time for a late dinner. All her siblings were already there: Joel, Joan and their children had made the drive from Kamloops, Will had flown in from Vancouver, Mary and her husband Carter had come in from Williams Lake, and

Brent and Carol were cooking in the ranch house kitchen for a change. Well, Carol was cooking, but Brent was helping out by tasting.

The family was anxious about Justine's chemo, but over dinner, they talked about the food instead.

That evening, before a blazing fire in the great room, they continued not talking about it. Justine looked at her photo albums and Alice texted a friend while Elizabeth, Joel and Brent talked about ranch management. Whatever Will and Mary were talking about was too dry for anyone else to even think of joining in. Suddenly, Justine yawned.

"I think I'll go to bed," she announced.

Noah, half-asleep in his easy chair, got up with a start.

"Yes," he said, dazed. "I'll go with you."

"Are you still having trouble sleeping, Mum?" Elizabeth asked.

"Not since your dad started reading Cervantes to me. *Don Quixote*. He started a month ago and I'm asleep within ten minutes every time. He's got such a sweet, relaxing voice."

The family said their goodnights and watched as Noah and Justine left the room. There was a moment's silence before talk of ranching resumed.

Both Noah and Justine were determined to put on a brave face. Noah puttered about the ranch that weekend. Since Justine's diagnosis, he hadn't had the heart to paint and had yet to go back to his studio.

On Sunday, Mary and her family left the ranch after lunch and returned to Williams Lake. The others had an early supper as Elizabeth had to pick up the boys from Anahim Lake.

"So, Dad, are you painting yet?" she asked Noah as he was taking his first bite.

"Let him eat," Joel chided.

"Your father will paint when he's ready to," Justine answered for her husband.

Elizabeth's cellphone rang. She checked the display.

"It's Leonard," she announced, getting up from the table and going into the kitchen.

The rest of the family exchanged knowing glances and listened as best they could from the dining room.

"Yes, Leonard?"

"Elizabeth, Clint's got himself into some trouble."

"What sort of trouble?" Elizabeth's alarm bells were ringing.

"Looks like," Leonard answered laconically, "he's going to be charged with assault with a weapon."

"I'm leaving now," Elizabeth said through gritted teeth. "I'll be there in an hour."

"Yeah, well, the RCMP have taken him and Jeremy to Williams Lake."

"Why didn't you do something?" she exploded.

"Like what?"

"Like go with him. You know, act like his father."

"Well, I thought you live in Williams Lake. You could sort it out."

"Thanks, Leonard," she muttered as she hung up, "for nothing."

She filled the family in on the news. Elizabeth immediately phoned Mary and asked her to go see Clint.

"I'll get down to the jail tonight and speak to the police and the boys," Mary said. "I won't be able to get bail tonight, but I'll apply for it first thing tomorrow. I'm sure I'll get it."

It wasn't everything, but it was enough to calm Elizabeth.

Every Detail is a Story

F red arrived in Williams Lake, the centre of the Cariboo Chilcotin, nearly broke. He booked himself a cheap room in a cheap motel on the outskirts of town. Using hiding software, he deleted all his social media accounts. He was completely off the grid.

He nosed around the city to get the feel of the place, spending his days walking almost aimlessly, trying to learn every nook and cranny. Ranchers in black Stetsons peopled the streets. They were in town mainly for supplies, the cattle auction and gossip. In Fred's first few days, it seemed the ranchers were not as obviously different in dress or manner from the townspeople. As he grew accustomed though, he began to notice the difference in their rolling walk, direct talk and look-you-in-the-eye attitude.

Fred knew he stood out, not a good thing for a reporter. He listened to the tone of the townspeople's speech and the words they chose, doing his best to mirror it. He realized that, even were he to pick up a new wardrobe, he'd be marked as an outsider by the lack of wear in his clothes. On the plus side, he still had some older jeans and work shirts from his time in Wyoming.

He decided to become a regular at the Rendezvous Café on First Avenue, a hangout for ranchers and their wives to meet up with friends who lived fifty miles apart in the bush. There, they mingled with First Nations people and professionals from the town. The banter between the waitresses, Hazel and Nancy, and their regulars was his way to take the temperature of the area. On his second morning at the café, Hazel recognized him.

"What'll you have, darling?" she asked. "Black coffee and a danish like yesterday?"

"I think I'll have a roll in the hay with Nancy if you don't mind," he grinned.

It was a risk, but a calculated one. His cadence and tone was friendly, joking enough. A few heads at nearby tables turned.

"Hey, Nancy, we've got a live one here!" Hazel called across the café.

And that was all it took. With that bit of down-home humour, he started to warm to the Cariboo Chilcotin and it to him. None too soon, for the temperature dropped that night — the locals had warned him it was coming, but he had to feel it to understand what 2° Celsius meant. Nothing that serious for the locals, but he was still a Georgia boy, no matter how much he affected the local accent. He started to do the conversion, but then decided that, either way, it was cold enough to stay indoors whatever the numbers.

It was only mid-November, shirt-sleeve weather in Georgia, when Fred went to Morrison's Men's Wear to get outfitted for winter.

People around town remarked on his new fleece-lined coat. At first, he basked in the praise, then realized that the locals were still wearing T-shirts and it would get much colder. He'd probably need to buy longjohns. He was running low on cash and had wasted too much time. He needed money and resources if he was going to work on his story and there was only one way to get both.

72

Back at the Rendezvous, Fred was reading the *Williams Lake Tribune* while drinking coffee. He noticed Nancy had taken his table, even though he was sitting in Hazel's section. He figured she didn't want anything beyond flirting, but that a big tip was expected. The size of his danish made that clear. He sighed, pulled a five out of his wallet and slid it under the plate even before taking his first bite. Better to get it out of the way. If breakfast was going to be this expensive every morning, he definitely needed to find work.

He'd scanned the *Tribune* earlier while getting his bearings, but now he devoured it. He took special care reading what no one ever did. From the fine print in the masthead, he noted that their offices were just a few blocks away on First Avenue. Since they only published three times a week, they probably had no room for a new reporter, but he was sure that he could drum up a story or two to impress them, just like he had with the *Herald*. If worst came to worst, he could always sell ads. The editor's name was Muriel Steeves and, from her picture in the masthead, she looked tough but honest.

He found out quickly how right he was.

At the *Tribune* office, he'd barely finished saying why he was there before she started grilling him.

"Accent's Southern," she began. "*Southern* Southern, right?"

"Georgia, to be precise, ma'am," he replied in his finest drawl, grinning even though he was a bit deflated that his attempt at the local accent needed more work.

"Came here straight from Georgia?" she asked, chewing her lip. "Or parts inbetween?"

"Well, I spent the summer in Wyoming," he dodged.

"Let me see what you've got."

He handed her his CV and a copy of a letter of reference from a *Herald* editor.

"How long you been in town?" she asked, scanning him carefully, paying no attention to the sheets of paper in her hand.

"Just a week or two."

"Make up your mind," she chided. "One or two?"

"Uh, eleven days."

His cheeks flushed. He was in a newspaper office looking for work and had been vague about the facts.

"How'd you know where our office is?"

"It was printed in your masthead."

"So you didn't think to ask Hazel? Or Nancy? Girl thinks you're sweet on her. You're not, of course."

Fred nodded. *Right. This isn't the big city.*

"No, I'm not."

"And you're out of money."

"How'd you know that?"

"You're staying in the cheapest motel in town and you've got new clothes. You're on a budget in a place you weren't ready to be in," she said matter-of-factly. "How'd I know? I talk to everyone and I've got eyes. I've heard about the newcomer whose dad spent time in the Chilcotin but has no other reason to be here. I'm a journalist, kid. How about you?"

"I am," he laughed. "I had four or five stories printed in the *Atlanta Herald.*"

"Four or five...?"

"*Four* stories," he laughed, at himself this time. "And a sidebar piece for someone else's story."

"Not that important to me anyway. Williams Lake isn't Atlanta. I need to know if you can write *our* stories. A degree doesn't mean jack if you can't connect with the locals. I'm hoping you know what yours *does* mean. That it's not a coupon for a job."

"I know."

He was impressed by Muriel. She'd sized him up in no time and was dead right. He had expected to rest on his laurels — his degree and his grades and the *Herald* articles — and hadn't bothered to really think about the approach of a local reporter. He knew what was considered news here, but not the ways and methods of the place. He suddenly realized he couldn't even ask for references if he wanted to stay off the radar.

"So tell me what else you know. You've been here eleven days. Show me you're a reporter. Convince me before I yawn or go to lunch and I'll give you a shot."

Fred felt like he was having the dream about standing in front of the class in his underwear.

"Don't worry, you get a little reprieve. I'm going out for a smoke. You have an answer for me when I get back."

After Muriel left the room, Fred went from uncertain to real concern. He calmed himself, remembering his first-year journalism prof's advice. *Every detail is a story in itself. See everything. Hear everything. You can't know everything, but you* can *understand* any*thing.* The office was furnished in a Spartan way, but paintings on the wall overshadowed the plaques and awards — their colours were brilliant and understated at the same time, the style Native and local, one he'd seen around town. Some, though, were much more polished, more precise. He noted a signature in common on these and one other feature, a small sparrow in the right-hand corner.

She doesn't want a story on her own office, he told himself.

He looked out the window, up and down the street, nodding as pieces started clicking into place. He looked at the tops of the buildings and a mental map emerged. Flashes of things he'd seen and snippets of conversations he'd overheard came back to him. Then the cornerstone piece was in his hands. The topography of this map was the *people.*

He'd barely had the thought when Muriel swung the office door open with a thrust of her palm.

"Well, what've you got for me?" she demanded.

"I like the paintings. Local artist. Native?"

He knew she knew he was stalling for time.

"Yep. He kind of pulled away from doing media some time back, but he was selling his work in the big cities not too long back. Was going to refuse the Order of British Columbia out of protest, but his wife convinced him to accept it. Good woman she is, if in hard times these days. You're not telling me anything I don't know. Or showing me you know how to know things I don't. When paintings are signed 'Wawant'x', it's not hard to guess the artist is Native. We know him as Noah Hanlon."

On hearing Noah's name, Fred looked up again at the paintings. Muriel noticed.

"Want to tell me his nation or the specific stories in the paintings?"

"I can't. But you don't need me to, anyway. This is what I *can* tell you."

"Shoot," Muriel perched on the edge of her desk. "I'm listening."

"That side wall at the market? It needs repair, probably more than Betty can manage or Frank can fix on his own. They're in some trouble there. Let's see. Cass and Jonah have been fighting. I can't be sure, but he's been flirting with someone she knows. Oh, and the bar a couple blocks over is getting their liquor cheap somehow. The beer, they're obviously paying full price for."

Fred couldn't tell if Muriel was smiling or frowning.

"Uh, and Molly," he added. "I think she's pregnant."

Muriel roared with laughter.

"Betty's cousins," she said, "are going to come into town and help fix up that wall and Frank's not happy about it. Cass and Jonah, well, they're always fighting, but yeah, something different there this time. As for Jack's place, that was someone making good on an old debt — expect those specials to run out soon. Molly, well, you may be right there. You know none of that's anything I can print, right?"

"Of course."

"It's enough, though," she nodded. "Shows me you've got the eye."

"I was hoping."

"I *hate* hope," she replied. "Horrible thing for a reporter. Gets you focused on what you want to see rather than what there *is* to see."

"Yeah, that's fair."

Fred was smiling now. Muriel cocked her head and returned the smile, if with a wry twist.

"Amanda," she said meaningfully. "You don't know her, but she's *definitely* pregnant. Taking a long maternity leave. I was going to juggle her stuff between the others, but an extra pair of hands in the mix would be good. Can't put you on staff, but there'll be a fair amount to cover."

"What kind of stuff?"

"Good, you ask questions," she replied. "I'd be regretting my decision if you'd just said 'yes'. Amanda had just started a series on local notables and now we've got to continue it for her. Never finishes anything, mind you. I'll be surprised if that kid doesn't come out half-baked."

Fred chuckled.

"Oh, that sounds great."

"Hold your horses," she warned. "You might have the eye but I haven't seen how that looks on paper yet. Amanda also covered provincial court here and there for us. How are you on criminal law?"

"I covered cases in Atlanta."

"Good enough. The Lalula plea — charge of assault with a weapon — is coming up tomorrow and Ken Lamb's busy. After that, I'll throw you some human interest stuff and some business profiles."

"That'd be great!" Fred jumped in.

"So I'll put your name up on the board. Fred Scully, right?"

"Well, 'Frederick' when I publish, but," Fred hemmed and hawed, "I've been thinking of going by something different."

"Well, I'm not hiring you for your name recognition. What's your pen name?"

Fred thought about it. He looked up and realized he needed an answer before the favour of time Muriel was giving him turned to impatience. He was here to prove he was a reporter, the least he could do is figure out his own name.

Fred flashed on a strong memory of playing with other kids in shallow rapids dotted with large stones smoothed by the flow of the water, which was a vivid blue where it pooled.

"Stone Clearwater," he said firmly.

It had the ring of the area, he thought, as he'd already gleaned the significance of stone in the Chilcotin culture. Muriel just stared at him silently.

"It's a bit over the top," she finally sighed. "But it'll do."

"Well," Fred stammered, "I could…"

"No, no need. But there's the other reason I agreed to give you work. Amanda's series is popular and monthly. Give you a presence in this town. If you pan out."

"Thanks for the carrot. Now about pay…?"

Muriel was pleased Stone recognized she was giving him a plum job. She had other reasons though, like avoiding the clash between her other reporters, both of whom wanted the job. Also, since she was giving him a shot with the assignment, she wouldn't have to pay him as much.

"Yes, your pay. That's the stick," she chuckled. "Four hundred dollars a week. I don't suppose you have a work permit in your hip pocket. It's a starting wage so I can see what you're made of."

"Four hundred in cash," he swallowed hard.

He nodded and took her outstretched hand. He could exist on that. He turned to go.

"I hope you find what you're looking for," she said.

He was taken by surprise by Muriel's parting shot, which seemed clairvoyant. He hadn't told her he was looking for anything.

Regina v. Clint Lalula

Ken Lamb seemed like a nice enough guy. Fred ran into him at the diner and invited him out for a beer at the Legion. He hoped getting to know Ken would give him some insight into Muriel.

Ken arrived dressed almost exactly the same as at the diner. He wore a loose tie over a dress shirt, the top two buttons open and the sleeves rolled. He had sunglasses on, even though it was already dark outside.

"She'll accept that a reporter can't spell, but your punctuation…" With that, Ken drained his third beer. "She's obsessed with commas. Watch your commas."

Fred nodded, noting the empty glass more than the advice. He signalled the bartender for another. Considering his finances, he figured he may as well cut to the chase.

"I hope you won't hold it against me that Muriel offered me Amanda's series."

"No," Ken smiled. "Muriel and I go back a long way. She has a good reason for everything and a sixth sense about people. I don't often question her judgment. My main beat is city hall and provincial politics, more than enough to keep me busy. We also share the editorial."

"Good to know. By the way, I first heard of the Chilcotin from my grandpa when I was a kid in Georgia. Now I'm seeing it spelled with a 'T'. I should get it right."

"Yeah. Pronounced by the Indigenous people, it's 'Tch-co-*teen*' and spelled with the 'T'. 'Chilcotin' is the whites' pronunciation, spelled with a 'C'. Use the 'T' spelling for the tribe, 'C' for the land. She might not care much about spelling, but you should know stuff like that."

Fred nodded thoughtfully, then drained his beer. He signalled for refills, slapping a twenty-dollar bill on the table.

"Who's this Regina?" he asked.

Ken doubled over laughing.

"She just bought the next round," he replied, pointing to the portrait of the Queen on the banknote.

Fred laughed along with Ken. Still, he wondered how many beers it would take for Ken to fill him in on the basics of a Canadian court case.

The next morning, Fred forced himself to focus on the court rather than his hangover.

He was covering a plea on a charge of assault with a weapon arising out of a shooting in Anahim Lake. He had covered lower court cases in Georgia and presumed little public interest in this case, especially as the RCMP corporal he'd phoned had said the injury was minimal. This hearing being a routine legal matter, he hadn't expected a courtroom already full when he arrived at ten a.m. He had a good look at the crowd from the seats reserved for reporters. They were mostly First Nation people, but seemed to have divided themselves into two groups.

The case was called: *Regina v. Clint Lalula*. An Aboriginal youth walked into the prisoner's box. Fred scrawled a description: "slight, wiry, dark skin, straight black hair". Clint turned and looked directly at Fred, the unfamiliar face in the room. Fred smiled at him. The boy's dark, expressive eyes seemed to take his measure.

Presiding Provincial Court Judge David Hardy, known for his practical approach to justice, walked into the courtroom and counsel stood. Clint wasn't sure whether or not to stand until Mary motioned him up. Fred made a note of that.

"Mary Kent for Mr. Lalula, Your Honour."

"Timothy Sanders for the Crown, Your Honour."

The clerk read the charge.

"Clint Lalula, you are charged under section 267 (b) of the Criminal Code with assault with a weapon in that on November fifteenth, you shot Norman Twoshoes in the foot with a rifle. How do you wish to plead? Guilty or not guilty?"

"Not guilty, Your Honour," Clint loudly affirmed.

The strong tone of the young man's voice made His Honour take a closer look at the accused.

"What are the particulars, Mr. Sanders?" the judge asked.

"An altercation between two young men occurred on November fifteenth at Anahim Lake, Your Honour. There is bad blood between two families, the Twoshoes and the Hanlons. Two young men representing each side of the divide, Jeremy Hawthorne and Norman Twoshoes, had a physical fight. Later in the day, outside the local hotel, they met again to settle unfinished business. This time, there were reinforcements and guns. Clint Lalula, the accused, shot Norman Twoshoes in the foot. Fortunately, Corporal Wilson of the RCMP came on the scene and prevented any further hostilities."

Fred was startled by the name 'Twoshoes'. Bull had mentioned 'two shoes' in the library. So, it was a person's name, not a description of footwear. He scrawled a note in the margin of his notepad and circled it.

The gallery was anything but quiet. As the prosecutor spoke, the sides supporting each young man glared at each other and muttered throughout the summation. The judge looked up from his notes and spoke to the gallery.

"Please, folks, this is a courtroom, not a bingo hall. Please, no talking."

The crowd settled, now glaring at each other quietly.

"Ms. Kent," the judge asked, "how does your client elect to be tried? By judge alone or by judge and jury?"

"My client wishes to be tried by judge alone in the provincial court."

"Very well. What dates are available?"

After consulting their calendars, they settled on April 30th at Anahim Lake.

Bail was set on Clint's own recognizance and on condition he be denied the use of firearms, unless hunting while supervised by an adult family member.

"From what I've heard," the judge cautioned the gallery's two factions, "these young men are caught up in a feud. You must sort out your differences peacefully or instead of charges there will be funerals. It's up to the elders to settle these disputes."

"Order in court," the clerk called.

Everyone stood as the judge left the courtroom. Fred noticed a group of spectators surrounding Clint as he stepped down from the prisoner's box. He assumed they were the young man's family. He walked up to Mary.

"Ms. Kent? I'm Stone Clearwater with the *Tribune.* I understand that you are Clint's aunt. Will you be taking the trial?"

"I don't intend to. We hired a QC from Vancouver, Terry Laliberté." She smiled warmly, adding, "You must be new to the *Tribune.*"

"Yes," Fred nodded. "This is my first assignment. Tell me, are these people family?"

With his hand, he indicated the group of people surrounding Clint.

"Yes. They're Clint's grandfather and grandmother, Noah and Justine Hanlon, and my sister Elizabeth Henry, Clint's mother. Excuse me, I have to speak to my client."

Fred was scribbling furiously. It never occurred to him that a lawyer could represent a relative in a criminal trial. Nor would he have connected the accused to the painter whose work he'd seen in the *Tribune* office — Muriel was trusting him with a more relevant case than he'd thought. He noted that Justine looked very pale and drawn, but nonetheless she was there with her arm around her grandson. And what was a 'QC'? Would he have to go drinking again with Ken to find out? His head throbbed.

"I'd like to get a statement from Clint," he told Mary.

"No. He has pleaded not guilty to the charge. I've told him not to speak to the press. That goes for my parents too."

"Thank you. One last question: what's a 'QC'?"

"A Queen's Counsel," she replied, eyeing him carefully. "A distinguished senior lawyer expert in his field. In this case, criminal law."

He thought it ominous that his first contact with the people he had come to the Chilcotin to see was through a trial for a criminal charge. He would have to meet Noah some other day.

Canadian Whiskey

Fred filed his story and Muriel read his final draft with him in her office. There hadn't been much in the courtroom to cover, except the names of all the family members. He included in his story the continued hostility between the two factions outside the courtroom where, ignoring the advice of the judge, they jostled and gibed at each other on the way outside and into the parking lot. Muriel told him she liked that he didn't leave before the story did. He didn't say that he'd first heard the name Twoshoes in the library at Copper Beech.

"Clearwater, I couldn't find a punctuation error in your piece," she noted. "You were probably warned that I'm a comma Nazi. Oh, and watch the American spellings. In Canada, we spell 'defence' with a 'c'. Otherwise, your article is fine. It's gone to press."

In the weeks leading up to Christmas, Fred worked hard at establishing himself as reliable. He helped when needed on circulation and advertising, came in sober and promptly, and showed a talent for telling a good story. In December, Muriel rewarded him with the series on Chilcotin notables.

On his way to his motel from Ginty's Bar one night, he noticed Muriel's light was on in her office. He let himself in to the main office and knocked on her door. She was alone with a bottle of rye and a cigar. Fred couldn't help thinking she was one of the last of a breed in this digital age.

"Come on in, Clearwater. Would you like some rye to go with that name?"

She was jovial, not drunk, as she half-filled a water glass with Canadian rye whiskey, a liquor that Fred had yet to acquire a taste for but wasn't about to turn down.

"Thanks, Muriel. Bottoms up!"

He took a swig.

"Don't suppose you'd like a cigar?"

"One in the room is enough for me, thanks."

"Figures, but I don't have any pot for you. Keep quiet about it, though. I know it's against the law, but one after-hours stogie once in a while…" She took a puff on her cigar with genuine enjoyment and switched from her bantering tone. "You know, Clearwater, I checked you out. You are what you say you are, but for some reason, you gave up your connection with the *Atlanta Herald.* Two months later, you show up broke on my doorstep, willing to live on the scraps from my table. I have to ask myself why?"

"How about a broken heart? Or maybe a chance to see my dad's world before I get serious about earning a living?"

"How about you're onto a story and you won't tell old Muriel what it is."

"If I am, as you say, 'onto a story', you'll be the first to know if I find it. You've been damn good to me."

"It's a deal, then. Let's drink to it."

They clinked glasses and drank.

"Now that all that sentimental crap is over," Muriel fixed him with her gaze, "what did you come to see me about?"

"I saw Noah Hanlon at the Lalula hearing. I couldn't speak to him there. His daughter Mary said not to. I want to go out to Tatlayoko Lake and interview him for the series."

It was past time for Fred to follow up on his hunch. Interviewing Hanlon would get him out into the far reaches of the Chilcotin where he could investigate.

"It's not a good time for that. I'd like you to do your first interview with Robin Redford."

"The Robin Redford who sang 'Backroad Nights'?" Fred asked, stunned.

"You know her?"

"Hey, I'm from the South. I know my country classics. Used to play that album all the time. She should've had more hits from that alone. Didn't know she was Canadian though."

"Don't make me have second thoughts," Muriel cautioned him. "Her husband Vlad Volk's a recluse. I figure they would open up to a Georgia boy who wouldn't likely screw up a country music story. How about it?"

"Definitely," Fred answered. "Could you give me a bit of background about Volk?"

"Vlad was shot, and Noah Hanlon stopped the bleeding. Saved his life. An ambulance arrived and the paramedics gave Vlad a blood transfusion. It was a life and death thing. He had every reason to go back to Vancouver where he would get better care, but he stayed. I covered the story. Along with everyone else, I thought that after Vlad was discharged from the hospital, he would cut his losses and move back to the coast. But the community misjudged him. He stayed, began ranching his property on the Chilcotin River and married Robin. Vlad and Noah never spoke to each other after Noah saved his life."

"That's a long time to hold a grudge," Fred volunteered, thinking that old Muriel was leaving a scented trail for him.

"And you know it's a long time because it must've been a long time ago that I was a cub reporter, right?"

"Uh…"

Fred searched for something to say, but Muriel saved him.

"And you'd be right." She raised her glass. "And I'd much rather you be right than polite. So don't fret about calling me old. I am and I don't have time for any reporter who can't see that."

"Okay, then," Fred laughed, raising his glass in return. "So the grudge has been going for a long time."

"That's for damn sure, but feelings ran deep. The Chilcotin country changes people, sort of stamps them with a sceptic's view of the world."

Gang of Three

T he snow was higher than you'd expect only a week into December.

Brent used the plow on the tractor to clear the long driveway from the ranch house to the main road. He looked up with a satisfied grin when he finished and waved to the crew cab pick-up with Noah at the wheel, Justine in the passenger seat and Elizabeth in the back seat. They were heading off on their early morning journey to Kamloops to speak to Justine's oncologist about how she was responding to her treatments.

Justine was in a happy and talkative mood. She called her troop the 'gang of three', remarking how they were off on an exploratory expedition, even if it was the same one they'd been making for eight weeks. Noah tried to follow the banter as Elizabeth and Justine talked about him.

"Lizzy," Justine asked, "if you were to describe your father in one word, what would that word be?"

"'Scout'," came her quick response.

"Like your horse? How so?"

"You know he's always thinking ahead, planning the next turn in the road or for the next pitfall. On trail rides, he's always in the lead. On road trips, he knows the direction. Now it's your turn. Pick a word for Dad."

"'Sentinel'. Because at night, he is always alert to the slightest sound. Like when you were in your teens coming home after your curfew."

Noah laughed.

"How would you describe yourself, Dad?" Elizabeth teased.

"Well," he drawled, "I would say 'delightfully charming'."

"That's two words."

They arrived in Kamloops from the west on the Trans-Canada Highway. Noah drove past the turnoff and travelled for three miles beyond. Elizabeth looked up from a book she had been reading,

"Dad, remember, we're going to the hospital."

"Yes, of course. I was thinking of something else."

"Some scout," Justine shook her head. "You know, your father is getting absentminded."

In her office, the oncologist looked serious.

"The chemotherapy treatment hasn't been effective in controlling the cancer and it's spreading. Radiation is a possible further treatment."

"No."

Justine was adamant. Noah was silent and Elizabeth bit her lower lip. Both of them looked at her, the same thought forming.

"I want to spend the last days at Tatlayoko with my family," she said, answering their unspoken question.

She reached out to Noah and Elizabeth and held their hands.

"We can control the pain with morphine," the doctor offered, her voice filled with compassion.

Noah looked down at Justine's hand clasped in his. He had no Aboriginal herbal substitute for that powerful a pain medicine. They rose to go.

"Thank you, Jill," Noah said softly. "We appreciate all your help."

Backroad Nights

For the first time since arriving in Williams Lake, Fred was driving west across the Fraser River over the Sheep Creek Bridge. He was heading into the Chilcotin, another step towards finding the truth behind Bull and Billy Joe's conversation. His directions said that the Volk turnoff was a mile past the Larson Lake exit. He drove past a patch of prairie where, in the distance, smoke rose from the chimneys of the Toosey Reserve. He turned off the highway and, within a quarter-mile, came up to the ranch house.

Fred was excited to be knocking on the door of Robin Redford, one of his teenage heroes. He had spoken with her by phone to make arrangements and she still had that raspy voice he knew so well. The door was opened by a wisp of a woman with long blonde hair and crinkly eyes.

"How you doing, Stone?" she asked warmly.

"I'm doing fine, Robin," he grinned. "Now that I've met my high school heartthrob."

She let out a hearty guffaw and they shared a quick embrace.

She showed him around her house, in particular the sound studio. They settled in her living room, which overlooked the Chilcotin River. He asked her about her early years.

"My ma and pa were itinerant log-house builders. Just like robins: building a house every spring."

"Is that why they called you 'Robin'?"

"Nah, they called me that because I chirped a lot. Redford is a stage name. I don't suppose your mother named you Stone Clearwater."

Fred raised an eyebrow. He decided that there was no point in covering well-trod ground. Or being trod on.

"Muriel filled me in on your husband. I understand he's quite reclusive and I might not be able to speak to him."

"Yes, he likes his privacy. The important thing for you to know is that I wouldn't have gotten a hit without his support. He financed my career and opened a lot of doors for me in Memphis."

"I'd like to meet him."

"Well, there he is with our son, Noah." She pointed out the window into the field. "Driving that tractor. They're feeding his prize herd of black angus."

Stone couldn't hide his surprise on hearing their son's name. He looked out on the pasture, watching as the hay-cutting machine cut up the bales and laid them out in furrows for the feeding cows.

Robin picked up on his interest.

"That gives you some idea how much we are indebted to Noah."

Robin served tea. They talked about music and her career for a few hours. Fred was about to pack up his tape recorder when Vlad came into the house. Robin excused herself. She was away for a few minutes and returned with a weathered white-haired man smartly dressed in ironed jeans, a white starched shirt and a brown houndstooth jacket. He put out his hand.

"I'm Vladimir Volk. Glad to meet you."

"Nice to meet you, sir. Your wife and I have had a good talk. I'm looking forward to writing up her story."

"Yes, she told me. I look forward to reading it. She tells me you're also going to do a story on Noah Hanlon."

"I hope to. Maybe we could talk some more later. About Noah, but you'd also make a good subject for the series."

"Please let him know that Robin and I are thinking of him and Justine, praying that she will get better," Vlad replied, ignoring the comment. "I'd tell him myself, but I just remind Noah of some bad times and wouldn't want to upset him. Especially now."

A Famous Person

In late December, Noah's phone rang.

"Mr. Hanlon," an unfamiliar voice said, "my name is Stone Clearwater. I'm a reporter from the *Williams Lake Tribune*."

"Why are you phoning me now?"

Noah's voice was strained.

"We're doing a series," the voice on the phone replied uncertainly, "on famous people of the Chilcotin. I'd like to come out to your ranch and interview you."

"I'm not a famous person. Thank you for the call."

He put down the receiver and turned to Justine.

"What was that about? Another award?"

"No, just a reporter who wanted to interview me," he said with some disdain. "The *Tribune*."

"You should speak to the reporter," Justine frowned. "It's important to us and to our nation that your paintings be honoured."

"Well, you talked me into accepting one award. I figure that's enough."

"This is the local paper," she protested. "You should support them."

Noah left it at that. He didn't get back to Stone.

Goodbye

The day after New Year's, the whole of Noah and Justine's family — five children and ten grandchildren — gathered in the ranch house at Tatlayoko Lake to each in their turn say their goodbyes to Justine.

When Elizabeth went into the library, her mother had a special request for her.

"Dear, look after your father. He's getting very absentminded."

"I promise, Mum."

Elizabeth tried not to cry, but couldn't stop the tears welling in her eyes.

When Mary approached her bedside, Justine, too weak to say much, said everything between them in her serene expression.

"Thank you," Mary softly said to her stepmother, "for being there for me when my mother died. For loving me as your own."

"You were," Justine whispered, squeezing Mary's hand. "I only wish I had known it sooner."

Mary left the room at peace. It was a gift that Justine was able to bestow even this close to the end.

When it was the boys' turn, they went together. As the oldest, Brent stood by the head of her bed. Will and Joel lined up beside him.

"Mother," Brent said, speaking for them all, "your three boys…"

Brent had had to be strong more than the others, living next door. He faltered, a tear running down his cheek, but with a smile. His eyes dropped, unable to say more.

"Your boys are here to wish you goodbye, Mother," Will jumped in, placing his hands on his brothers' backs.

Brent leaned down to his mother's forehead and kissed it, then stepped back. Will did likewise, then Joel.

"I will plant a tree, Mother," Joel assured her.

Justine smiled.

Justine died with no regrets while holding Noah's hand.

Coming Together

Among the Tŝilhqot'in, the funeral of an elder brings the nation together.

Justine was an elder that all six bands had honoured and they were all present in the great room at the ranch on this early January day. The Twoshoes family were there, headed by their matriarch, Sara, and her son, Ray. Clint and Jeremy kept at a safe distance, but Norman couldn't resist needling Clint.

"You're going down for ten years on that assault charge," he said.

"I don't think so," Clint answered coolly.

He grinned at his adversary and winked at Norman's cousin Bonny, who was standing nearby. She turned away quickly.

"Lay off it, boys," Mary jumped in.

Will had come up from Vancouver, Joel from Kamloops, Mary and Elizabeth from Williams Lake. After lunch, Brent organized the close family to dig their mother's grave by hand. All took part, including the grandchildren. When they had finished, Noah walked up and stood looking at their work. They waited for him to say something.

"Yeah, it looks big enough," he said in a whisper. "You know Justine's brother, Peter, was my best friend. He's lying next to Justine on her left. I want to lie beside Justine on her right."

Alice winced at the thought. Noticing, Will couldn't leave it at that.

"You'll have to live with us a while yet, Dad."

"Your mother kept you boys and girls in line. I'll probably spoil you if I'm around much longer," Noah said.

He looked over his gathered family, overwhelmed with pride.

"No fear of that, Dad," Elizabeth quickly replied. "You'll live a long time and be just as ornery as ever."

She and Alice walked over to where Noah was standing, hat in hand, and both hugged him.

The great room was full, the crowd spilling into the dining room and entry hall. The surroundings and the ceremony overwhelmed Noah as Justine was honoured and her spirit commended to the Creator. Justine's children recalled her life in anecdotes. Clint remembered her quiet determination and love of family in a poem he had written. Noah was deep in thought throughout the ceremony.

At the graveside, the members of the family each placed a shovelful of dirt on Justine's coffin. Alice added a friendship bracelet she had braided.

Noah made a point at the reception afterwards to thank each of the mourners for attending. Muriel was there with Ken Lamb to pay their respects. She pulled Noah aside for a quick word.

"Elizabeth told me that you got a call from my new reporter, Stone Clearwater, about an interview. I'm sorry. I told him it's the wrong time. He's a keener. He saw your painting in our office and wanted to speak to you."

"Maybe I'll speak to him later."

Noah looked around for Vlad and Robin, who he'd seen at the service, but they'd left before the reception. He went upstairs and took to his bed with a cough.

In the morning, Noah had a raging fever and was delirious. Dr. Rogers diagnosed severe pneumonia and made arrangements for Noah to be transported to the hospital. Elizabeth refused. She knew how much her father disliked hospitals. Instead, she hired a nurse and took time off from work for the first week of his illness. It was she who insisted he set up his bed in the library, where Justine had spent her last days. She was beginning to think of it as an infirmary.

After a week, Noah wasn't better, so Elizabeth rallied the other children to alternate spending time with their father. She had promised her mother she would look after her dad and was determined not to lose him. After a month, Dr. Rogers declared him cured, but the declaration seemed empty.

Noah would remain in a depressed state for months following Justine's death.

Real Estate

Over Christmas, away from his family and the woman that he loved, Fred had spent the days feeling sorry for himself. He hadn't been sleeping, and when he did, he had nightmares featuring O'Connor. He'd gotten a copy of *The Secret Agent* from the Williams Lake Library and read it. It was foreboding, reminding him of the perfidy of man, in particular Bull O'Connor.

Fred and Harriet exchanged loving texts. Her texts were from all over the US as she accompanied Billy Joe on his campaign. They were gearing up for the first primaries in Iowa on February 1st and she had very few spare minutes to think of him.

In the new year, Stone Clearwater was taking over Fred's life.

He began making inquiries about the Northrop Green Trust and Northrop Oil buying up ranchland that came up for sale. He connected with Reg Bragg from Parson's Realty, a long-time Williams Lake real estate agent who dealt almost exclusively with ranchland. Fred told him that his family back east was interested in buying a place. He'd created social media accounts with a pictureless profile to support his backstory but keep him pretty nondescript. Reg had some quarter-sections of land for sale to show him.

"What do you want to do on the land?" Reg asked.

"Maybe I'm looking to subdivide it into smaller parcels."

"You can't. In BC, the Agricultural Land Protection Act prohibits subdividing farmland."

"What about logging?"

"Sure, but trees grow slow in this country. If you don't hobby farm, you could lease it to a local farmer."

"You know, Reg, and this I want you to keep between us, my family are interested in buying a big cattle ranch on the scale of the Gang Ranch. We could put up some serious cash if you could find us a property."

"Heh, heh. Well, sonny, the market for them ranches is pretty tight."

"Are there any ranchers out there who are thinking of selling?"

"There may be, but I can't represent you as I would be in conflict."

"Oh, who are you representing?"

"Can't say."

Through January and February, Fred saw every agent in Williams Lake and all but one gave him the same answer. Over coffee in the New World Tea and Coffee Shop, Kathy Jenkins, an independent agent, filled him in on what was happening.

"If a large acreage comes up, Bragg and his friends make a bid that the seller can't refuse. Some deep pockets in the States behind that, if you ask me."

It seemed that the Chilcotin was experiencing a real-estate boom with buyers out there ready to outbid each other to raise cattle. Cattle prices were high, no doubt, but were they *that* high?

Oiling the Message

I owa was called a triumph for Billy Joe by the press.

It was a vindication of Bull's political strategy. He had found the path to the sweet spot in the Republican electoral process: a politically oppressed, mad at politicians but actively voting, protectionist right wing. With every press release Bull wrote, with every talking point he came up with, the poll numbers had increased. When Bull had Billy Joe announce he'd ban all Muslims from entering America, his lead over his nearest opponent had doubled. No one pointed out that Lincoln had talked about freedom and equality for everyone in the Gettysburg address which Bull was so fond of quoting.

The New Hampshire primary was even more convincing. Billy Joe's numbers were surprisingly good for a hard-right candidate in a northern state.

There was little time for celebration as the 'Northrop for President' campaign team began planning for South Carolina and then Nevada while gearing up for Super Tuesday. Bull spent sixteen-hour days in his war room, on his phone to people in those eleven states, texting, emailing and tweeting, or in his words 'oiling the message'. The message being hate the government, love the gun and protect our borders, a message that Bull not only had Billy Joe foment, but one that Bull believed in.

Harriet was busy working the phones and press herself, much more visibly. On the ground in South Carolina and Nevada, she was planning their next stops as they led up to March 1st. The campaign chief in Georgia noted that Harriet had told him she'd gone to school there three times. She was on the hustings with her father in his private jet twenty-four/seven.

Bull, meanwhile, had the mansion mostly to himself. Bull thought his strategy of pairing father and daughter was not only brilliant for voter appeal, but also would get her out of his metaphorical hair. He didn't trust Harriet in the first place, but now her boyfriend was the viper in their camp. Canada was a fitting place for him, a haven for pot smokers and bleeding-heart liberals. Harriet still believed he was writing a novel in Wyoming.

Which meant he only had to tell her the truth to end the relationship.

Trading Stories

F red set up a map of the Chilcotin in his motel room and invited Ken over for a beer. The senior reporter on the *Tribune* had become a close friend.

He cracked a Moosehead and handed it to Ken.

"So you want to follow the results, I presume?" Ken asked, opening up his laptop.

"What?" Fred asked, stunned. "What results?"

Ken raised an eyebrow instead of his glass for once.

"Super Tuesday," he said, half a question. "The Republican primary. Georgia."

"Oh. Right."

Fred couldn't believe he'd forgotten about it.

"I've been busy with other things. I forgot. Yeah, let's check it out."

They checked out results and traded links when they found some interesting video. Ken went to grab another beer anytime he figured Fred was too caught up in the news. If he'd stayed and paid attention, he might have noticed Harriet on the screen each time it happened.

104

Once Georgia went to Billy Joe, they turned to other topics.

"Muriel is old school," Fred remarked.

"Stone, you have no idea of how old. Muriel was taught by Ma Murray of the *Bridge River–Lillooet News*, a legend in BC. Ma died in 1992 at the age of ninety-four."

"How old *is* Muriel?" Fred asked.

"She's getting on. The highlight of Muriel's life was when she won the Ma Murray BC Community Newspaper Association award for excellence two years ago."

"Well, good on the old bat."

"So far, you haven't got on the wrong side of her."

"Thanks. I don't get much feedback from her."

"You won't until you screw up."

Ken saw Fred wasn't laughing. He'd been down ever since Billy Joe started winning state after state.

"Hey," he ventured, "I just read your piece on George Robinson and the widening of the Chilcotin Highway. I liked where you quoted that article about his great-grandfather."

"Yeah, I got that from the archives. He was the superintendent in charge of the stretch between Alexis Creek and Anahim Lake when it was a dirt track."

"What are you working on for the series?"

"For March, I interviewed a lesbian bronc rider. She was on the circuit competing and winning against men. She not only won in the corral, she also competed in the bars. Stole her male friends' girlfriends. I'm hoping to interview Noah Hanlon for April. What about you?"

"I'm writing a retrospective of the *Roger William* Supreme Court decision. I wrote the original story. That's when I interviewed Noah Hanlon."

"Hmm. Does that have anything to do with the name of the city?"

"Williams Lake was named after Chief William of the Shuswap Nation. Roger William from the case is a chief of the Tŝilhqot'in

Nation. You know, one of the biggest property owners in the Chilcotin is the Tŝilhqot'in First Nation?"

"Really?"

The Indigenous peoples hadn't figured into Fred's thinking about the land. In the US, in particular Georgia, it was the blacks who seemed to cloud the profit picture and they were land-poor. He had assumed the same held true for the Native people here.

"How's that?" he asked Ken.

"After a long court battle, the Tŝilhqot'in won certain rights to a large chunk of land in the area around Brittany Triangle and Potato Mountain."

"Do they run cattle on it?"

"Some, but this is their traditional hunting and fishing ground, the same land that sustained them for centuries before Europeans came on the scene."

"Show me on the map where it is."

Ken Googled the Supreme Court case and showed Fred the map at the end of the decision.

"The Aboriginal title land is nineteen-hundred square kilometres. That's the size of Tokyo or London. Bigger than Metro Vancouver."

"Do you think the First Nations would be willing to sell?"

"You're kidding. This land is owned in trust by their people to be passed on to generations yet to be born."

"Would they allow cattlemen to lease the land?"

"Some of the land's under lease."

"Would they allow logging?"

"The *William* case came out of a logging dispute."

Fred nodded. Ken smiled at having distracted him from the primary results.

"What about mining or drilling for gas?"

It was the only really important question Fred had.

"Mining," Ken mused. "Ah, there's an application for mining near Fish Lake. They're opposing it. There's no oil or gas in the region. But the Ministry of Energy and Mines register shows a large number of mineral claims staked in the area of Potato Mountain, Tatlayoko Lake and Chilko Lake. Come to think of it, a lot of those old ranches have titles from the province that include subsurface rights."

From what Bull had told Billy Joe in the library at Copper Beech, Fred figured that those numbered companies were all owned by Northrop Oil or some subsidiary. He had to contact Noah about the seismic tests, but Noah was seriously ill. He didn't know if there was time to wait until Noah recovered. Or if he would.

Sparrows' Song

Still in the library a few months after his brush with death, Noah reoriented himself with the printed word. He started sampling and discovered that the books gave him, a man who had ranched and painted his whole life, new tastes of what others thought about living. His adoptive mother Belle and her third husband Stan Hewitt had been the readers — it had been their library, filled with the classics. His library had been the land, the plants and the animals on the Chilcotin plateau.

Had he been healthier, he would have gone to Antoine's cave. There, he would have fasted, sought visions and divined what the ravens said of the Tŝilhqot'in Nation's future. Convalescing and recovering from both pneumonia and depression, he wrestled with the written words and reasonings of others. In his life, he had sought ways to express his connection to the silent and timeless through painting. As *deyen*, he told his stories orally, to be passed down to his children and the nation. Well into the third month of his slow recovery, with these ideas stirring his brain, he began considering the question.

Who would he name as the next *deyen*?

The sparrows were chirping in the bushes outside his 'cave', as he called his recovery room. The sparrows were a sign from Ta Chi, chiding him for feeling sorry for himself. She wouldn't have lain in bed with dark thoughts, she would have gotten up, gone onto the land and let its powers cure her sickness.

The telephone rang and Noah picked it up.

"Hello, Mr. Hanlon. This is Stone Clearwater of the *Tribune*. I was very sorry to read about the death of your wife, Justine."

"Thank you," Noah replied hesitantly.

"By all accounts, she was a remarkable woman."

"Yes, yes she was. She was an elder. What did you say your name was?"

"Stone Clearwater, sir. I'm a reporter with the *Tribune*. I phoned you last year. I'm writing articles on famous Chilcotin people."

"You don't say," Noah replied. "Why are you phoning me?"

"You *are* a famous person, Mr. Hanlon. I would like to interview you if I could."

If Noah hadn't heard the sparrows' song, he would've said no, but Ta Chi was telling him to get on with his life. And Justine was always telling him that he should be getting more attention for his painting. She'd told him he should speak with the reporter.

"Come along Saturday morning before lunch," he said.

He went to the calendar on the wall and circled the date.

The Interview

Noah shuffled to the kitchen to make breakfast for himself and Joel. When Joel came down later, he was surprised to see his father there.

"Hey, old man. I smelled coffee, but I thought it was Carol being nice. Then I remembered she took the twins to kindergarten. You should be in bed. You aren't out of the woods yet."

"I'm not dead yet, either. I've got an urge to paint."

"The doctor says to take it easy."

"Doctor? Hmm. He can treat only part of me. The rest is up to the Creator."

"I'll catch hell from Elizabeth for letting you get up without the doctor's say-so."

"I'm expecting a reporter from the *Tribune*. I won't let him see me laid up in bed. Besides, I want to paint."

"Have it your own way."

"You sound just like your mother."

Joel got up from the table and refilled Noah's coffee.

110

"You never told anyone you were being interviewed by a reporter," he said in a puzzled, questioning voice.

"I don't have to get your permission," Noah replied in a hurt tone.

"No, but you have been laid up for close to four months and suddenly you act like Lazarus."

They finished their breakfast in silence. Joel cleaned up while his dad had a third cup of coffee.

"I think I'll check on my experiment on Potato Mountain," Joel said. "Probably won't be back till after supper. Elizabeth is coming this afternoon for the weekend. Take it easy."

Noah sat by himself at the kitchen table, listening intently.

"Hell, Justine," he said to the air, "that's the second time the boy said to take it easy."

"Our boy is forty-six. You shouldn't quarrel with Joel," she answered in her always calm voice.

"The boy is getting on my nerves. Treating me like an invalid," he replied, annoyed.

"I'm glad you're on your feet and talking about painting. The time for grieving is over. You have your work and your family to care for. I'll be with you."

This appeased him.

Later, he sat on the porch soaking up the sun, feeling it warm his chest and breathing the spring air into his lungs. His thoughts were of his family and just as warm. His children had rallied around him and nursed him through his sickness. He could thank Justine for that. She was all about family while he had his head in the clouds thinking more about his painting than his relationships. He wanted to do something to honour Justine's memory.

On the drive west to Tatlayoko Lake to interview Noah, Fred went over it all in his mind again.

Was it investigative journalism or fear that had brought him here from Atlanta? Probably both. Why had he become a reporter for the *Williams Lake Tribune*? It sure wasn't the money. The question was what exactly had driven him out of Georgia in the first place. He had continually thought in quiet moments about that time back in September when he'd left, but his recounting of that day was detailed and accurate only up to a certain point. Past there, his mind still refused to go.

Fred was jolted from his reverie on noticing that his gas tank was registering empty, with a ways still to go to the Hanlon ranch. He stopped at Tatla Lake to gas up at the West Chilcotin Trading Company store and station.

He'd worn a shirt with the sleeves rolled up and a loose tie over it, with sunglasses to complete the look. The effect was calculated, mirroring what he'd thought was the look of a Chilcotin reporter, a Ken Lamb look, so that anyone would think that he belonged in this country. Even so, when he went to pay his bill, the clerk took him for a salesman and directed him to the owner in the office.

"Mrs. Graham's in the back if you want to see her."

He went on through, thinking that he might get a handle on Noah from the storekeeper. In the office, Betty Graham was staring at her computer and swearing under her breath when he appeared at her door.

"The people in the East," she said without looking up, "are so damn rude."

"I'm from the East and I agree."

"Sounds to me you're more from the South," she said, eyeballing him.

"Okay, but now I'm from Williams Lake. I'm Stone Clearwater, a reporter from the *Tribune*. Here to do a story on Noah Hanlon. Do you know Mr. Hanlon?"

"He's been a customer and friend of mine for the last thirty years."

"Do you mind if I ask you some questions about Noah?"

"Depends on the questions."

Fred took out his notebook and pencil.

"I want to know what sort of man Noah Hanlon is."

"He's a man who pays his bills on time," she replied.

Fred had noticed in the months that he had been in the Cariboo Chilcotin that the people were not given to verbosity.

"Is that all he means to you and to this community?"

"In this country, that says a lot about a person," she nodded. She seemed to reconsider her curt answer and added, "He's brought a lot of pride to our community through his paintings and his status as an elder. The Hanlons go back four generations on Noah's father's side. On his mother's, she's a Tŝilhqot'in back to time immemorial. His wife Justine died a few months ago. He's taking it hard. I haven't seen Noah since the funeral, but his family say he hasn't left the house."

Fred was scribbling away. *Betty suddenly caught a verbosity virus*, he thought.

"As much pride as, say, a star hockey player might?" he asked.

"You could say that."

"Thanks for your time, Ms. Graham."

"I'm Betty."

Back at Frederica's wheel, Fred attempted to resume his musings. In his recollection of what had happened at Billy Joe's plantation, he found it difficult to face the reason he left Georgia. He believed that, for some time now, he had been suffering from post-traumatic stress disorder. He put it out of his mind as he was too busy winding his way down the Homathko Valley toward Tatlayoko Lake, watching the land as he went. He would have plenty of time to explain to the world why he left. Now, he had to concentrate on interviewing Noah Hanlon. The Hanlons had helped his family back in the seventies. He had a hunch they would help him now in his investigations.

Fred slowed his Subaru on the gravel road near the unmarked entrance to a ranch he believed was the Hanlons' Bar 5. An Aboriginal man was rambling down the dirt road towards a barn in the distance. He looked up at Fred's car. Fred stopped and shouted through the open window.

"Hey, is there an artist living hereabouts?"

"Follow this road," the man shouted back. "You'll probably see an old man sitting on a porch dreaming of the Creator. He's an artist."

"How do you know what he's dreaming?"

"His art is pretty well all he thinks about. The Creator inspires him."

The man appeared to be a cowhand, by the way he dressed and walked. He was wearing what the locals call the 'Cariboo tuxedo': blue jeans and a blue denim shirt with a bandana tied about his neck. A brown Stetson topped his six-foot frame. From the exchange, Fred knew he had the opening sentence for his article. He stopped the car and scrawled quickly in his notebook before looking back up and taking in the scene.

"So this is Noah Hanlon's place," Fred murmured to himself, "I'm finally here in the country that Grandpa and Dad praised."

Fred drove up to the cowhand and got out of his car, notebook and tape recorder in hand. He held out his free hand.

"I'm Stone Clearwater from the *Tribune*," he said.

The cowhand took his hand in a gentle grip, looked him in the eye and nodded, then continued walking to the barn in silence.

"What should I call you?" Fred shouted after him.

"Joel," he said without looking back.

"I guess I won't get any more quotes from Joel," Fred muttered.

He got back into his car and drove toward the house.

Joel stopped to look at the herd. His brother Brent was a good rancher. The cows had pretty well calved out, except for some mistakes where the bull had got into a few late in the year. It would be another month before the cows would be put out onto the range. He carried on, his mind wandering to his mother and father.

Joel had always thought of Noah as an optimist. You could see that in his paintings — it was almost as if his landscapes were alive with movement and freshness — but he hadn't put brush to canvas since Justine took sick and died. Then his father had just crumpled. It had been pneumonia and then depression, but 'crumpled' best described the sickness. That's why he'd been surprised to see Noah up. He wouldn't have left the ranch without knowing that someone was around to keep an eye on his dad. Now that the reporter was here, he could go.

Joel entered the barn and began saddling his horse, Sugar. Since his mother's death, Joel's immediate concern had been his father's health, both physical and mental. He had taken some time off from his job at the university to nurse Noah through his sickness, along with his brothers and sister. Now that the old man was rallying, he had to pick up his botanical research.

Botany hadn't been Joel's first career choice. He'd wanted to be a veterinarian. Since his family was in ranching, being a vet had seemed a logical choice. By his second year at Cariboo College, the importance of understanding what cows ate had been brought home to him. Grasslands are a precious asset. The Chilcotin had grasslands. He'd approached the dean about his doubts around continuing on in animal husbandry, noting he was thinking of going into botany with an emphasis on grasslands. The dean had wanted him to stay the course. After his second year, he'd been flying to Williams Lake for the first time and looked down at a rare sight in a province known for mountains and trees. Spread out before his eyes were the meadows, lakes and pastures of the high plateau country, fringed with forests of fir and pine. But the pine was tinged with a deathly red from an infestation of pine beetles. This plague had been one of the early visible indicators of global warming. He'd made up his mind right there on the plane that his life's work would be to preserve this grassland.

Justine had met him at the Williams Lake airport.

"Mum, I'm not going to be a vet," he'd told her when they were driving down off the airport hill into town.

Justine had braked hard and pulled off the road.

"Oh, fuck," she'd said. "You're going to disappoint your granny. She and I want you to finish university."

Joel's grandmother Belle was a Scottish lady who had outlived three husbands. He probably wouldn't have made it this far without her financial support and certainly wouldn't make it further.

His mother had the patience of a nurse, the deep knowledge of an Aboriginal and the love of a mother for her son, so when she used profanity in his presence for the first time, it had shocked Joel.

"I'm not quitting," he'd countered. "I'm going to be a botanist."

"Have it your own way," Justine smiled.

Belle had been in her ninetieth year when she'd attended Joel's graduation from the master's program at the University of British Columbia, the halfway marker on his way to his doctorate.

By the time Joel reached the base of Potato Mountain, it was after lunch. Noah would be answering the reporter's questions. The reporter seemed awfully young to Joel and didn't have a Canadian accent. Joel wondered if he'd be able to get a story out of Noah.

Halfway up the mountain, Joel realized he should have left a note for Elizabeth to explain that he'd left Noah with the reporter. He probably should have questioned that young reporter more about the article. His experiment would have to wait. He turned Sugar around and headed back down, riding back to the ranch. It was getting on to suppertime when he arrived. The reporter's beat-up Subaru was still parked where he had left it six hours ago. Elizabeth's truck was parked beside it.

Elizabeth was ten years older than Joel. As a social worker, she acted as den mother to displaced Aboriginal youth. With nothing to occupy their days, many of them turned to petty crime, drugs and gang fights between the three nations: Carrier, Shushwap and Tŝilhqot'in.

The role was a natural one for her. She had also felt a responsibility for her siblings. Not that her concern had ever seemed to be appreciated. That hadn't prevented her from continuing to give them advice on how to live their lives. From time to time, she asked her brothers' families to take in her more troublesome clients in order to keep these young Aboriginal men and women out of prison. That they did, every time she asked, was the only hint she had that her concern for them hadn't gone unrecognized.

On her mother's death, Elizabeth had taken over Justine's role as head of the house, which included managing her father. She had wanted to stay at the ranch and would have, if the demands of her job as a shit-disturber and interface between the authorities and her young clients, while being a mother to three children, had not been so pressing. She'd had to leave her father's day-to-day care to Brent and Carol, with Joel relieving them when he could take some time off from his research. Will, a bachelor in Vancouver, wasn't as reliable.

She arrived at the ranch at lunchtime. There was no sign of Joel. A beat-up Subaru was parked in the yard.

"What's going on here?" she grumbled.

She got out of her truck and walked quickly to the back door, swinging it open.

"Dad, I'm here," she called out.

There was no response. She went into the library where she'd ordered Noah to stay.

"Damn that Joel. Dad shouldn't be up. And where *is* Joel?"

The sun shone directly on the front porch. Noah sat in an easy chair, a rug around his shoulders and a mug of coffee in his hand. Opposite him was a slight young man who couldn't have been more than twenty years old, yet looked wise. He had longish hair and a trim beard. His eyes were alert, inquisitive, blue, circled by thick-framed glasses. Elizabeth almost laughed at his owlish appearance.

"Who're you?" she demanded. "What are you doing getting my dad out of his sickbed?"

The young man stood up, ungainly, flustered.

"That's my daughter, Elizabeth," Noah said in a raspy voice, "She's the boss. Now Lizzie, before you run this boy out of the house, you should know his name's Rock and he's a reporter from the *Tribune*."

"Sorry, Rock, but Dad shouldn't be up. I'm going to get him to bed, then I'll find out why you're here."

"Ma'am, my name is Stone."

She nodded, then turned to Noah. She eased his frail frame out of the chair and escorted him into the den. He didn't protest. He was tired after his first day out of bed. Fred tried to help, but Elizabeth didn't give him the chance. In the den, Elizabeth tucked Noah into his bed and fussed over him. Fred stood at the door.

"We'll have a talk after my nap," Noah spoke past Elizabeth to Fred. "You stay overnight. We can talk some more tomorrow."

Fred followed Elizabeth into the kitchen. She looked around the large room. There were washed breakfast dishes piled on the sideboard and dirty lunch dishes in the sink.

"I see he made you lunch."

"I rustled up something for us."

"Did you see my brother?"

"No, but I did see a ranchhand headed for the barn."

"That would be Joel. How about explaining yourself?"

"As your dad said, I'm a reporter. I'm doing a story for the *Tribune* on your dad. It's part of a series we're doing on famous Chilcotin people."

"If he's not careful, he'll be a dead Chilcotin person. Then you can write his obit. You've been here a few hours. What have you talked about?"

"Justine."

She shook her head at his answer.

"What did he say about my mother?"

Fred looked at his notebook.

"Well, his exact words were that 'in the beliefs of the Tŝilhqot'in, who are part of the Athabasca Cree, the soul is not attached to any one part of a man's body — not his nose, not his heart, not his penis. And that goes for the woman's body too, except the vagina and the womb. That's where the soul resides in all humankind.'"

She raised her eyes in astonishment.

"Is this what you're going to write?"

"I haven't finished my interview."

"You'll stay the night," she ordered. "I'll tell you about my father."

While Noah was napping and Elizabeth was cleaning the kitchen, Fred had some time alone. He wandered down to the lake, sat on the shore and every once in a while skipped a stone into the lake as if casting a bit of himself onto the waters.

Last September, at the graduation ball, Harriet had been the only thing on Fred's mind. 'Chilcotin' had been only a word uttered by his father and grandpa.

The sun dipped behind the mountains at about four, bringing Fred back to the present and the shores of Tatlayoko Lake. He wasn't ready to face those ugly Copper Beech thoughts just yet. He stood, skipped another stone into the lake and walked back.

Vindication

Super Tuesday hadn't been everything Bull had hoped it would be, but it had been enough.

The party's backroom brass had rallied to try and stop Billy Joe, with some success. Massachusetts had gone to a different candidate, Minnesota to yet another and other states likewise split, but that split had still left Billy Joe in the lead. He'd taken Texas, Georgia and Tennessee, which left him well on the path to the presidency.

The rest of March and April had been the same power struggle: Billy Joe against all other contenders. A different candidate would rise here and there, but Billy Joe still led overall. The other candidates didn't stand a chance against Bull's weapons — in this battle, lies and deceptions were more powerful than bullets and guns.

The hope was to take the delegate count outright and avoid a contested convention, especially with the rumours of party brass looking to field a new candidate to gather up all the anti-Billy Joe vote, but the last crop of states for April wasn't cooperating.

California alone should be enough to take Billy Joe over the top, but now it looked like it would be a fight all the way to the end. The campaign would have to split its resources rather than focusing primarily on the Golden State. California would still be the jewel in the crown, but maybe not enough.

Bull would have to call in some favours.

Ray Twoshoes held the map up in front of the surveyors from Northern Drilling, pointing out the various features of the landscape. They needed his knowledge of the land, he told himself, so that they could drill in the best places. They assured him that the seismic testing to date in the Brittany Triangle and on Potato Mountain showed huge reserves of natural gas. They would require further seismic tests in the coming months to show where to drill.

This was good enough for Ray to go to the tribal council with positive news, but he cautioned the surveyors.

"Tell Mr. O'Connor that I'll get our tribal council to approve the next phase of seismic drilling. Don't start work until I give you the green light."

He was starting to speak their language.

"Bull won't like that. He wants to get started, like, yesterday."

Ray had the final word.

"He has to wait."

Bridging the Divide

Elizabeth was dealing with her own demons.

While Noah was napping and the reporter took a walk to the lake, she tried to assess just how much she should tell the young man about her father. She had followed Stone's series in the *Tribune* and it was well-written. Stone showed the human side of his subjects, with faults presented in a way that gave depth to a person.

Elizabeth considered the interview possibilities. Noah was Tŝilhqot'in, Stone was American from the South. What, if anything, did Stone know about their people?

Maybe, Elizabeth thought, *he shouldn't be writing about us at all. What angle would he use? I was so proud when Dad pinned the Order of BC on Mum. How can you express the feeling of an Aboriginal about our values unless you are one?*

Elizabeth understood that her father bridged the divide between two cultures. She could tell the reporter that Noah wasn't well enough to give an interview, but he had already spent a few hours with the old man and Noah had said he was anxious to tell him more. She decided she would speak to Stone to find out what else Noah had told him and that she would be present at the next interview.

Elizabeth was in the kitchen readying a roast chicken, when Joel returned from his ride. She fixed him with a steely look.

"Why did you leave Dad with that reporter?"

"He seemed harmless enough. And so what? Dad can speak for himself," Joel said in a flat voice.

"He shouldn't even be out of bed," she snapped back.

"That was his decision. I think it was a good one. It's a sign that he's getting better." Joel kept his cool under cross-examination.

"You were gone most of the day. What if something happened?" Joel threw up his hands.

"Elizabeth, Dad is not one of your gang members. You don't have to be his advocate and mother."

Noah wandered into the kitchen where the two of them stood toe-to-toe.

"My, my, look what the reporter stirred up. You two hornets just going at it. Reminds me of when you were young."

Noah had dinner in the dining room for the first time since his illness had struck. It was a relatively peaceful meal. Elizabeth politely questioned Fred about his background. She was familiar with men his age. Her clients ranged from their early teens to late twenties. She looked at most men through that lens, including her male partners. They were all liars. She smiled at Fred as he took a large bite of a chicken leg.

"You're a long way from home. Dad tells me you're from Georgia. What brings you to the Chilcotin?"

"My dad's family lived at Tatla Lake back in the early seventies. He told me so many stories about it that after I got my degree in journalism, I thought I would see for myself. I was lucky enough to land a job with the *Tribune*."

"If your dad's family lived in Tatla Lake in the early seventies, they would have known the Hanlons."

"Yeah, he did mention Noah. Although he was about eleven years old at the time, he helped my granddad with the haying at Eagle Lake."

"Dad," Elizabeth asked, "do you remember the Clearwater family?"

Noah was preoccupied with his own thoughts. The last time he sat there at the dining room table, Justine had been alive. He asked himself, *What would Justine say or do?*

"Justine would probably have remembered them," he answered.

Joel's mind had been on Potato Mountain. He should have checked his experimental plot. After all, Elizabeth was already fussing over Dad before he could get back. At the mention of his mother, though, his thoughts shifted.

"You were talking the other day," he ventured, "of painting a portrait of Mum. Why didn't you paint her while she was living?"

"I had the real Justine before me every day. I didn't need a substitute."

Elizabeth wasn't finished with her inquisition of Stone.

"Where'd you get your degree?"

"Georgia State University."

He answered confidently, forgetting that the school wouldn't know him as Stone if anyone tried checking his credentials. He was more focused on trying to get the interview he'd come all this way for. He wasn't here to be interviewed himself. He changed the subject.

"I was lucky to land this reporting job in Williams Lake. It's experience for my résumé."

Elizabeth relented then, as Noah seemed to have fallen into a trance.

"You all right, Dad?" she asked, worry in her tone.

Noah had been acting strangely since her mother's death.

124

He'd recovered from the pneumonia over two months ago, yet until today he had been bedridden. And he was always talking to Justine as if she was alive in the room. The doctor said that he was still grieving but that in time he would come to terms with his wife's death.

"Are you all right, Dad?" Elizabeth repeated herself.

"Uh-uh. I'm thinking about that portrait I'm going to paint of Justine."

Dessert was Noah's favourite, sopalali berries whipped into froth. Fred thought it a good time to raise the question that brought him to Tatlayoko.

"Mr. Hanlon," Fred asked, "a reporter at the *Tribune* is doing a story on the Green Trust. Are you familiar with that trust? It owns some property around Lonesome Lake. Is it involved in any lands around Tatlayoko?"

Noah didn't answer. His eyes were closed.

Joel noticed his father was tired. He took a closer look at Fred. Something had been puzzling him. Over the last year, the Green Trust had been actively buying up good farmland and then letting it go fallow. He would have welcomed a green belt, but this seemed to be without purpose and the cattlemen were getting restive at the lessening of their grazing range. Contacting the local Green Trust representative to find out what was in the works, Joel had been told the trustees were in the process of developing a plan. Maybe the reporter could offer a clue.

"Green Trust," he said thoughtfully. "They're buying up a lot of land in the Chilcotin. I haven't gotten any satisfactory reply about their plans. It's not like Ducks Unlimited. We know how they operate. They've been here since the fifties, buying up wetlands as habitats for migrating birds. They often work in conjunction with the Nature Trust of BC, which has a reserve in the Chilcotin marshes near Puntzi Lake. These trusts cooperate with the ranchers. Green Trust, I can't figure out."

"What's Ducks Unlimited all about?" Fred asked.

"It's a charity, an American hunters' group, which preserves wetlands for the sake of their sport. It does have the advantage of keeping the bird populations healthy."

"Thanks. I've got a lot to learn about this country."

There was a pause in the conversation. Joel couldn't figure out if Fred knew nothing or was hiding something.

"Do you run this ranch?" Fred asked Joel.

"My brother Brent does. I'm a botanist at Thompson Rivers University. You're here to talk to Dad about his life. I'd like to sit in."

"So would I," Elizabeth insisted.

"Now, I have something to say about that." Noah's eyes were closed, not his ears. "You'll know what we have talked about when you read this young man's article in the newspaper. Thanks for dinner, Elizabeth. He and I will have coffee in the great room."

He rose from his chair and walked carefully to the other room, motioning Fred to follow.

Once settled into his recliner, positioned facing the lawn with the lake in the distance, Noah gazed out at the Canada geese having returned from their winter in the States and shitting on his lawn again. In the background, the loon's call echoed in the mountains. Fred sat on a chair opposite the elder and took in the silence. He didn't interrupt the old man's thoughts but did wonder what he was thinking.

Noah's thoughts drifted back fifty-five years. Back then, he had burst into this very room through the double doors and confronted his dad, Bordy. They'd had words about Justine and fought. A rifle had spoken in the twilight that night. He'd had his first dance with Justine in this room, listened to Belle playing Beethoven on her Beckstein and celebrated many a birth and wedding here. Inevitably his thoughts clouded when he remembered that this was also where they had honoured Justine's life.

Fred looked around the room. It was immense, two storeys with a balcony around the second floor. There was a grand piano in the room. Fred went over to it and softly picked out a tune, Billy Joel's "Piano Man".

It was then that he saw in the half-light a mural of the Chilcotin spread all along one side of the room. Seeing that Noah was still lost in thought, he got up from the piano and took a closer look. It was centred on a great snowcapped mountain which seemed to radiate calm. Circled around this was a majestic landscape of lakes, hills, plains and peaks. Cutting through the landscape was something Fred assumed must be the Chilcotin River. Elizabeth came in with coffee as he was taking it in. She walked up beside him.

"Dad did the mural from sketches he made back when he and Ta Chi, my grandmother, were evading the law and traversing the Chilcotin. The original is in the museum in Victoria."

"The mountains seem human."

"Lendix'tcux, the half-man half-dog mythological transformer, changed himself and his three sons into Mount Ts'il?os soon after he performed the miracles. Dad is a deyen with the right to tell you the full story."

She set down the coffee.

"Dad has to be in bed in half an hour," she said, turning to leave the room. "If you're not finished, you can talk after breakfast tomorrow."

Fred was about to question Noah about his painting when the old man held up his hand.

"Tell me, son, why are you here?"

Fred had spent enough time earlier in the day with Noah to see that the elder's memory was slipping.

"I'm here," he explained slowly, "to interview you about your life as a significant artist who is renowned in the region and known to the outside world."

"Yes," Noah said, still watching the fading light on the lake. "But why did you come to the Chilcotin?"

"I wanted to experience what my father experienced back in the seventies when he lived in Tatla Lake."

"But what forced you out of the States?"

Noah turned and looked Fred in the eye while he waited for an answer. Fred was suddenly concerned. Sleepy, faltering, sick Noah had divined Fred's backstory.

"What makes you think that I was forced out of the US?"

"When you arrived, you asked about the Chilcotin. Not about the spirit of the land, more about the wealth. You know nothing of art or of painting or of our people. Your false interest was clear. At dinner tonight with my family, there was a chance to talk to them about me for your story. You asked instead about the Green Trust. The Green Trust is headquartered in Georgia. But more than any of these, which are as clear to me as a deer trail to Ta Chi, it was Justine who told me. She put me onto your track."

"But sir," Fred blurted out, "your wife is dead."

"Yes," Noah nodded. "Her human form is no more. Yet she is as alive to me now as when she lived. I think of her as away, preparing a place for me. She is continually on guard for our land and our people and speaks to me of dangers. Tomorrow, I will start to paint her portrait."

Fred was confused. Noah's mind seemed both insightful and clouded. He decided that honesty was the best road to where he needed to be with a *deyen* who had picked up on his hidden fears. He removed his mask and spoke to Noah the painter as Fred Scully the fugitive.

"My name is Fred Scully," he sighed. "My dad was Earl Scully."

"Yeah," Noah replied. "I remember the Scullys. They were good workers."

Fred noted that Noah's long-term memory seemed to be good.

"My girlfriend," he continued, "invited me to her father's house in Georgia. I didn't know that her father was Billy Joe Northrop. I overheard a conversation between him and Bull O'Connor, his political strategist. A politically damning conversation that involved the exploitation of the Chilcotin, among other things. Bull found out that I was eavesdropping and… threatened me. I decided to come here to see if I could find any proof of what I had overheard and expose the secret."

Noah nodded while Fred spoke, as if telling Fred to come clean.

"All right," Noah said, suddenly animated and alert, speaking in determined tones. "Our secrets are out. We are the living guardians of the Tŝilhqot'in standing beside Lendix'tcux and his three sons transformed into stone. My inspiration is Justine, yours is Justice."

He paused. Fred felt the silence was intentional and didn't dare break it.

"We shall speak more of this in the morning," Noah announced. "I feel like I'm rising from the dead. Like Odysseus returning home to Ithaca to reclaim Penelope. Yet maybe I'm just Don Quixote."

He rose. Fred followed suit.

"Sir," he ventured, "I would appreciate it if what I have told you about my true identity would remain between us for now. I'm still looking for proof. The reach of a Fortune 500 company is long and American politics are dangerous."

"Of course. Remind me of your name again, son. What was it that you told me?"

"In the morning, sir. In the morning."

Fred walked with Noah to the library. Noah chuckled to himself and turned to Fred as he was about to close the door and leave.

"I've been doing a lot of reading while I've been lying here feeling sorry for myself. Now is the time to kick out the Tŝilhqot'in's false suitors, mount Rocinante and charge windmills. Good night, Rock."

Fred closed the door quietly. Perhaps Noah had forgotten his name. His secret was more than safe.

Chasing Ideas

Fred went into the kitchen carrying the empty coffee cups he and Noah had spilled their thoughts into. Elizabeth lay in wait for him.

"How did you find Dad? Did he give you what you wanted for your story?"

Fred emptied the coffee dregs into the sink and rinsed them out.

"Yeah," he answered cautiously. "We made a start. We spoke mostly about your mother. And the portrait he wants to paint of her. From the way he spoke, it seemed like she was in the room."

She motioned for Fred to sit. While he fished in his pocket for a pen, she sat opposite him.

"Dad and Mum got along," she began. "She lived with his mistakes and he always let her ride with him wherever he went. Of course, she was the better rider. I think, though, that the reason they got along was that they both had their retreats from each other. Mum through her nursing at Tatla Lake and Dad, his painting. We're worried about Dad's lapse of memory and his dialogues with Mum."

Fred nodded.

"I've read your other articles. Seems you're looking for an angle. Have you come up with one on Dad?"

"I'm chasing an idea. I'll let you know when I catch it."

"That's pretty cute for a twenty-two-year-old reporter."

"I'm twenty-four. What would you like me to say about Noah?"

"You know," Elizabeth sighed, "I'm a Native youth social worker in Williams Lake. My life is torn apart during the week fighting the system, the police, the district, the city. All the time fighting for my clients' rights. I may win battles but I'm not winning the fight. I'm even having trouble with my own kids. Sure, a few young people get off drugs or alcohol. Many don't. Some of them know about Dad being a painter. I tell them, 'He spent five months in the same jail you're in now, when things were a lot tougher. And he escaped and found his spirit in the land.' Then I get Dad to make the rounds with me. I take the kids out to the ranch and he talks to them and gets them to go hunting with him or on a sketching trip for a week."

"What were your dad's mistakes?"

"Dad is mixed-blood. He has a certain attitude towards First Nations people and whites alike. Sort of studies them, judges them. Some people take offence. But he doesn't care what they think."

"Why doesn't he care?"

"Why?" she laughed. "He thinks that the whites haven't taken the trouble to learn from the First Nation peoples who have lived on this land for a long time. Likewise, we have to learn some more of the white ways of thinking. He tells Aboriginals and whites alike the truth through his painting and visions."

Elizabeth went silent. Fred's question got her to thinking some troubling thoughts about her dad. Thoughts she would rather not have.

"We can talk some more tomorrow," she said abruptly. "I'll show you your room."

With that, Elizabeth brought Fred to a second-floor bedroom with an attached bathroom.

"What *does* your father care about?" Fred asked, before she could leave.

"Three things. The land, my mother, and Ta Chi. In his mind, they are all the same."

"Who *is* Ta Chi?"

"She's Dad's mother," Elizabeth offered with reverence. "My granny. She roamed the Chilcotin night and day in all weather, as if it was house and backyard. She was part of the landscape, one of the revered ancients."

"Thank you. I would have liked to have known her."

It had been Fred's intention to travel on and spend the night at Anahim Lake after his interview with Noah, so he had a bag in his car. He went out to fetch it at about nine in the evening. When he closed the car door, he saw Joel walking up from the barn.

"Has the old man told you the secret to his life yet?" Joel called out.

"Justine," Fred replied.

Joel smiled as he walked up to Fred.

"Mum wasn't his secret, she was his salvation. You know Dad drank a lot when he was in his sixties and early seventies. That was after some bad business with Vladimir Volk. He also spent a lot of time in his studio working on a series of paintings of the Tŝilhqot'in transformation story. He finally finished it, to great applause amongst the white community, but the effort almost finished him. Mum got him dried out. Since then, he's been acting a bit philosophical. He's been taking on the role of an elder."

"What about the Order of BC? Did that affect him at all?"

"No. He accepted it for Mum, not himself. That's what he said at the ceremony. He would have liked to have the approval of the Tŝilhqot'in people."

"Did he get that approval?"

"Some Tŝilhqot'ins liked it. Most thought it would have been better if a full-blooded Tŝilhqot'in had painted it and gotten the award, but there aren't too many of those left, if any. The most important person Dad wanted to please was Mum. And she thought it was grand."

"At dinner," Fred ventured, "you mentioned that the Green Trust is active in the Chilcotin buying up private land. Do you know who represents them?"

"I met someone in a coffee shop in Williams Lake last summer who seems to know something. He has a strange name." Joel thought a moment. "Bull. Bull O'Connor. He claims that his mother is a First Nation Cree from Manitoba."

Fred gagged.

"I've met Bull," he said in a suddenly heated voice. "And God help me, O'Connor is Texan to the bone. There's not an ounce of Native in him and he's full of bullshit."

He thought, but did not say, *God help the Chilcotin.* It seemed to Fred that O'Connor was holding all the cards: the strong smell of a large profit in shale gas, the power of the Empire of the United States of America, the Northrop money and name, the Green Trust and now, the First Nations.

Joel had assumed Fred was a meek and deferential young man eager for a story, but now found himself surprised at the conviction in his voice.

"Whoa! I've struck a nerve. Why do you hate this guy?"

"Let's just say we've crossed swords. Does O'Connor have any dealings with the First Nations?"

"Yeah. When I saw him, he was meeting in the Rendezvous Café with Ray Twoshoes."

"Have you met anyone else from their head office?"

"A woman came with him to Williams Lake. She had a clipped drawl like yours. Her name is Harriet. Last fall, she invited me to speak about climate change effects on grasslands at a conference in Atlanta at the end of June. Do you know her?"

"Yeah," Fred gulped, forcing himself to be nonchalant. "She's a friend of mine. I'll let my colleague know. Maybe he'll want to speak to her directly. Well, tomorrow comes early. See you then."

Joel nodded, but noted the shift in Stone, from questions to letting things lie. *Americans,* he thought.

Fred headed up to his room. His hands were damp. He was sweating. He entered his room and collapsed on the bed. He'd had these panic attacks before, but never this acute. He lay on the bed, hyperventilating. The thought of Joel meeting Bull in the Chilcotin unnerved him beyond reason.

Thoughts and Dreams

By ten that night, Noah, Elizabeth, Joel and Fred were each in their rooms behind closed doors, each turning over in their minds the events of the day and thinking about tomorrow.

Fred found himself praying, reverting to his father's Baptist faith in a crisis, despite never practicing it.

God, I could be living with Harriet, the love of my life. You've got to help me through this one so I can get back to her. And, if I succeed in proving Bull O'Connor's deal with her father, help Harriet forgive me.

When he and Harriet had left for her father's house last September, he'd thought they were on their way to bliss and the promise of a more permanent relationship. Then Bull showed up. Harriet had no knowledge of what Bull was doing and he couldn't tell her. Not then, not yet. He had told Noah, though. Noah had seen through his disguise — despite his age and confused state, the man could be helpful to him.

Elizabeth tossed and turned, punched her pillow and fretted. She had promised her mother on her deathbed that she would look after Noah. Even with his physical strength seemingly returning, it was Noah's mental condition that worried her. Noah was understandably physically weak after his bout of pneumonia, yet he had stayed in bed for another two months, talking to Justine. Elizabeth couldn't get to sleep without making a plan for tomorrow.

I'll spend the day with Dad. Perhaps take him for a walk and talk about Mum and her portrait.

Joel had spent one week of each of the last three months at Tatlayoko, arranging his research work around the western Chilcotin. With the coming of spring, his graduate students would soon be conducting field experiments on Potato Mountain and the Brittany Triangle. Yet, looking out on the land, he wasn't thinking about that. His dad was on his mind.

My father sees everything that grows or moves on our land. It is there to be interpreted by him in his paintings, in colours and forms. Mom's persistence steered Dad's greatest work, The Tŝilhqot'in Creation Story, *without which the world outside wouldn't have seen our culture and spirit.*

I look at the land of my ancestors and, unlike Dad, I don't see beauty. I see degradation, not heroic transformation but insults, not caresses but blows. I saw all that in my youth working summers as a tree planter. The land is treated by non-aboriginals as something to be used, abused, cut down, ripped up or sucked out and thrown away. The Indigenous peoples have been treated by the non-indigenous in the same way. Dad knows *this. Most First Nations people know this too. Dad protests against the disrespect by keeping the First Nation culture alive and idealizing the land through his paintings. I use science to restore the land after the inevitable degradation by the colonizers.*

136

Now that Dad is feeling better, I'll get him out on the land. Perhaps a ride through the Chilcotin. The same ride that he and I took when I was sixteen, if he's up to it.

Noah's mind was fixed on painting a portrait of Justine, who had shared the creation of their children with him. When he was painting the Tŝilhqot'in creation story, he was both creator and transformer, as Lendix'tcux was when he, with the help of his three sons and with advice from their mother, transformed the monsters of the land into birds, fishes and animals that sustained and gave joy to his people.

It fell to me, with the urging of Justine, to paint scenes of the story Antoine first told me over fifty years ago. I have told the story to my people on ceremonial occasions. My painting was a pictorial re-creation, a changing of the land to a new form, function and structure.

"Tomorrow," he said into the darkness to Justine, "I'll go to my studio and begin my portrait of you, my love."

That belief — I remember now — it was told to me by a Cree from Northern Manitoba, a learned and very spiritual man. I think I told it to the reporter? Or was it him who told me? In the beliefs of our Athabasca ancestors, the Cree — the belief I think I told that reporter — the soul is not found in a man's finger, nor his heart, nor his penis, nor is the soul found in any woman's parts except her vagina and her womb. That is where the soul resides. Justine is in the air that I breathe, the venison I eat, the water I drink.

I'll sleep now.

And so he did, dreaming of Justine.

At three-thirty, he woke with a start as the old often do, then couldn't get back to sleep. He told himself some more stories to the accompaniment of coyotes howling outside in the moonlight. To Justine, he repeated something that he had heard before. He might even have said it himself.

Now that they know I'm not going to die anytime soon, what the hell does my family have planned for me today?

This time, lying in his bunk at four in the morning, he had a response for it.

Me, I'm going to my studio in the morning with that reporter. Then, after a nap, I'm going out to Eagle Lake to see Clint and Jeremy plow the land the old way with a team of Clydesdales.

At six in the morning, Fred had a nightmare. He was running on a flat open prairie, being chased by Bull, riding a Percheron stallion. He tried every dodge, every move to evade the charging beast and rider. He had no place to hide, no protection. He had only his quickness, his wits and his will to survive keeping him from being trampled by the huge horse's hooves. Then the scene changed. He was on the Williams Lake Stampede grounds. The stands were full of people urging Bull to ride him down.

"Crush Fred!" they were chanting.

"I'm not Fred! I'm Stone!" he screamed.

Bull jumped off the horse to land on him. Fred came to on the floor with a scream that woke up the house. The covers and sheets were strewn about, wet with sweat.

Awakened by Stone's scream, Joel recognized it as a nightmare.

Unable to sleep, he lay in bed thinking of the nature of the people of the Chilcotin, both white and Aboriginal.

He remembered, when having coffee at Tim Horton's in Hope a few weeks back, having seen a couple in their sixties quietly having coffee and a doughnut. They'd exchanged the odd word, comfortable and contained, different from the mill of people surrounding them. The man wore a cowboy hat and string tie. She was in jeans and a colourful checked blouse. Joel had gone up to them, knowing where they were from without ever having seen them before.

138

"Howdy. It's a nice day," he'd said, thinking these people would appreciate it.

The woman had looked him up and down.

"What are you selling?" she'd asked, flatly. She didn't say 'sonny', but her expression said it for her.

"I just thought I would give you a Chilcotin hello," Joel had said with a smile.

Sure enough, they were your usual Chilcotin sceptics. It turned out Joel and the couple knew the same family, the Sheriffs, from near Redstone.

With coffee on his mind, he flung the covers off and headed down to the kitchen to make breakfast.

Faith in Reason

Joel was making his specialty, waffles, as well as bacon, sausages and eggs when Fred entered the kitchen. He was met with a raised eyebrow from the cook.

"Your demons were after you this morning," Joel teased. "I thought a bobcat had attacked you."

"It must have been something I ate."

"Better not tell that to Elizabeth — she made supper last night. By the way, who is 'Fred'?"

"What do you mean?"

"You were shouting in your sleep. 'I'm not Fred, I'm Stone.'"

"Fred's my alter-ego," he replied without thinking.

Elizabeth came down next. She looked fresh.

"Good morning," she greeted them cheerily. "Thanks for waking me this morning, Stone. I needed an early start."

Brent, Clint and Jeremy came through the back door. Brent shook Fred's hand.

"Morning, Stone. I'm Brent. Elizabeth told me you were here from the *Tribune* to interview Dad. These two lads are Clint

140

and Jeremy. They've been working hard all yesterday with the Clydesdales and this morning on the tractor. I promised them a big breakfast."

Both boys nodded and looked at the floor. Fred recognized them from the provincial court bail hearing last fall, though he hadn't realized Jeremy was family, considering how different he looked from his half-brother. He didn't say anything and Clint showed no sign of remembering his face.

"Sit down, boys," Joel said. "I know you like waffles."

Once they had settled, he served them each a waffle fresh from the iron. Without a word, they started eating.

"Good morning, boys. Remember me, I'm your mother," Elizabeth said sardonically.

"Good morning, Mum," they said in unison.

"Have you guys worked with Clydesdales before?" Joel asked.

Their mouths full, they shook their heads.

Fred watched them while sipping his coffee. He had seen boys like these hanging about Williams Lake with seemingly nothing to do. They would be on the streets and parks in groups in the afternoon and move to the library around six to play video games on the computers until closing. After closing, he didn't know where they went. The reporter in him wanted to ask, but he decided against that.

"What do you like best," he asked instead, "the tractor or the horses?"

"Tractor," Jeremy mumbled.

"Clydesdales," said Clint, a little louder, more certain. "They're like gentle people. Grandad told me last time I was out here that the first horse he ever rode was a Clydesdale. He was four."

Fred smiled and nodded. *There's something to this boy*, he thought. *I'm going to cover his trial.*

"Brent," Elizabeth teased, "will my boys make good ranchhands?"

"Sure. They're learning to look after the horses and service the tractor. When they can do that well, I mean with understanding and compassion, they can call themselves cowboys."

"How can you show compassion to a tractor?" Clint asked, looking up from his plate.

"By maintaining it and treating it like it's important," Brent replied.

Clint chewed on that a while.

"When are we going hunting?" he finally asked.

"It's not hunting season," Brent replied.

"I thought First Nation people could hunt anytime."

"Well, here on the ranch, we hunt in season. I'll tell you what, when we finish the plowing and seeding, we'll do some target practice. Maybe shoot a few gophers."

Noah walked into the kitchen while Brent was talking. Everyone at the table looked up. He took his regular seat and Brent welcomed him.

"Good to see you up and about, old man."

"My time's not up yet. I have a few things to do before I leave you for good. Like have a cup of coffee, if it's not too much trouble."

"Oh, you've got your humour back," Brent replied.

He poured Noah a cup and placed it in front of him.

"How're you doing, young men?" Noah addressed the boys. "I haven't seen you for a while. Look at you, Jeremy. You're taller than your big brother. We'll have to call him your older brother from now on."

Joel served Noah a waffle and sausages. Noah dug into his breakfast with an appetite.

"How about another one, Joel?" he asked.

"It'll be ready in a minute."

When the waffle came, Noah smiled as he poured on maple syrup.

"You've finally perfected the art of waffle-making, son."

"Coming from you, Dad, that's a great compliment," Joel said playfully.

Noah was too busy eating to reply. He signalled he had finished his meal by wiping his mouth with his napkin. He replaced it in its silver ring, a detail that Justine had always insisted on.

"I'm going to do some painting and jawing with Rock here this morning," he announced. "Then after my nap, I'm going out to the Eagle Lake Meadows and watch these young fellows work the field."

"I'll go with you, Dad," Elizabeth said, clearing away his dishes.

He smiled at his daughter before turning his attention to Clint.

"Say, Clint, my calendar tells me that your trial is coming up soon. Remind me of the date?"

"Not for two months, Grandad," Clint said, clearly agitated. "It was adjourned to just after the Stampede weekend. Norman Twoshoes is talking around town saying I'm going to jail for a long time. I didn't mean to shoot him. Just wanted to let him know we're not scared of him."

"Yeah, Norman started it," Jeremy held his head up and with fire in his eyes.

"Well, I believe you. Your grandmother and I plan to be there. Give you some support."

"Thanks, Grandad," the boys said in unison, looking a bit uneasy with their grandfather talking about Granma as if she were alive, hoping he would forget the date.

Fred walked with Noah towards the barn where his studio was. He turned his recorder on and looked about the homestead, thinking of questions. He was caught up in interviewing Noah, a complex and intriguing First Nation man, even though he realized it would never have happened without his ulterior motive of proving Bull's involvement in Chilcotin natural gas. It was Joel he had to speak to about the gas exploration. Noah broke the silence.

"Joel believes that since humans are endowed with reason, we should use reason like a tool to solve the riddle of life, the mystery of it all. He says, 'If you must have faith, have faith in reason.' My son has answered many questions in his field of botany. The one question that has occupied him lately above all others is the symbiotic relationship between the species."

"What does that mean?" Fred asked.

Noah motioned with his hand to the home pastures surrounding the ranch.

"In his particular field of grasslands, he's trying to prove that the more diversity in species, the higher the biomass up to a certain point, then production falls off. It's illustrated in a graph he calls a humpback curve."

He waited for Noah to make his point, if there was one, as they ambled toward the studio. The old man seemed sharper in the morning.

"There's a lot to be said for science. I never studied it myself. I know it has its place, but how can it measure genius or creativity or the passion that will see one man grow grass on rock and another who can't grow in loam?"

Where is he going with this? Fred wondered.

Noah opened his studio door. They entered a large room flooded with light from the western sky. He brushed away the cobwebs around the windows.

"I haven't been in my studio since Justine took sick. It seems a long time ago," he said in a sad voice.

He placed a canvas on the easel.

"Is it good to be back?" Fred was hoping to pick up the old man's spirits.

Noah didn't respond. He waved a paintbrush at the canvas.

"You see this brush in my hand and the blank canvas on the easel? I have in my head the image of Justine's portrait and in my heart the intention to transpose that image onto that canvas.

144

This is art — the portrait will have form and beauty. It will have no use whatsoever and it is not what nature created. It is what nature's creature has created and maybe it will be part of who we Tŝilhqot'in are long after the memories of Justine the person have faded into nothing. Like those cave drawings in France. Science has its place. Its truths improve our lives. But so does art have its place. Its truths are beauty and it also improves our lives. The artist is the link between the seen and the unseen world."

Noah seemed to tire after his speech and sat silent on a chair.

"You're mostly known," Fred broke Noah's reverie, "for your landscapes."

"My big commissions have been my landscapes. A copy of my first is in the ranch house. The rest I've painted for money are reproductions of that. They hang in the lobbies of office buildings in big cities: Vancouver, Toronto, maybe even Atlanta. In my mind, the painting of our transformation story was my best work."

Fred nodded politely.

"I have painted portraits for friends, like Johanna and my adoptive mother, Belle, but I have never painted Justine."

"Do you regret that? That you didn't paint her while she was alive?"

"No. I had her with me."

"Is there anything in your life that you've regretted?"

"I've not loved enough."

"You loved Justine."

"Yes, but with conditions. I put her on a pedestal. I didn't love what she loved, what made her who and what she was."

Fred was put off-balance by the sincerity of the man. He had been accepted by Noah and his family on the premise that he was to write an article about the artist for the local paper. He hadn't expected to be drawn into the warmth of the Hanlon family in such an intimate way. He found the experience captivating. He also found himself conflicted, for his main purpose had been to question Noah about Northrop Oil and the Green Trust. Noah was recovering from his sickbed and the most traumatic event of his life — the death of his wife.

"Who did your wife love?"

This made Noah pause for a moment.

"Besides me?" he smiled disarmingly. "Of that, I have no doubt."

He paused to give the question some thought.

"She loved others," he finally said, clearly speaking from the heart. "Her love was universal. I think my grandson Clint put it best. He wrote her a letter. I have it here."

Noah pulled a folded piece of paper from his pocket. He smoothed it out on his desk and read it aloud.

"'Granma, you approach your cancer with a brave heart. You spend time with the family and are the strongest spirit in the room. Thank you for being Granma.'"

Noah wiped a tear from his eye.

"He's a very caring young man," Fred said with feeling.

"Yeah. You wouldn't think so with all his swagger and bragging, but he's sensitive."

"Have you been up on Potato Mountain in the last while?"

"Before Justine died, I went up there alone to be in the presence of my Creator, to see the sweep of the Chilcotin and remember the first time Justine and I made love."

"Did that give you some peace?"

"Yes. I returned from the mountain no longer angry at the thought that I might lose her."

"While you were up there on Potato Mountain, looking down on the world, did you see any activity or disturbance?"

"No, I don't think so. Well, maybe that time a helicopter landed nearby. It disturbed my peace."

Fred noticed Noah shudder when he mentioned the machine.

"I understand," Fred responded sympathetically.

"Potato Mountain is sacred. Helicopters have no place there. They bring death and destruction."

Fred had to keep reminding himself that the story on Noah the painter was part of his assignment, yet it was expanding into Noah the person, the mystic. How could he capture him in a short article?

"Why are you asking me these questions about helicopters?" Noah asked anxiously.

"A colleague of mine thinks that Northrop Green Trust and Northrop Oil are conducting tests for natural gas. I'm thinking of riding up to Potato Mountain to see for myself if there's a connection."

"I see."

Noah continued to look closely at Fred, a half-smile stretching the lines on his face. Could it be that Noah remembered what Fred had told him the night before and saw Fred's real reasons for being there? If he did, he said nothing about it.

"Perhaps Joel will take you up there," he suggested instead. "He has an experimental plot he wants to check."

With that, he picked up an old print. In the Northwest Coast Native style, it showed a raven, perched on a branch and looking down intently at something out of frame.

"Is that your work?" Fred asked.

"It was."

Noah pulled out a pencil. He turned the print over and began drawing the face of the woman he loved.

Fred, seeing that Noah was lost in his work, left him alone with Justine. He went back to the ranch house to replay the tape and write up his notes on their conversation.

The house was empty, Elizabeth and Joel having gone with Brent, Clint and Jeremy to Eagle Lake. Fred went to his room. After putting his thoughts and observations of the morning on paper, he made a start on his piece on Noah.

It was eleven o'clock when he opened his email to find something from Harriet.

Hi Fred,

I haven't heard from you in a while. I miss your cynical humour as you toil away in the wilds of Wyoming on your "Secrets". I wonder if you're getting inspiration from the foothills of the Rockies. Let me know of your progress.

The campaign's heating up to the point in the debates where the candidates are calling each other names and talking about their privates. We never learned this in our PoliSci courses. I'm sure you're following it all. I wish Dad would cool his rhetoric. He's leading in delegates but it's going to be a fight to the finish. Urged on by Bull, he believes plain talking, as he calls it, is one of the reasons for his success. He's catching his wind after doing so well. As Assistant Campaign Manager, I'm very busy helping to coordinate the Regional Campaign Managers you met at Dad's place.

I'm hoping that we can get together in Wyoming when Dad campaigns there next month.

I'm seeing a lot of Mr. O'Connor. He seems to always talk about Christian morals as he strikes out at the other candidates. It's hypocrisy and it bothers me. He has a foul mouth and uses dirty tricks against Dad's opponents. Just the other day during a primary, he wanted our state chairman to place an anonymous false story about one of Dad's opponents avoiding the draft. Since you warned me against him, I'm keeping a close watch on him. I even told Dad that I was offended by O'Connor's lack of morals, but he wouldn't hear of it. He's mesmerized by the favorable polls and primary results. He actually told me that sometimes you've "got to get your hands dirty to succeed." This may apply to farmers or oilmen, but it shouldn't be followed by politicians. I'm starting to have my doubts.

I'm thinking that I would like to join you in your cabin in Wyoming. We could have a long weekend with just the two of us. Anyway, you have my good wishes and love. It would be nice to hear from you soon.

Love,
H.

Fred felt a warm rush of tenderness until he remembered his present life was based on a lie. Bull couldn't know where he was or what he was up to — and Bull would know if Harriet were to join him in the Chilcotin. He decided that he would wait until evening to reply to Harriet. It was getting to lunchtime and he could hear some noise in the house. He decided to go down and be social.

Over lunch, Joel agreed to take Fred up Potato Mountain the next day. Fred professed an interest in Joel's experiment, but really wanted to question Joel and see if the helicopter Noah had seen was related to Northrop.

Clearly pleased at the prospect of a Sunday with her dad, Elizabeth agreed. Her father had been recovering nicely, but she didn't know how much time they might have left together.

Spring Beauty

They saddled up early Sunday morning. Joel rode Sugar. Fred took Elizabeth's horse, Scout.

The mist rising from the lake gouged out of rock by retreating glaciers spread into the lowland, creating the illusion that their horses were walking on clouds. Rising out of the mist, the Potato Mountain range girded the lake's eastern shore and the Chilcotin range its west. The Homathko River fed the lake from the north.

Noah watched them go, wishing he was out there with them so he could give thanks to the Creator for allowing him life enough to paint Justine's portrait. He had decided to paint her in pastels as a seventeen-year-old bride.

Angus was alert to the sound of the horses leaving the ranch. The dog whimpered, torn between loyalty to his master and its instinct to follow the departing men and horses. Noah signalled Angus to go and the border collie loped after the ghostly figures receding into the distance.

There was no idle talk between the men. They were thinking of what lay atop Potato Mountain — Joel about his experimental plot and Fred, tipped off by Noah's mention of a helicopter, about proof of exploratory work by Northrop Oil.

Within a half-hour, the path led them from the lakeshore to the lower slope of the mountain. The horses, well used to the trail, picked their way at their own pace for the three-hour climb through the forested upland.

A quarter of the way up, Fred broke the silence.

"Why is it called Potato Mountain?"

Ever the scientist, Joel seized on the question.

"We First Nations have been coming here for centuries in late spring and early summer. We call it Chunezch'et. We harvest a small starchy tuber that has some food value and can keep for the winter. With the similarities to the potato and the coming of the non-aboriginals, the name stuck. It's not related to the potato family. It's in the lily family — the Spring Beauty, a perennial that grows five to fifteen centimetres tall with white flowers and one or more stems arising from a shallow corm which might be five centimetres or more in diameter."

"Will I be able to find and eat these potatoes?"

"We're too early this year."

Now that Joel had surfaced from the depths of his thoughts, Fred pressed him with more questions as their horses laboured up the steep slope.

"You said yesterday there had been some talk about exploration work."

"I believe it was Dad who said that. I'm interested in checking it out."

They reached the northern edge of the flat ridge above the treeline before lunch. To the south, wild grasses covered the shallow bowl-shaped mountain ridge stretching out before them. Two small lakes were in the centre of the bowl. To the west was a rocky ledge that looked down five hundred metres to Tatlayoko Lake.

They dismounted and let the horses graze. Joel went to the lip of the precipice and shoved a good-sized boulder off with his boot. They watched it bounce down to the treeline.

"What's the hypothesis for your experiment?" Fred ventured.

Joel only signalled that they would ride on. They remounted and cantered down into the grassland.

"I fenced off a nine-square-metre plot of grassland," Joel said eventually. "Later in the year, my students will identify the species and harvest all the plant material in that plot. We call it 'biomass'. This will be dried and weighed. This experiment is being repeated worldwide on six continents to show there's a link between plant biomass and species richness. It's important to establish a pattern and data that will advance the science in this field. Here's my plot."

They reined in. Joel checked to make sure the fence was secure and the grass had not been disturbed.

"Damn," he muttered. "Someone's pulled out some posts and exposed the plot to the animals. Lucky I came when I did."

"I can help," Fred offered.

On Joel's signal, they dismounted and reset the fence. The wind blowing from the southwest and funnelling through Waddington Canyon drove grey rainclouds from the coast and emptied them onto the two tiny figures on the mountain. They remounted and rode through the deluge toward Echo Lake to the shelter of a stand of fir.

"I haven't been here for a year. There's a cabin on the shore of Echo Lake. We'll get in out of the rain until the storm blows over."

As they approached the cabin, Joel reined in Sugar.

"I'll be damned," he shouted into the slicing rain. "What's going on here?"

The firs on the lee side of the stand had been felled. The land had been marred with signs of construction. The cabin had been modified and enlarged. Garbage littered the site.

They dismounted and entered the cabin. Angus followed, shaking the rain off his shaggy coat.

"Who's responsible for the damage?" Fred asked.

"You tell me. We'll have a look after the rain blows over."

Joel lit a fire in the stove as the storm raged outside. They unpacked the lunch they'd brought and ate in silence. Fred felt Joel's questioning eyes on him but felt it best to respect his silence. Questions of his own were on the verge of being answered once the rain let up.

Joel drank his tea as he did some hard thinking about the damage to his plot and the activity on Potato Mountain. He wondered about this reporter called Stone, who showed up and wanted to ride up the mountain. Could he be connected to this outrage? Or maybe he's onto a story?

"Where'd you say you're from?" Joel asked.

"The state of Georgia."

"What brought you here to the Chilcotin?"

"My dad lived here in the seventies. He talked so much about it, I had to come and see for myself."

So far, Fred hadn't lied.

"You came to the ranch to interview Noah."

"Yeah."

"Noah's still down at the ranch. Why in the hell are you up here?"

Fred had reached the shores of his Rubicon, which the Latin teacher had said he must cross, not halfway, but completely. He had already taken Noah into his confidence, and now he had to decide whether he was going to cross that mythical river by telling Joel, who would, unlike Noah, remember what Fred had said.

"Have you heard of Billy Joe Northrop?"

Poses

Noah was torn between going back to his bed or fighting his depression by being active. He remembered that he had begun the preliminary sketches of Justine's portrait and walked to his studio. Inside, he sat down and looked at the pencil lines that were the beginnings of Justine's face. The act of imagining the finished painting calmed him and gave him a sense of pride. He worked for an hour outlining her pose, then sat down for a breather.

Elizabeth found him asleep in his chair by his sketch. She gently shook him.

"Dad, come for lunch."

"Justine?" he asked, looking up into Elizabeth's face.

"No, Dad. Your daughter. Elizabeth. It's time for lunch."

"Elizabeth, would you sit in this chair and pose for me? I need to get your mum's arm just right."

"Sure, Dad."

As she posed for her father, she wondered if he was seeing her or her mother.

Northern Drilling

"Yes," Joel nodded. "I've heard of Billy Joe Northrop. Probably the most recognized name in America these days. Yeah, he's the one who wants to build a wall along the Mexican border to keep out what he calls 'the rapists'."

"That's him. Well, his company, Northrop Oil, also intends to drill for natural gas in the Chilcotin."

"I haven't heard of that." Joel raised an eyebrow at Fred. "And I know what's going on in this territory."

"I have it on good authority that Northrop Oil or its subsidiaries have conducted seismic surveys in the Chilcotin and identified large gas fields. Your dad told me he was on the mountain before your mother died and a helicopter landed in the area of Echo Lake. I was suspicious and wanted to see for myself."

"You don't say," Joel said, getting to his feet. "All right. The rain's let up and the tea's drunk. Let's go see."

They left the shelter of the cabin. The afternoon sun had broken through the cloud cover, steaming the moisture off the plants and shrubs. Within a hundred metres, they came across a helicopter pad built from logs of the felled trees. There was the imprint of a large machine, empty fuel barrels and wooden crates with the words 'NORTHERN DRILLING CORP' stamped on them.

They mounted up and began following a pattern of drill holes. Fred took pictures of empty dynamite boxes strewn about, which confirmed his suspicions of seismic testing. He would show the photos to a geologist for confirmation, but that would be a formality. In the bagged garbage ripped open by animals were papers further identifying the seismic company as Northern Drilling Corp.

Joel kept his thoughts to himself about this sacred ground where his ancestors had met in council, where his grandmother Ta Chi had been buried and where his father and grandfather, both *deyens*, had spoken. Further on, atop a knoll overlooking the smaller lakes, they came across a grave marker that had been pushed over.

Joel dismounted. He turned the marker inscription-side up. The words seemed to burn into his eyes.

HERE LIE THE BONES OF TA CHI
RETURNED TO HER CREATOR

Joel righted his grandmother's gravestone. Hat in hand and head bowed, he stood before her grave then, raising his head to the heavens.

"Enough!" he shouted. "They have desecrated our land, messed with my experiment and disturbed the bones of our ancestors. That's enough."

Fred was struck by Joel's obviously deep-seated anger. Coming from a scientist and a man of reason, it had an even greater impact. Joel abruptly shook off his flare-up and became a man of action again.

"If we don't start down the mountain now," he said, mounting Sugar, "we'll have to spend the night."

156

As they cantered past Joel's experimental plot, they were startled by a crack of a rifle and a buzz in the air. A tuft of ground jumped beside the horses. Joel dug his heels into Sugar's flanks.

"Ride!" he yelled.

Fred needed no other encouragement, nor did Angus who ran hard on the horses' hooves.

Another shot struck and splintered a rocky knoll. They rode full gallop for cover behind the shelter of an outcropping. They dismounted and Joel took his rifle from its scabbard.

There was no more shooting, only an eerie silence.

"Who are you?" Joel shouted.

There was no answer.

"Why are you shooting?"

After a while, a distant shout responded, "You trespass on First Nations land."

"I'm Joel Hanlon. With me is a guest from Williams Lake."

"How do I know you're Hanlon? Take off the hat. Stand in the open."

"I don't need a haircut. How about you asking me a question that only a Hanlon would know?"

Another long wait.

"Who was your grandmother?"

"Ta Chi."

"Okay, I'll come out. Soon as you see me, you both come out without any firearms. I'll put down my rifle and we'll meet."

"Okay."

Angus came close to Joel, not knowing what to do. He'd heard Joel's tone soften and a familiarity in the man's voice. The man was well-built, young and First Nations, with a two-week beard. Angus bounded toward him, barking and attempting to herd the man, which he ignored. Joel and Fred approached and the man nodded.

"Angus, heel!" Joel commanded.

The dog did as he was told.

"I'm Norman Twoshoes," the man said.

Joel sized up the young man.

"Yeah, I know you. Your father's Ray from Anahim Lake."

"Who's this guy?" Norman pointed to Fred.

"Stone Clearwater. He's a reporter from the *Tribune*."

"I thought you were the guys who fucked up our land. I was scaring you off," he snorted, with an accompanying hand gesture of pulling a trigger.

Joel took a good look at Norman, the young man who'd picked a fight with Jeremy. He could see Norman was alone and not looking forward to a chilly night on the mountain.

"Say, Norman, it's getting too late to head down the mountain. Why don't you come over to the cabin and have a drink with us?"

"Yeah, okay."

He mounted up and the three rode back to the cabin in silence.

Whiskey Talks

In the cabin, Joel built a fire. Once it was going, he produced a bottle of whiskey from his pack, pouring a generous helping for Norman and smaller amounts for Fred and himself. Norman took his glass and had a swallow. Fred turned on his recorder.

"I'm not allowed to have alcohol when I'm on guard," he grinned. "But since you offered…"

"Oh? Who says you can't drink?"

"My dad. He sent me up here to keep an eye on these holes. To make sure the markings weren't fucked with and challenge anybody who comes on this land."

Fred could see that Norman had no idea what was going on and was only doing a job.

"I guess the pay is good."

"Yep. Damn good."

"Who would have given permission to drill these holes?" Joel asked in an offhand manner, trying to appear more curious than inquisitorial.

"I guess my dad did."

"Do you know why the holes were drilled?" Fred asked.

Norman finished his drink. Joel poured him the dregs of the bottle. Norman, seeing that the source had dried up, was ready to leave.

"All he said was that they were going to make us all rich," he finally said.

"Are there other areas in the Chilcotin that have been surveyed?"

"Yeah. Some on the Brittany Triangle." Norman drained his glass and rose to go. "I guess I'll be moving on."

"Where you staying, Norman?"

"Oh, I got a bivouac down the way."

After Norman left, Joel warmed up some stew he had brought up the mountain. As they ate, he and Fred talked over what Norman had told them about his father's involvement in the Northern Drilling seismic tests. They concluded, before they got into their sleeping bags, that Norman's dad had an agreement with the exploration company and, for a large amount of money, Ray had given the company permission to conduct seismic surveys on the land.

The next morning, Joel and Fred rode down off the mountain, arriving at the ranch house in time for lunch. They told Elizabeth and Noah what they had discovered.

"Ta Chi's grave," Noah muttered, a fierceness in his voice his children hadn't heard before.

"What are you going to do, Joel?" Elizabeth asked, pacing the kitchen floor.

"I don't know yet," Joel replied. "Alert the tribal council, I guess."

"Ta Chi's grave," Noah repeated.

He left the room. The others finished their lunch in silence.

Fred left for Williams Lake late in the afternoon. The deadline for his story on Noah was Wednesday if he was to make the Friday edition and he had lots to do before then. In the company of a bottle of rye, which tasted like warm piss to a bourbon drinker, Fred met the deadline.

After, he thought about the hard evidence he had unearthed of Northern Drilling surveying on Potato Mountain with the agreement of a First Nations chief. He was that much closer to breaking the story of the Copper Beech secret meeting.

With proof almost in his grasp, he thought of Harriet. He hadn't answered her email and felt ashamed as she was having doubts about her dad's candidacy. He composed a response and sent it at midnight before falling exhausted into bed.

Beat Your Feet

At three in the morning, Harriet heard music.

It's a treat to beat your feet on the Mississippi mud.

Her phone was heralding an incoming message. She turned it over. It was Fred. She frowned at his waking her, especially since it had been three days since she'd poured her heart out to him in her last email.

Dearest Harriet,

I love you more than anything. Sorry not to get back to you sooner. The thing is I went on a trail ride into the mountains for two days with an Indian guide to get more background for my novel. There's no wi-fi in the wilderness. It was quite an adventure. We were challenged by an Indian who said we were trespassing. It was tense until my guide was able to prove he was Native too.

My novel is turning into a mystery. It's all about two
lovers whom fate has separated — one to devote herself to
her father's ambition and the other to devote himself to
"Secrets," the great American novel. Despite their divergent
interests and the distance in space between them, they are
connected electronically and emotionally.

Harriet laughed out loud. Even from a distance and through
emails, Fred amused her.

She lives in hope that her father will win the nomination and
the chance to become president, and he that his mystery will
be published to great acclaim so that they can renew their
physical and spiritual bond. My mystery has a subplot that
raises the question of political morality. I agree with you that
dirty tricks should have no place in the America that we live
in.

She sobered on reading this, remembering Bull. Sadly, she
knew he was a man who got his way and who had a great influence on her father. The more primaries her father won, the more
dependent he was on Bull's strategies and the more outrageous
those strategies became.

To be with you is my fervent desire. It won't be long before I
finish my novel and I'm in your arms. I know you love your
dad and will try to be a good influence on him.

You continue to be my inspiration.

Love,
Fred.

She knew she had to speak to her father and Fred's email was just the push she needed.

In the morning, she was to accompany her father to Indiana, a winner-take-all state. Its primary was May 3rd with fifty-seven delegates up for grabs.

Billy Joe's daily exercise when he was at Copper Beech was doing laps in his Olympic-size pool. He usually swam before breakfast, using the exercise to clear his mind of politics. Harriet chose this time after his swim, when his mind was fresh, to talk to her father about Bull. And of course, she timed her entrance perfectly.

"Morning, Happy," he shouted from the far side of the pool, pulling on his terrycloth robe. "Are you coming for a swim?"

"No, Dad. I came down to talk about something that's been on my mind for some time."

"Will it take long to get it off your mind?" He was in a cheery mood. "We should be heading for Indiana in a half-hour."

She walked up to Billy Joe. He kissed her on the cheek and motioned to the table. They sat down and Billy Joe leaned forward.

"I haven't," he stumbled, "taken the time recently to tell you how much your support and work on the campaign means to me. You're one of the reasons I'm doing so well."

He smiled broadly at his daughter.

"Thank you, Dad," she blushed. "I think you'd make a great president and I want to see you elected."

"What is it you want to talk to me about?"

"You know that I loathe Mr. O'Connor," she spoke bluntly.

"You've made that perfectly clear."

"Well, Dad, I'm not the only one. O'Connor's strategy is to insult women. When you speak the words he writes for you, calling women dogs, pigs and slobs, I know you don't mean it. You don't mean that about me."

"Of course I don't, dear. It's just… it's just an approach to get the nation's attention. To get in the headlines, to steal the show."

"Well, it's time to change tactics, Dad."

"What are you suggesting?"

"You should let O'Connor go. You're in a position to win the Republican nomination. But if you continue insulting women and minorities, you may not become president."

Billy Joe nodded his head as if he understood what his daughter was saying.

"We haven't," he answered in a kind, lecturing voice, "locked in enough delegate votes to win the nomination. Our strategy has been successful and I won't change it at this stage. I hope you'll remain by my side. I need your support."

Harriet looked sadly at her father.

"Okay, Dad," she said, in a resigned voice. "But I don't trust O'Connor. Nor should you."

Rendezvous

Fred slept in. He got out of bed at eleven, squinting in the midday light. In the bathroom, he dropped the tumbler he used for water and gritted his teeth at the pain the sound of it hitting the sink caused him.

Rye was not his friend.

He took a double-strength Tylenol and grabbed a shower. He was in no shape to make his own breakfast, let alone eat it. He boiled some water and laced it with Nescafé. Fortified, he wandered over to the *Tribune* to get copies of the new issue with his profile on Noah Hanlon.

Muriel was in her office.

"Clearwater," she called out. "Come on in."

She had the paper open to Fred's piece. The headline trumpeted "Noah Hanlon, Artist and Elder" above a picture of Noah and the Stone Clearwater byline.

"I liked your opening," she said.

This was the first praise he had received from Muriel.

"Thanks," Fred smiled. "I tried for a bit of spontaneity."

She pulled the paper close and cleared her throat.

"'*Follow this road*,'" she read. "'*You'll see an old man sitting on a porch dreaming of his Creator. He's the artist.* Those were the directions I got from a cowhand on my journey to find and interview the First Nation artist Noah Hanlon. I met him at the back door to his ranch house on Tatlayoko Lake.'"

She turned the page.

"Your ending was quite good, too," she said, reading on. "'Although Noah is convalescing following the death of his wife, he has begun a portrait of her. Despite painting many portraits during his illustrious career, likenesses of the humble and the famous alike, sometimes for free for his friends and sometimes for reward for the rich, he has never painted her. *I had the real Justine before me every day*, he told me at his ranch. *I didn't need substitutes.* The Chilcotin shall look forward to seeing Justine once again, this time through the eyes of her husband, Noah, the artist who loved her.'"

Fred suspected that this was the end of the praise and said nothing.

"It was the middle," Muriel continued, setting the paper down. "It was a bit flabby. I thought it needed a little more of Noah and a little less of Stone. Don't forget the golden rule: let the subject reveal himself. Show, don't tell. I learned that from Ma Murray, editor of the *Bridge River–Lillooet News*, a woman of strong opinions and that's for damn sure. Otherwise, I see some promise in your writing."

She didn't smile, she just nodded.

"Thank you, Muriel," he mumbled, feeling dismissed.

"Just get some coffee," she said with a wave of her hand. "Or learn to drink."

Fred felt damned by faint praise. He needed that coffee and time to lick his wounds. Nancy looked up from behind the counter when he opened the door to the Rendezvous Café. She held a copy of the *Tribune* in her hand and a big grin on her face.

"Well, look who's here! The great reporter, Stone Clearwater, who wrote the article on Noah Hanlon. We know him as Fred. Let's give him a hand."

The customers, a full house, most of whom knew Stone, clapped. Some younger Natives shouted "Ya!" Some others responded with "Hoo!"

"To think," Hazel chimed in, "he was just a penniless bum when he first walked in here a few months ago."

"Thank you kindly, ladies. I'm still penniless."

A few ranchers stopped by to introduce themselves.

"How's Noah?" one asked.

"We miss him," said another. "If you see him, tell him we asked."

"Thanks for the profile," said a third.

Fred kept smiling for the crowd, but rubbed his head between sips of coffee.

In the weeks that followed, Fred couldn't believe the response to his article on Noah. For the most part, it was positive — letters to the editor wishing Noah 'godspeed' and phone calls, tweets and emails from artists and politicians who'd read it online. Many were looking forward to Noah's portrait of Justine as if it was the Chilcotin *Mona Lisa*.

Noah missed all the hype, not being connected to the internet age. He thought the telephone was a huge innovation over the radio phone — that had been his only concession to modern communication. Suddenly Stone, by default, became Noah's accidental agent and press secretary with people within the region and elsewhere enquiring about Noah via Stone's *Tribune* email. He felt it necessary to answer all the questions and, from time to time, give an account of Noah's health.

Just Vote

Indiana was unexpected.

As far as Bull was concerned, Oregon and Washington were hippie states and he never expected success there, but he was sure he'd worked all the levers for Indiana. Billy Joe's lead was still there, but now, even California wouldn't likely be enough to avoid a contested convention. The Republican brass were going all-out and he certainly couldn't count on Minnesota or New Jersey.

Much as he hated to lose, Bull wasn't worried. When it came to convention time, he'd have to beat the establishment brains at their own game.

With the tribal council now aware of the drilling on Potato Mountain, Ray had been forced to reveal there'd been a survey of the land. Another ripple was circulating among the First Nations people, about Norman Twoshoes' encounter with Joel and Stone on Potato Mountain. Ray was clearly deep in the thick of things.

Even so, he'd already put in his time lobbying heavily. It was time, as he saw it, to win over the Tŝilhqot'in to progress and wealth. He started over coffee with an elder of his band.

"Albert, how would you like to buy that sorrel horse you've had an eye on?"

"Ray," he laughed. "I don't have the money for that."

"What's the price?"

"Two thousand."

"Tell you what. I'll loan it to you."

"What the hell, Ray? Stop messing with me."

"I'm not. I'm going to be rich soon and so are you. This is just a taste."

"Yeah? How's that?"

"The survey found natural gas on our lands and there's a company that'll pay us millions for it."

"Okay," Albert nodded. "What do I have to do?"

"Just vote for the contract."

"Sounds good."

"If you vote for the deal, I won't ask for repayment."

"Okay."

"This is just between you and me now."

The two men shook hands. Ray counted out twenty hundred-dollar bills and handed them to Albert.

Twin Purposes

The excitement of the last two weeks had been tiring, but in mid-May, Noah was gaining strength. Brent, his family and the cowhands were at the ranch. That was enough human company. Alone and bereft in the spring, when the pollen was blowing off the aspens and the bees were after the wildflowers, he felt the need to go into the mountains on a retreat. There were many questions that needed reflection and contemplation. Noah walked to the lake edge every day, breathed the air his ancestors and Justine had breathed and felt winter's icy grasp being loosened by the warm winds coming from off the coast.

This day, sparrows, his mother's bird, flitted in the budding lilac that bordered the lawn. A raven, Antoine's bird and his own, perched on a pine to survey the land, cawing and scanning for its next meal or an opportunity to create some mischief. Then, there above the walking and crawling and flying creatures, was a bald eagle soaring and waiting for its opportunity to strike. All of nature's energy aroused Noah and reminded him of his goal — to paint Justine's portrait.

Her features were so fixed in his mind that he didn't need a photograph of her. He remembered the young woman he first kissed, sitting on a hay bale by the barn. That kiss had sealed his fate. Together they had faced happiness, infidelity, family, laughter, sadness, tragedy and, in the end, peace. The only way he knew how to honour Justine's memory was to paint her portrait. He walked slowly toward his studio.

The room was cold. Brent had set tinder and wood in the potbelly stove. Noah lit a match and touched the tinder, which flared into life. He sat in the chair, took out his sketchpad and began drawing the image that filled his mind.

After an hour, he stood and stretched, looking out the window at the cattle feeding on hay. He turned back to his sketch to see Justine's face emerging. It was time to start applying colour, but that would wait for tomorrow. He was hungry.

He walked to the ranch house to be greeted by Brent's twin preschoolers, Luke and Joseph. Their mother Carol had barley soup simmering at the back of the stove. She ladled out a bowl for Noah.

"How's Justine's portrait going, Noah?" she asked in a cheery voice.

"Hmm, you know Justine. She's camera-shy and refuses to sit still for her portrait."

"I know." Carol had decided to play along with her father-in-law speaking as if Justine still lived.

"Well, she hasn't changed any."

Noah hungrily slurped his soup while Luke and Joseph chirped away.

"I'm going to kindygarten, Grandad," Luke spoke up proudly.

"Oh, where is that?"

"At Tatla Lake."

"What's 'kindygarten'?"

"Grandad, everyone knows about kindygarten. We get told stories, we learn to add and we have a nap at our desks."

"Do they teach you how to trap and hunt?"

"No, Grandad. You do that," Joseph chimed in, giggling.

Noah finished his soup and bread and pushed himself away from the table.

"Well, boys, Grandad's going to have a nap," he announced.

He headed for the den. Carol looked up from writing a grocery list.

"Noah, I've been getting more phone calls from friends, even some strangers, wanting to come and see you. I've told them that you're not well enough. Do you want to see anybody?"

"Yes. I would like to see Chief Littlejohn from Nemiah. And Vladimir."

Before settling down for his nap, he re-read the *Tribune* article about him written by that Stone fellow. It reminded him that now he and Justine had twin purposes in life: the fate of the people and the land, the Tŝilhqot'in and the Chilcotin.

The Right Place

Noah thought Justine would have been embarrassed about all the fuss. People were anticipating his portrait of her. Stone's article had vibrated throughout the Cariboo Chilcotin. Noah was told it had even created comment in social media throughout the province. He was proud.

Where was he going to unveil the painting that would immortalize his wife, though? Over sleepless nights at the ranch, he thought it through. There were so many places which, in one way or another, simply weren't right. Finally, he decided it would be on Potato Mountain at harvest time in July. That was where, years ago, the Tŝilhqot'in had recognized him as one of theirs and where a circle of elders had acquitted him of a crime most heinous. Most importantly, though, it was the place where he had married Justine. It would be the right place to commemorate her.

The Hanlon family gathered in the great room after dinner. The grandchildren who were old enough to mount a horse were exhausted after sorting and branding the cattle, then turning them out onto the range. They played board games. The adults, except Noah, played poker.

Noah sat by the fire. He saw faces from long past flicker in the flames, allowing his thoughts to go back as far as old Antoine, the storyteller. Antoine probably had the most influence over Noah's Indigenous life. Well, that might not be accurate. In different ways, Antoine and Ta Chi had both taught him to read nature's book on the Chilcotin by observation of the flora, the fauna, the landscape and the seasons. Antoine was the storyteller; Ta Chi was the silent guide and teacher. It was on Antoine's deathbed that he named Noah the next *deyen* of the Stoney.

Eventually, there was a movement by the adults to bed.

"Goodnight, Dad."

"Goodnight, Noah."

"Goodnight. Don't stay up too late."

Noah, lost in his own silence, noticed the stirrings. He held up his hand to stay them. His children circled him.

"Your mother is in the studio," he announced.

It took them a moment to realize that he was speaking of Justine's portrait, that Noah meant the spirit of his wife captured for time immemorial.

"I've been secretive about her portrait. I want to get it right and I don't want to show you something partly finished."

From the top of the stairs, Luke spoke up.

"I saw it, Gran'dad. It looked cool."

"Go to bed, you," his mother scolded.

"I want to unveil it on Potato Mountain at the harvest where many of our friends and our nation will be enjoying themselves. A happy time."

"Do you think you'll be able to get up the mountain on horse-back?" Will asked.

"Well," Noah smiled, "Antoine did it when he was eighty or more. With Justine's help."

"Don't worry, Noah," Mary chimed in. "We'll get you up there."

Joel recognized the optimism that defence lawyers sometime develop, and smiled slightly, but still looked a little doubtful.

"What's bothering you, boy?" Noah called him out.

"I'm concerned," Joel replied. "Ray Twoshoes has a proposal for the Tŝilhqot'in Tribal Council. He wants our nation to enter into an agreement with Northern Drilling, an American company, to develop our natural gas fields. I didn't know we *had* gas reserves until Stone Clearwater told me."

Elizabeth smacked her hand on the table. All eyes turned her way.

"That damn agreement will never pass the council."

"Don't be too sure," Joel sighed. "Ray's been lobbying hard after Stone and I discovered those drill holes. He's spreading around a lot of money and big promises for the future of our nation. Ray has a lot of support. The debate may get heated around potato-picking time."

"All the more reason," Noah stated flatly, "I should be on the mountain with Justine."

Most of the family silently nodded.

"We'll see if you're ready," Elizabeth offered.

Grizzlies

Bull watched Billy Joe give his speech live on TV after winning the California primary. He preferred the comfort of his war room at Copper Beech to being out on the hustings and he at least trusted Harriet enough to stage-manage the proceedings. The jewel of the primaries, California with its 176 delegates, was now Billy Joe's. They'd even done better than Bull had expected, though some of the other candidates had surprised him in other states. Billy Joe was now positioned as the leading candidate with only the last set of primaries left before going into the conventions on July 18th.

June was going pretty much the way Bull had written it. By attacking the Democratic frontrunner and belittling his competition among the Republicans, Billy Joe came across as the presumptive nominee — and most people want to jump onto the team with momentum. All the press about accusations of the Democratic hopeful being a criminal kept Billy Joe's name in the public eye, with five stories to one for his nearest opponent. Every latte-drinking late-show host was feeding the frenzy, joking about Billy Joe, keeping his name in the public eye.

Billy Joe didn't have the needed 1,327 delegates, nor were there enough delegates in the last three primaries to give him a majority at the convention. Still, there was no doubt in Bull's mind that lobbying and promises leading up to and during the convention would gain Billy Joe enough votes to push him over the top, provided that Harriet's boyfriend wasn't a crisis in the closet. Each candidate that had dropped out had pushed their delegates to go with someone other than Billy Joe, but each time, Bull knew how to catch a few strays. That was simple phone work, wheeling and dealing of the sort Bull did in his sleep.

The convention would be something else entirely, though. He'd need to be running full-out when that came around, so he thought he could stand to take a break. Checking on the progress in the Chilcotin would be good too. Last time he was there, Ray Twoshoes was talking about grizzly bears. A grizzly bear hunt would be just the thing to get him in shape for the last sprint to the finish line and Twoshoes was the man to arrange it for him. After that, spurred on by the scent of blood, he would work full-time massaging the message and the delegates right up to and during the convention.

He phoned Ray that night.

"How the hell are you, Twoshoes?"

"Okay, Mr. O'Connor. What's up?"

"I'm flying up to your country on the twenty-third. I'll be checking on my claims."

"Yeah, well, I've guided your geologists and looked after your survey crews over the winter."

"I want to see the sites for myself."

"Okay."

"Has your council signed the agreement?

"Not yet. I'm working on it. Most of them want to vote for progress, but there are a few holdouts. When it goes to a vote, they'll sign."

"If you need more money to help convince them, just call."

"Okay."

"Listen, while I'm up in your country, I want to shoot me a grizzly."

"The season's closed, Mr. O'Connor."

"Look," Bull laughed, "I can only get away for three days from the twenty-third to the twenty-fifth. I'll fly into Williams Lake on the twenty-third, take a helicopter to wherever the bears are and I'll shoot one."

Ray had learned to say only one word when dealing with Bull: 'okay'. He knew Bull would overpay him in cash. A normal grizzly bear hunt in the Chilcotin would cost $10,000, but a hunt out of season without tags was another matter. Besides, it seemed to Ray that Bull was in good humour.

"Cost you fifty thousand up front." He had a sudden thought. "American," he added.

"I'll pay cash when I see you in Williams Lake."

Huge Reserves

R ay checked himself in the mirror. His trademark white Stetson was sitting right and gave him presence, adding almost six inches to his 5′7″ height.

Ray figured he could win a vote on a partnership deal with some strategic spending. The only strong opposition would be from the Hanlon family and the Nemiah band, whose reserve was closest to the drill sites. Ray was using all of his powers of persuasion, and Bull's money, to influence the other five bands.

He stepped forward to make a motion at a tribal council meeting in Williams Lake.

"As you know," he told the council and chiefs, "over the winter, I gave permission to Northern Drilling to conduct seismic surveys to test for natural gas around Potato Mountain and in the Brittany Triangle. These surveys didn't harm our land. I gave permission without taking it to council 'cause, until the tests were done, there wasn't enough information about the size and extent of the gas reserves to make it worth talking about. Now the good news. The tests have proven up huge reserves and we'll get a royalty on all of it."

Two men stepped forward, handing stapled sheafs of paper to members of the council.

"I'm circulating a draft agreement," Ray announced. "This would give Northern Drilling the right to drill our land in exchange for a sizable percentage of the profits, which will make our nation rich."

The debate that followed was heated. It mainly centred on Ray bypassing council and secretly testing on Potato Mountain. Charlie Littlejohn put it best.

"Ray," he asked, "why did you go behind our backs?"

The question was rhetorical. They all knew why. It was because there was a dollar in it for Ray Twoshoes. Ray's answer was different.

"I did it because without the testing we would be talking to you about the *possibility* of gas. I am coming to you with a certainty. I spared you the worry. Northern Drilling is prepared to enter into an agreement now and we need the money."

Charlie Littlejohn made a motion.

"We need time to study this proposal. I move that we adjourn the discussion until we meet on Potato Mountain in July and vote then."

Even Ray Twoshoes was in favour of the adjournment. He wasn't quite sure of his support and this would give him more time to lobby and, if necessary, buy it.

Spiritual Guidance

The May branding at the Hanlon ranch had seen the whole family in attendance.

It went so well that Noah, whose energy was improving every day, had decided he should make the journey to Antoine's cave. He would broach the idea with Joel first. He knew his son would be up for a trip on horseback into the mountains where Joel could keep a scientist's eye on the effects of changing climate on plant life.

He got Joel alone after breakfast.

"Son, I'm feeling better physically, but I'm in need of some spiritual guidance."

"What are you thinking, Dad?"

Joel was sceptical of his father's spiritual guidance, which he interpreted as Noah's goal-oriented will.

"I'm thinking I'll go to Antoine's cave to breathe the air and to commune with the ancestors."

Joel wasn't surprised. Noah retreated to Antoine's cave at least once a year, particularly when he was unsure of the future.

182

There was an unkindness of ravens in the area that Antoine and Noah had consulted about the future, not unlike how the ancient Romans examined crows, except that Antoine's ravens could survive the consultations.

"That's a bit of a journey." Joel was worried whether Noah was physically up to the journey on horseback over rough terrain. "Take you a day on horse just to get there in your condition."

"That's where you come in, Joel. I would like you to go with me."

"I'll see if I can free up some time."

Joel was not a person who made up his mind quickly. His philosophy on family life was like his philosophy on science: try to find consensus based on data. His family in Kamloops hadn't seen much of him for the last five months. He called Joan and they decided, their children in mind, to spend some time with Grandad for a nature ride into the mountains. After, he went to speak with Noah.

"All right, I'll go and so will my family. We'll all travel with you to Antoine's cave, leave you there, do some hiking for a few days, then pick you up on the way back. Now you better clear it with Elizabeth."

Noah cornered Elizabeth that evening when she was relaxing with a drink in one hand and pencil in the other, working on a Sudoku. He sat down beside her on the sofa in the great room.

"You know that pemmican that you made last fall?"

"Yes," she said, still absorbed in her Sudoku.

"Well, I've found a use for it."

"What's that?" she asked, still working on the puzzle.

"I'm planning a trip to Antoine's cave in the next few weeks."

She bolted upright and shook her head.

"What? I don't think so."

"Joel's family has agreed to come with me."

"You're too old and too sick." Elizabeth immediately regretted putting it so bluntly. "I mean, I don't think you're up to it."

"I've been riding a horse around the ranch for the last month," he reassured her. "I'll be fine."

He patted her on the knee.

Noah thought it was a bit much to have to negotiate his freedom with his daughter and he complained about it to Justine in bed that night. She, as usual, tamed his anger.

"Now, dear, I did tell her to keep an eye on you. Perhaps you *should* wait a while."

Neither Elizabeth nor Justine agreed to his going, but they didn't try and block Noah from doing so. Noah, along with Joel's family, left the ranch on June 17th, heading southwest into the mountains.

The journey was in easy stages, so as not to tire Noah. What would normally take a half-day stretched into the late afternoon. For the children, it was a history lesson from Noah about the survey and roadbuilders massacre by the Tŝilhqot'in war chief Klatsassin at the sandbar below Waddington Canyon. Their father's lessons were tamer, explaining the flora and fauna on the ride. As they were descending from mountain to the river, they approached a clearing. Noah noticed an anthill had been freshly dug up. He called Angus to him, ordering the dog to heel.

He started shouting and making noise.

"There's a bear nearby," he yelled. "Let her know you're here."

"How do you know it's a she-bear, Grandad?" Hugh asked.

"There are some fresh low scratch marks on a fir tree back a bit. Seems like the cubs are imitating their mother."

"All right, kids, stop here and listen," Joel ordered.

They heard some crashing in the bush below. They came out onto a rocky promontory and looked down on a clearing. There, a huge humpbacked sow foraged with her two cubs. She hadn't gotten wind of the onlookers and the bears were taking their time seeing what nature had provided.

Joel trained his binoculars on the animals.

"Looks like they've wintered well. Momma is a bit lean, but the cubs are fat."

"It's Big Momma," Noah whispered loudly to the children. "We Tŝilhqot'in honour that grizzly. Your Granma was really connected with the spirit of that bear. Anyone who sees her tells the rest of us. We've followed her since she was a cub. She's a survivor."

The bears ambled off and the party continued their descent to Antoine's cave.

Arriving at suppertime, they made camp. Around the fire, the children toasted marshmallows on sticks. Noah sat quietly, watching them and scratching Angus's ear, flashing back to a similar scene with the children's father, uncles, aunt, and an earlier Angus. Hugh lifted a burnt marshmallow from the fire. Seeing the boy on the verge of tears, Noah spoke.

"Have I told you two," he asked, "about your grandmother Ta Chi and how she saved my life?"

"No, Grandad," they said in unison.

"Tell us," Rebecca asked. "Is it a scary story?"

"It all started after I escaped from jail."

"Why were you in jail, Grandad?" Hugh asked.

"Well, son, it's because I was accused of murdering your great-grandfather, Bordy."

Both children's eyes widened. Noah smiled on seeing them shake off the sleepiness of a long day.

"Did you kill him, Grandad?"

Noah noted Rebecca's wide eyes.

"No," he answered firmly. "But a white jury was about to say I did. I didn't wait to hear their opinion. I skedaddled."

"What happened then?" Hugh was engrossed enough that he set down his burnt marshmallow.

"Then I threw myself on the mercy of the Chilcotin by jumping off a truck, before the RCMP caught me, and into the arms
of Ta Chi, your great-grandmother, although I didn't know it
at the time. She and I were fugitives from the law for about five
months until, on Potato Mountain, a circle of elders cleared my
name and I married your grandma."

Rebecca grinned. Hugh made a sour face. She clipped him on
the ear and he forced a smile to match hers.

"Ta Chi tended to my wounds, hid me from the posse and
taught me how to survive in the Chilcotin. Just like your dad is
teaching you."

Joel, tending the fire, looked at his watch.

He stabbed at the fire's edges with a stick. As orange embers
drifted up onto the breeze, the children gasped and turned his
way.

"Okay, kids. You have a big day tomorrow. Especially if I have
to teach you how to survive. Time to get to sleep."

"Ahh," Rebecca protested.

"Do we have to?" Hugh grimaced.

"You'll hear the rest of the story some other time," Noah
assured them.

The children made their way to their tent. Noah and Joel
exchanged looks.

"You can finish the story," Noah said to his son.

"I can't tell it as well as you can, Dad."

He turned and followed his children to the tent.

In the morning, Noah dreamt that Justine was alive.

"Noah," she called out to him. "Help me, help me."

The wind was up. Hearing its whistle, he thought she was
outside. He stepped out of his tent, sure her call was coming
from Antoine's cave. He faced it, resolute.

"Help me."

186

Her voice came from another direction. He stumbled his way through the dark to the edge of the river until his gaze was locked into her penetrating eyes.

"Tell me, my love," he said, "what troubles you?"

"Tell the hunters that I am sacred to our nation."

"It's not hunting season."

"That matters nothing to poachers. Save my spirit, for the sake of the nation."

"I can but pray to the Creator."

He woke with a start before light.

In the early morning light, before the others awoke, Noah told Joel of his dream. Joel, already busy packing the horses for the trip, tried to calm the old man before the family left him alone. Joan and the children made their way out of their tents.

"I know Justine's spirit is in danger," Noah said suddenly.

He crumpled into Joel's arms. Joel tried to comfort him.

"It's only a dream, Dad. Mum's spirit is safe."

"I will pray for your mother's spirit. Leave me now. I'll be fine."

He straightened himself as Joan and the children rushed over.

"Is there anything you need, Noah?" Joan asked.

"Tell us more of the story when we get back," Hugh implored.

"Won't you be lonely?" Rebecca asked.

"I'll be fine," Noah assured her. "I've had a bad night."

At ten that morning, they were saying their goodbyes. They mounted their horses. Joel looked down on the old man, the elder, his father, sitting cross-legged in front of the cave with Angus at his side. He had some misgivings, but time for meditation was an important part of Noah's life and shouldn't be denied.

"We'll be back in two days," he shouted as they rode from the clearing.

"Keep a lookout for Big Momma," Noah shouted after them.

He sat cross-legged at the mouth of the cave.

After Joel's family said goodbye to Noah, they headed to the alpine meadows below the snowcap of Mount Waddington where they collected wildflowers and looked for mountain goats. Joel taught them how to snare rabbits as he had been taught by Noah and as Noah had been taught by Ta Chi. Rebecca was squeamish about eating rabbit, but she was hungry and Joel hadn't brought extra food.

When she finally bit into the roasted rabbit, she found it quite tasty.

"We should save some for Grandad," she announced.

Windfall

At three in the afternoon, six men in dark suits deplaned from a Northern Drilling private jet and walked as a group to the Williams Lake airport terminal. In the middle of this phalanx, one man, distinguished by his height and bald head, was immediately recognized by Ray Twoshoes.

Ray turned to his companion, Clarence Lafrance.

"Let me do the talking. This Bull guy is nasty."

A commercial flight had come in at the same time and the terminal was buzzing. Still, once inside the terminal, Bull quickly spotted Ray. Shadowed by two bodyguards, he walked up. He grabbed Ray by the arm with one paw and squeezed his hand with his other.

"Twoshoes. All the arrangements made?"

"Yeah. I've got a small bus outside to take you to your hotel. Tomorrow, the helicopter'll take you out near Homathko Canyon. A guide located what you're looking for." Ray raised his eyebrow as if to say that no one would mention the bear.

The bodyguards took the luggage off the carriage. Ray figured the large wooden crate which needed two men to carry it contained the hunting rifles.

He arranged to follow the two taxis into town in his pick-up, where he would see the group settled into their rooms.

After dinner, Ray knocked on the door of Bull's room.

"Who's there?" Bull shouted.

"Twoshoes."

"Come in. The door's unlocked."

Ray entered.

"Have a seat."

Bull was at his desk, emailing his office in Atlanta. Another man was standing in the room and Ray elected to remain standing. Bull soon turned to look at Ray as if to ask why he was being disturbed.

"Ray," he said, indicating his companion, "this here is Sam Coulson, my lawyer and shootin' buddy."

The two men nodded at each other.

"Everything okay, Mr. O'Connor?" Ray asked.

"You looking for your money, Ray?"

"That was the deal."

"Here it is. In real money."

Bull showed him a large envelope full of American hundred-dollar bills.

"There's an extra two grand in there," he continued. "I need a favour."

"Oh. What's that?"

"When we get back from our trip, we'll want to party. I want you to line up some young girls and boys to party with us."

"I guess I can do that."

"Good." Bull handed the envelope to Ray. "When do we leave?"

"The taxis will pick you up tomorrow at nine and drive you to the helipad."

Ray went to his truck to count the money. It was all there. He'd never had more than $5,000 in his hand at one time and felt empowered. He took a stack of bills and put it in his pocket, putting the envelope in the glove compartment. He headed back into the hotel.

Clarence was waiting for him in the coffee shop. Ray peeled off fifteen hundred-dollar bills.

"What's this for?"

"I want you to round up fifteen street kids for a party on Friday night at the Blue Moon."

In the morning, when the taxis picked up Bull and his group from the hotel, he had already put in three hours of work on the phone and internet. As far as the campaign knew, he was still in his war room in Georgia. Yet here he was, dressed in camouflage, with a blackened face and a Tilly hat on top. He looked more like a beast in the disguise of a man. Ray was hard-pressed to hold his laughter. The bodyguards remained behind, but the rest of the entourage accompanied Bull: his best friend Coulson, a cameraman and a writer from a hunting magazine.

At the waterfront, Ray crowded them into a helicopter and they headed west. An hour later, having flown over the Brittany Triangle and Potato Mountain test sites, the helicopter landed on a gravel bar near the junction of the Homathko River and Mosley Creek. There, the party met with the guide outfitter.

"Hi. I'm Jesse Pollock. You must be Bull O'Connor."

"Jesse, Ray here tells me that you've located a grizzly."

"Yeah. He just came down from the mountain there and is making his way to the river valley, looking for green grass and any other grub he can find."

"What do you suggest?"

"We don't want to scare him off so we'll have to leave the helicopter here. We can ride horseback for a few miles and get within a mile of where we last saw him. Then it's straight climbing from there. Have you sighted in your rifles?"

Bull pulled out his rifle and Sam Coulson unpacked his. Bull loaded his, a Winchester Model 70 Alaskan (.375 H&H) with a six-shell magazine. Bull was particularly fond of this gun, one of his prize possessions. He regularly rubbed the mahogany stock with linseed oil and broke it down to lubricate the metal parts. He prided himself on his marksmanship and paid regular visits to the rifle range.

Jesse pointed out four empty soup cans he had placed on a log at two hundred metres.

Bull aimed at one of the cans, braced himself for the recoil and pulled the trigger. It blew apart. He fired at the next can and there was another clean hit.

"Yeah. I figure it's well-sighted."

Coulson aimed his Marlin 1895 (.450 Marlin) .45-70 at a soup can. He fired and missed the first shot.

"Damn."

He turned and glared at Ray Twoshoes as if it was Ray's fault. He took his time on his second shot and nicked the can. The rifles were declared functional.

"Twoshoes," Bull barked, "you stay here and set up camp."

Ray nodded. He was glad to have less time with Bull and his friends.

Bull, Coulson, the cameraman, the writer and Jesse mounted the outfitter's horses and headed off into the mountains.

The horses could only take them so far, so they dismounted to continue. On the climb by foot, for a man of such bulk, Bull was surprisingly nimble, keeping up with the guide as they trudged through the brush and melting snow. The intention was to circle the draw where the grizzly was last spotted, keeping downwind and gaining a height advantage. This took three hours with a break for lunch.

Three sets of binoculars scanned the draw, looking for any movement. It was Bull who saw a small sapling sway at the edge of a clearing when there was no wind. Five minutes later, the snout of the grizzly came into view five hundred metres from their position. It would take them another hour to climb down to get closer for a shot and the light would not be good. Jesse's advice was to go back to the camp, get up early in the morning, come back to this spot and track the bear from there. Bull agreed.

They woke at four the next morning. After breakfast, they left for the hunt, Ray opting to stay behind and clean up.

The wind was blowing off the mountain. They retraced their steps to where they last saw the male grizzly. They picked up the bear's tracks at nine — they were fresh. Bull placed his hand in the bear's pawprint. As big as his hand was, the bear's paw was three times bigger, not counting the claws.

They talked in whispers and signalled each other with their hands. The cameraman was the most active of the group, working to get Bull's every move and reaction, as well as his comments. Bull placed himself in the front of the group, turning back to the camera to explain the strategy to confront and kill the bear so it would appear that he was directing the hunt.

At ten in the morning, they approached a large windfall of a hundred trees near a mountain stream.

"Go around that side of the windfall," Bull ordered Coulson, pointing out the direction. "I'll wait here while you move the grizzly to me. Just like wild boar huntin' in Texas."

The guide, the cameraman and scribe followed Bull's every movement. Coulson marched out of sight. Bull tiptoed to the pile of trees and was about seven metres away when there was a crashing sound and a woofing grunt. Two bear cubs scurried into Bull's gunsights from behind the windfall.

They heard the discharge of Coulson's gun. He came running around the windfall toward Bull, a grizzly close behind him.

"For Christ's sake, Coulson!" Bull shouted. "Fall down! You're blocking my sight."

Coulson either didn't hear or was not going to offer himself as the bear's next meal. Instead, he veered hard left some thirty metres in front of Bull. With his experience of facing down wild hogs in Texas, Bull stood his ground and pumped three rounds of armour-piercing bullets into the bear's chest. The bear's momentum carried it to within five metres of Bull, who didn't flinch. The grizzly fell dead with a groan, as if its spirit was escaping back to the Chilcotin.

Bull turned and looked into the camera.

"Damn," he said, full of the excitement of the kill. "I saved Coulson's life *and* killed me a trophy bear. This is what life is all about, kill or be killed."

Although he didn't say it for the camera, this was a metaphor for Bull's approach to politics. Anyone who crossed him in the political arena would know what he meant. Jesse thought he understood what Bull meant as he took in the sight of a mule deer carcass behind the windfall. He said nothing, thinking it better to let the statement stand on its own.

The guide skinned the bear while Coulson, Bull and the others watched, reliving the moment in front of the camera. The writer took notes. No one mentioned the cubs who had fled down the mountain.

They headed back to the horses. Jesse was bowed over with the weight of the bear's skin. Bull, with his great bulk and light feet, danced back to the camp.

When they arrived back at camp, it was mid-afternoon. Jesse took Bull aside.

"I've got to tell you, Bull," he confided, "that wasn't the male we were tracking. You killed a sow grizzly which the First Nations called Big Momma, one they believe is sacred."

"So what? I got me a trophy."

Bull's belligerent reaction left Jesse speechless.

The helicopter picked them up at four-thirty and they were back in Williams Lake at six, in a mood to party.

Noah's Vision

At the entrance to the cave, Noah remained in a cross-legged position seeking a vision. In his mind, if anything happened to Big Momma, Justine would die another death.

His meditation was broken hours later by the sound, followed by the sight, of a low-flying helicopter. He feared the worst. He ate very little and drank some stream water over the course of the day while he thought things through.

It was one thing to be reading in a den full of books and another to be by oneself at Antoine's cave. In both cases, there is a silent discussion. In the den, the discussion is with the author, while in the cave, it's with one's conscience. The monks and nuns of the middle ages knew this and practiced it in their retreats and cloisters while they spoke to their god. So did Antoine, speaking to his Creator. At Antoine's cave, the resident ravens were to be watched carefully, for they were the omens who in the past had warned Antoine and Noah of the dangers to come to the Chilcotin.

As the helicopter flew by, the ravens cawed a warning and Noah was on guard.

196

In the late afternoon, a raven perched on a dead snag was look-ing down at Noah and failed to see the bald eagle soaring above. Noah saw it, but it was too late. The raven spread his wings in a futile escape attempt as the eagle plunged his claws in deep and began to slowly carry the raven away. The air around the eagle became full of ravens darting and diving at the winged predator. The eagle couldn't gain altitude, sinking as the weight of the one raven kept it from evading the unkindness that was attacking it. The eagle tried to release its prey, but its talons were too deeply hooked. Noah watched as the eagle and the raven plunged into the Homathko River to be swallowed by the waters.

Noah was left to interpret what had happened. The helicopter and the bald eagle were omens that came together. In his trance-like state, Noah interpreted this as an attack on Big Momma, on Justine's spirit, to be avenged by the ravens.

Again in his trance the next morning, Noah felt a short stab to his heart which then began to race.

Big Momma has been killed.

Towards dusk the same day, Joel and the children found Noah in the same cross-legged position they had left him in the day before. His head was bowed. He did not acknowledge their presence. Joel dismounted and walked up to his father. Noah straightened.

"The helicopters came," he told his son. "Eagle killed Raven. Big Momma's dead."

The Most Beautiful Girl in the World

On Friday night at the local dancehall in Williams Lake, the Blue Moon, the DJ was catering to the Americans in the crowd, warming them up with such offerings as Charley Rich's "The Most Beautiful Girl in the World". The small stack of folded American bills in his pocket kept him focused on the six middle-aged men at the round table in the centre of the room and their cheers told him that his efforts were appreciated.

People crowded around the men at the round table. The strangers had seemed out of place when they entered with their Southern accents, but all too quickly, they became friendly with the locals, buying rounds and holding court. A story about hunting hogs in Texas gave way to another about fishing for largemouth bass in Louisiana. Jesse, who had been through town enough for an occasional wave from a local, was thinking about the story they *couldn't* tell.

The crowd around the table thinned when Robin Redford took the stage. The locals had known her back when she first earned her chops in her daddy Paul Laboucher's band at church socials and then had followed her rising star. Her star in the US had waned, but she was still celebrated in the Chilcotin. She had gone through her k.d. lang stage, although "Crying" remained in her repertoire. Now, in her 50s, she sang mostly Dolly Parton songs, with an occasional hit of her own tossed in almost as an afterthought. She'd reached the point where she could do what pleased her and no one begrudged her that.

Even the visitors nodded and tapped their feet through her first set. They cheered along with the locals as she bowed and promised to return shortly.

The DJ jumped in with some Johnny Cash, trying to win more favour from the Americans, but their focus was on Robin now. Waitresses were consulted and drinks were sent over. She eventually made her way through the hangers-on to the table of strangers.

"Hi, Jesse," she winked.

"Should I introduce you?" he smiled back with a blush.

The men at the table all answered 'yes' with their eyes, trying to cue Jesse.

"Sure," Robin replied. "I'd love to meet anyone who thinks my voice is worth five drinks all at once."

The guide introduced the group to Robin. They tried out their stories on her. Robin had lived every kind of outdoor life you could imagine and she matched them exploit for exploit. As the drinks continued to flow and the young people listened to Bull recount the story of a duck-hunt gone wrong, the now-thoroughly-drunk *Hunting* magazine writer couldn't help but mention a charging sow bear in an attempt to gain Robin's attention and favour. Instead, her face went fiery red.

Jesse put his drink down and mouthed 'No!' at the writer. Over the speakers, Johnny Cash gave way to Stompin' Tom Connors and the opening strains of "Sudbury Saturday Night". The dance floor filled up.

"Are you telling me you shot Big Momma?"

"I don't know if it was *that* bear," he said, realizing he'd hit a sore spot.

Jesse tried to intervene, though unsure what to say. He'd realized there had been two grizzlies in the draw. Big Momma must have found the deer carcass behind the windfall and chased off the male they'd tracked. Coulson hadn't known the difference and had disturbed the *wrong* bear. Even so, everything came down to Bull, including the shot that killed Big Momma. It was Bull he had to talk to.

Robin got called up on stage to sing her next set. The writer breathed a sigh of relief and the others teased him as Jesse edged over to Bull. As the band kicked in, Jesse cupped his hands over Bull's ear and yelled over the noise of the party, trying to ensure that no one else could hear.

"Don't mention the hunt to anyone in this country." He pointed to the reporter. "And don't let him write in that magazine that you killed that sow grizzly."

Bull, however, wasn't in any mood to hear anything from Jesse if there wasn't something to shoot. More, he was indignant. He was proud of what he had done.

"Why should we cover your ass? The people who read *Hunting* are good Republicans. They don't give a hot damn if it's a sow or a boar."

"We're not in the States," Jesse replied in a panic. "We're in the Cariboo Chilcotin. Where Big Momma is sacred."

"You saw that grizzly charge us. If I hadn't killed the bear, Sam here would be hanging on my trophy wall instead of your Big Momma."

"While we were on an illegal hunt."

Jesse looked around frantically, trying to make sure no one had heard.

Fred and Ken came into the dancehall.

"So you interviewed your childhood idol," Ken teased, nudging Fred.

"Yeah. I wish you'd told me sooner that she would be singing tonight."

"This is Williams Lake," Ken laughed. "You'll get plenty of chances to hear Robin Redford."

"Depends," Fred shrugged.

Fred had lost interest in bantering with Ken. He scanned the room, past Robin at the bandstand and the whirl of dancing couples to the activity around the bar and the even bigger buzz at one table. There, young people surrounded a group of large men like bees drawn to honey. Fred tried to make sense of this. Suddenly, he understood. In the centre, Bull was orchestrating the show.

Bull surveyed his domain. As his gaze came to the doorway, Fred saw him and froze, staring. Bull noticed the stranger in glasses and locked into his gaze. Suddenly, recognition struck.

Bull turned away and spoke to one of his bodyguards, who motioned to the other. They both got up from the table and moved towards Fred.

Fred grabbed Ken by the arm.

"Let's get the hell out of here," he yelled. "I'll explain later."

Ken didn't ask questions. He trusted Fred's instincts enough to just follow. They ran out the door they had just entered, bumping into Elizabeth on her way in. Without saying a word to her, they tore out into a drenching night rain. They cut across backyards to Ginty's Bar down the street, making their way through the crowd and out the back door. Fred knew his cover was gone. There was no telling what would happen next.

Elizabeth had come to the Blue Moon, tracking one of her cases. As she came in the door, Fred and Ken Lamb ran out, followed by two thugs. Recognizing trouble, she rushed inside. No sooner than she was through the door, the girl in question, seventeen-year-old Rosie, ran up to her as Robin hit a high note and the band slid into their solos.

"Miss, miss, something terrible has happened." Rosie pointed to Bull's table. "Those men over there. They shot Big Momma."

Elizabeth saw some of her wards clustered around Bull's table, a few of them underage. She knew their lives, far beyond what they'd tell her, and knew how they made their money. Seeing Bull with his arm around an underage boy, she marched up to him.

"You fucking bastard," she yelled into his face. "You killed Big Momma!"

Her voice boomed over the drum solo. The fuse had been lit. Robin stopped the band, fire in her eyes. From the stage, her eyes fell on Elizabeth and the eyes of the crowd followed. A hush fell over the hall before hushed whispers replaced the silence. Word got around that Big Momma had been killed. The First Nation people began muttering amongst themselves and pointing to the Americans. Their white friends, conservationists and hunters alike, were as one concerning the preservation of Big Momma, their anger adding to the swell of protest.

All eyes on him, Bull pushed the boy aside.

The bodyguards, who hadn't had time to put on their coats, returned to the Blue Moon to report back, looking like wet beavers. They were greeted by cold stares. As they returned to the table, all eyes on them, Jesse disappeared into the crowd.

Bull rose and pushed Elizabeth away. Coulson grabbed her from behind. She was a squirming bobcat in his arms. Bull moved towards her, menace in his stance. There were audible gasps from around the room.

Elizabeth's lit fuse met the explosive charge of the crowd at Blue Moon who descended on the strangers. She kicked at Bull, he grabbed her leg, and the crowd stormed the table.

The RCMP broke up the fight. Later, they escorted Bull and his cohorts to the airport and saw them onto Northrop's private jet. They didn't charge Bull as they didn't have the hide or any other evidence who shot the bear, let alone that it wasn't in self-defence.

On the flight back to Atlanta, Coulson nursed his black eye with an icepack. Bull's head was bandaged from having a bottle broken on his skull.

"Remember when I agreed to go on this grizzly hunt with you?" Coulson asked. "You told me it was like a wild boar hunt in Texas. That I could act as the decoy so you could shoot it, just like you did the pigs."

"Yeah."

"You said there'd be something in it for me."

"I did say that, Coulson. But you roused the wrong bear. I was after the boar. You served up the sow."

"I think you owe me, Bull."

"Yeah, I saved your life. I could've let the sow get you and then gone for the boar. We're even, buddy."

"I don't think so, my friend," Coulson said coldly.

Quite the Number

"**S**tone Clearwater to see you, Mary," the receptionist announced into the phone.

Listening for a response, she eyed the young man as if to say he would look good on a horse.

"Mary will see you in a minute, Stone. Why don't you take a seat? We have the latest edition of *The Cattleman* on the stand over there."

Stone was flattered that the girl thought he was a local cowhand. He picked up the magazine and took a seat. The receptionist smiled at him while she was talking on the line to a client.

Soon enough, Mary came into the reception area.

"Hello, Stone. Come on in."

Mary's office looked more like a lounge. Two easy chairs and a low coffee table made for a welcoming feel.

"Some of my clients are intimidated by lawyers and this helps them relax," she explained, seeing the question in his eyes.

She sat behind her desk with a how-can-I-help-you look.

"Uh, thanks for seeing me," Fred replied. "I'm investigating some property transfers in the Chilcotin and I'd like you to do some searches for me."

Stone took a sheaf of papers from his briefcase and placed them on the desk.

"This is quite a number of properties," she said, ruffling through the pages. "Looks to be about twenty in all. Most of them large ranches that have been sold in the last year."

"Yes. I'm interested in tracing the buyers for an investigation and a story I'm working on."

"It seems that the buyers are all numbered companies."

"I'd like to find out the names of the person or persons who control the numbered companies, as well as Northern Drilling Corp."

"I'll do a search of the companies registry after the land registry search. I should have this done by next week."

"Thanks." That business over, Fred relaxed a bit. "I understand that you may be representing Clint Lalula at his trial."

"Yes," she nodded. "Mr. Laliberté has a conflict and probably won't be able to attend."

"I'm just curious. I take it there are no restrictions on you representing a relative in a criminal trial?"

"It's not recommended but isn't against the rules."

On the way out, the receptionist again smiled warmly at Fred. He smiled back.

"Stone," she ventured, "my name's Janice. It's almost five. How about a drink down at Ginty's?"

He had been asked for dates by Williams Lake women before, so wasn't surprised. In the circles in which he moved in Georgia, it wasn't the custom, but in Williams Lake, women could lasso at full gallop and throw a calf, jump off their horse and tie the calf's feet together, so they certainly had equal rights when it came to dating.

"Sorry, Janice. I've got a deadline to meet."

It didn't sound like a brush-off, so she took one of Mary's cards and wrote her number on the back.

"Give me a ring when you're out of deadlines."

He took the card.

"Thanks, Janice."

When he closed the office door, it occurred to him that Harriet was probably being hit on every day. Even so, he knew she was as loyal to him as he was to her.

Defending Your Territory

Clint and Jeremy had learned to survive on the tough streets of Williams Lake where gangs of youth from the three nations gathered to stake out territory and defend it. The boys also had to learn how to survive in the wilderness and amongst the factions in their own nation. Elizabeth considered it to their credit that the brothers were attending school and had not joined a gang like so many others their age. They were addicted to computer games and would commandeer the library computers until being politely asked to let others use them.

Elizabeth met them at the library door.

"You know, Grandad's starting to lose it," Clint said on the ride back home. "He's talking about Granma and Big Momma, the grizzly the Americans shot. He said Granma is telling him to avenge the killing of Big Momma by a bald American. He called him 'the Bald Eagle'."

"I know, son," Elizabeth nodded grimly. "I've noticed Grandad's moods. He's still grieving. I'll speak to him." As an afterthought, she added, "He's just talking nonsense. How can he avenge the loss of Big Momma?"

Exchanging Words

Mary steeled herself for grilling her nephew. Clint's lawyer from legal aid, Terry Laliberté, QC, had been called on to argue a case in the Supreme Court of Canada and was not available. It was now up to her to defend Clint, otherwise the trial would be put off again until the fall.

Mary had successfully defended Clint on lesser charges in the past, including possession of marijuana and possession of goods under $500. She would have preferred not to represent her own nephew, but he had to get on with his life.

"This is a serious charge, Elizabeth," she cautioned her half-sister. "The maximum jail time is ten years."

"I know, but Clint and I have faith in you. I think you're the best criminal lawyer in the county and I've seen them all."

"I'll need Clint's full cooperation, though."

In preparation, Mary reviewed the facts from the witness statements and the RCMP file with Clint and Jeremy. Last October at the Anahim Lake Stampede grounds, Jeremy had gotten into a fight with Norman Twoshoes. Mary asked Jeremy who started the fight.

"Norman did. His dad thinks he owns the reserve. They have money. His dad has a new Ram 250."

Mary read on from the RCMP summary: "'Clint was called away by his mother. In his absence, his brother had been approached by Norman Twoshoes, who taunted him.' What did he taunt you about?"

"About hassling a Twoshoes family elder."

"'Although Jeremy'," she continued reading, "'was younger by three years, he roughed up Norman. Rather than laying charges, Norman decided to ask his family to respond. Later that day, in front of the hotel and in broad daylight, the members of the Twoshoes family gathered to — quote, right the wrong, unquote. There, they met the two brothers. Words were exchanged.'"

Mary looked up from the summary, directly at her nephew.

"What words were exchanged, Jeremy?"

"You know, swearwords." His voice dropped off. "Like 'pussy' and 'son of a bitch'."

"Okay, don't be shy, you've got to say them in court."

"'Clint grabbed a rifle from his pick-up and shot Norman in the foot'," she read, then set the summary aside.

Four witness statements, all from the Twoshoes family, all said much the same thing. Crown counsel in Williams Lake had laid the charge under Sec. 267(b) of the Criminal Code — assault causing bodily harm.

"Clint," she asked, "why did you shoot Norman?"

"I didn't mean to. Just wanted to warn him off."

They continued until Mary was sure she was familiar with the boys' story and that they wouldn't be shaken under questioning.

"Okay," Mary asked, "so what are you going to do now?"

"I'm going back to the Stampede," Clint grinned. "In Williams Lake."

"Really? Now?" Mary raised an eyebrow.

"It's okay," Elizabeth assured her. "He'll be there for the trial. Right?"

"Right, Mum."

Hitchhiking

Late Monday night, Clint got a ride from Williams Lake to the Redstone Reserve where he bunked with friends. He woke at six-thirty in the morning with a hangover, walked to the highway and put out his thumb.

He had to be in court at Anahim Lake by ten that morning. Not many cars passed and those that did were mostly tourists who had no interest in giving a ride to an Aboriginal, while others were locals visiting friends on the reserve. He thought, with a sigh, that Jeremy wouldn't have a problem getting a ride.

One old Buick looked promising, driven by a well-dressed non-aboriginal man in his thirties with an empty passenger seat, but the car wasn't going very fast and there was some steam coming from the radiator. The car limped by him. Three hundred metres up the road, it stopped. The driver got out with a jerry can, lifted the hood, propped it up with a two-by-four, unscrewed the radiator cap and poured water into the steaming open hole. Clint decided not to run up and ask him for a ride. The man lowered the hood, clambered back into his car and carried on.

Time was short. It was more than two hours' drive to Anahim Lake and it was already seven. He began to walk, kicking up dust and looking back as he went, wishing for a car on the horizon. A newer-model SUV came into view, driven by another non-aboriginal man, grey-haired and dressed in a suit and tie. It passed by Clint's upturned thumb. Clint trudged on in defeat. The SUV stopped up the road. Clint quickened his pace and caught up with the car. The driver lowered the passenger window.

"Where're you going, son?"

"Headed to Anahim Lake."

The driver had a good look at the boy and unlocked the door.

"Okay, hop in. That's where I'm going."

"Thanks."

They didn't talk as they drove through the reserve, west on Highway 20 toward Tatla Lake. By the time they reached the reserve border, the boy was asleep. He woke when they slowed down through Tatla Lake.

"Good morning," the driver said. "You must have had a hard night."

"Yeah, you could say that."

"Visiting family in Anahim?"

"You could say that."

"I'm from Williams Lake myself. Did you go to the Stampede on the weekend?"

Clint sized up this formal, yet friendly, man and decided that he could loosen up a little.

"Yeah, I did. My girlfriend rode in the barrel races."

On the other side of Tatla Lake, approaching Kleena Kleene, they passed an old Buick parked on the side of the road with steam coming out of the radiator and the driver pouring water into it. Both of them chuckled.

"I might've got a ride from him," Clint volunteered, "but he was boiling over. I didn't want to risk it."

"Good call. He's a lawyer from Williams Lake. Fancies old cars."

They got into Anahim Lake at nine-thirty and the driver dropped Clint off in front of the hotel.

"Hope your day goes well. What are you here for?"

"Ah, I've got a court case. I'm told the judge is a real bastard. I'm not feeling good about it."

With that, he slammed the car door. He leaned into the window.

"Thanks for the ride."

"You're welcome. What's the judge's name?"

"Savage."

The stranger raised an eyebrow.

"That makes sense," he replied.

He drove off without looking back.

Final Briefing

Clint sauntered into the hotel and headed for the restaurant. Elizabeth and Mary were in a booth, staring at him as he entered. He dreaded the encounter. Worse, his grandad was there, sort of staring off into space. He'd hoped that Grandad had forgotten about the trial.

A waitress, a friend of his, was approaching Clint with a breakfast plate of bacon, eggs and hash browns. He hadn't eaten since lunch the day before. She paused in front of a tourist's table and was about to set the food down when Clint took the plate from her.

"Thank you, Chrystal," he said. "I'm starving."

"Hey! That's mine," yelled the tourist.

"Yours is coming up, sir," Chrystal smiled, surreptitiously kicking Clint in the leg as he walked away.

Clint carried his breakfast to the booth, sat down and began eating. His mother was all business.

"The trial is in half an hour. You should have been here an hour ago."

"I got caught up in the Stampede, had to hitch a ride," he offered, shovelling food into his face. "Where's Jeremy?"

"He's in the washroom."

"Clint," Mary said calmly, "we went over your evidence last week. Is there anything you want to add or to talk to me about?"

"No."

He stuffed half a slice of toast into his mouth. Noah sat looking off into space, saying nothing. Mary looked up from the table as a customer came into the restaurant.

"Stephen, I'm glad you made it," she smiled, waving. All the lawyers in Williams Lake knew about Stephen's undependable old cars.

He waved back. Still eating, Clint looked over his shoulder at the man and smiled to himself. It was the guy who was having radiator problems with the old Buick.

"Who's that guy?" Clint asked his aunt.

"Stephen Finch, the prosecutor."

Clint sucked in his breath and let it out slowly.

"Whew. I almost got a ride from him at Redstone."

Jeremy walked up to the table and sat down. He tended to slouch where Clint carried himself straight. They acknowledged each other's presence with a nod.

"Well, boys — and Elizabeth — let's go."

Mary rose from the table, the others following. Clint drained his coffee cup and was the last to get up. They passed the prosecutor, sipping coffee and picking at a bran muffin. He waved at Mary.

"See you in court," he nodded.

214

The Trial

In the summer months, the courtroom in Anahim Lake was a classroom in the elementary school. The clerk of the court had rearranged the furniture to resemble a court, with the teacher's desk for the judge and two tables with chairs for counsel facing the desk. There was a separate smaller table for the accused. A table with a lectern and Bible on top served as the witness stand.

Before Clint entered the courtroom, Noah called him over. Clint felt ashamed speaking to his grandad in this situation. Noah smiled at him almost shyly.

"Your mother told me yesterday that you were coming up for trial and your grandmother and I wanted to be here for you. From what I hear, you did the right thing and we support you, no matter what."

"Thanks, Grandad."

"Clint, I know something about courtrooms. I was in your shoes once. I had a good lawyer. His name was Stan Hewitt. He had… an upright piano in his office?" Noah caught himself.

"Well, in the end, it worked out all right. Your Aunt Mary is a good lawyer."

"Yes, Grandad."

They followed the rest of the family into the courtroom.

Elizabeth scanned the room for any sign of Clint or Jeremy's fathers. She sat where she hoped they would be. Ken Lamb was waving 'hello', his notebook open, but neither of her sons' fathers were there. She sighed and waved back.

Norman Twoshoes was sitting in the back of the courtroom surrounded by his whole family, including his father and the matriarch, Sara. When the Hanlons entered, they glared at them and were glared back at in return. The Hanlons arranged themselves on the other side of the courtroom and ignored their opponents. They all waited in uneasy silence until the prosecutor walked in and waved at his witnesses.

"Good morning, everyone," he called out good-naturedly.

His mood was not infectious. They greeted him with stony faces.

With all the actors in the drama in place, the clerk went into the ante-room and spoke to the judge. He then preceded the judge into the courtroom.

"Order in court," he called.

The lawyers rose and the gallery hesitantly got to their feet. In walked the judge. Both the judge and the accused eyed each other knowingly. The judge sat.

"Please be seated," he said.

Everyone sat. The clerk turned on the recording device.

"Counsel, are you ready to proceed?" the judge asked.

"Yes, Your Honour," the two lawyers said in unison.

Mary stood.

"Your Honour," she began, "Mr. Laliberté, QC, is the lawyer on record for Mr. Lalula. He is arguing a case before the Supreme Court of Canada this week, so I am appearing in his place."

"Thank you, Ms. Kent. Mr. Clerk, read the summons. Mr. Lalula, please stand."

Clint stood at the improvised prisoner's box.

"Clint Lalula," the clerk read, "you are charged under section 267(b) of the Criminal Code with assault causing bodily harm to Norman Twoshoes on the first day of August 2015. You have entered a 'not guilty' plea."

"Yes. I'm not guilty," Clint pronounced defiantly.

The judge cleared his throat.

"Counsel," he sighed, "you should know that I drove from Williams Lake this morning and, on the way, I stopped for a hitchhiker at Redstone. I drove him to Anahim Lake. The hitchhiker, who was unknown to me at the time, is the accused, Clint Lalula. I believe that Mr. Lalula did not know who I was. We did not speak about the case and the accused slept much of the way. Now, I want to know if you have any objections to my presiding today. I am prepared to proceed. I have not been influenced one way or the other by this accidental encounter."

Mary rose to her feet.

"I have no objection, Your Honour," she said.

Finch rose slowly, his brow furrowed.

"Your Honour," he finally said, "what makes you think that Mr. Lalula didn't know who you were?"

"It was an impression I got when we parted company."

There was a pause.

"Do you have an objection, counsel?" the judge asked.

"I am wondering what it was that gave you that impression, Your Honour."

Stephen Finch was a stubborn man. He favoured old cars that broke down and, when he was in a prosecutorial questioning mode, he dug to the root of the matter till it hurt. Out of instinct, he sensed the judge was holding something back. Had he been more sensitive, he would have understood that the judge, who he knew to be an honourable man, would not say or do anything that would taint his thinking.

Judge Savage, who knew Finch well, realized he would have to say what happened, much as he would have preferred not to.

"What gave me that impression, counsel," he sighed, "was that when I dropped Mr. Lalula off in front of the hotel, I asked him why he was in Anahim Lake. He replied, 'I'm the accused in a court case and I hear the judge is a real bastard.'"

The gallery erupted in stifled laughter.

"Order in court," shouted the clerk.

"Thank you, Your Honour," the prosecutor nodded. "I have no objection to your sitting on this case."

"Nor I, Your Honour," Mary reiterated in a light tone.

Elizabeth coughed. Mary turned and smiled at her, nodding to signal she knew what she was doing.

"For the record, Ms. Kent is appearing for the accused and Mr. Finch for the Crown. Your opening statement please, Mr. Finch."

"Your Honour, the victim Norman Twoshoes is a member of the Anahim Lake band and from a respected family. He was intending, with some members of his family, to enter a hotel restaurant in Anahim Lake when the accused, in the company of his brother Jeremy, stopped them."

Sitting in the prisoner's box, Clint squirmed on hearing the prosecutor's version of events. The prosecutor ignored this.

"Words were exchanged," the prosecutor continued. "The accused reached into a vehicle, pulled out a rifle and shot the victim in the foot. I will be calling Norman Twoshoes, his uncle, brother and two cousins."

"Thank you for your succinct opening, counsel. You may call your first witness. Oh, before you do, those persons who will be giving evidence in this trial, please wait outside in the hall until you're called."

There was a shuffling of chairs and mumbling while witnesses left. Norman Twoshoes stood to leave with the others.

"Norman," Finch called out, "you're my first witness. You can stay."

Norman sat back down.

"I call as my first witness," Finch proclaimed once the crowd quieted, "Norman Twoshoes."

Norman walked up to the witness stand and was sworn in by the clerk.

"You are Norman Twoshoes from the Anahim Lake band. You are twenty years old and work part-time for the band."

"Yeah."

"On August first, at about three in the afternoon, in front of the hotel, you were shot in the foot with a rifle."

"Yeah."

"Who shot you?"

Norman looked menacingly at Clint sitting in the prisoner's box.

"Clint."

"You mean Clint Lalula, the accused?"

"Yeah. That's him."

"Tell the court in your own words what happened."

"Okay. Me and some of my family drove up to the hotel and got out of the truck. We saw Clint and his brother Jeremy standing beside another truck. We walked toward the hotel entrance. Clint pulls out a rifle from the truck and shoots me in the foot."

"Was anything said between you and Clint?"

"What we always say. We don't get along much. Just the usual cursing and all."

"Tell the judge the words you used."

"Well, Clint called me 'a goddamn pussy'. And I said, 'Watch your mouth, you son of a mother.' That's when he went for his rifle and shot me in the foot."

"Would you describe your injuries?"

"I was wearing cowboy boots. The bullet went through the leather near my big toe. I took my boot off and it was full of blood. The doc sewed me up and I hobbled around for a month."

"Thank you, Mr. Twoshoes."

Mary Kent rose from her chair. She had no smiles for Norman.

"Norman, do you have a good memory of that day?"

"Sure."

"So you would remember that earlier, you and Clint's younger brother Jeremy had a fight behind the Stampede grounds stands. And that Jeremy, who was seventeen and three years younger than you, got the better of you in that fight. You threatened him. You said, 'Watch your back 'cause I'm coming after you.'"

"He didn't get the better of me."

"He gave you a black eye and a bloody nose."

"Okay, but I hurt him."

"You threatened him. You said 'I'm coming after you.'"

"I might have. It was just a saying."

"And you did come after him that afternoon."

"I met him and his brother outside the hotel, yeah. I wouldn't say I came after him."

"Norman, you and four members of your family were in a pick-up that came at speed to where Jeremy was standing and each of you, including your cousin Bonny, had a weapon."

"So?"

"You admit that."

"Yeah. I guess we were going hunting."

"You piled out, all except Bonny, with your guns pointing at Jeremy and you said, 'I've got you now, you motherfucker.'"

"I don't use that language."

"But you said, 'I've got you now.'"

"Yeah, I could have. But I meant I was going to fight him."

"Isn't that when Clint showed up and called you a pussy?"

"Yeah, like I said, he called me a pussy."

"And you and all your family pointed your guns at him and called him a son of a bitch."

"Something like that. But I didn't shoot him."

"And that's when Clint took a rifle from the truck and shot at the ground to scare you off?"

"He shot my foot."

"Did the police show up?"

"Yeah. Lucky for Clint they did."

"What do you mean by that?"

"Nothing, just that he's a lucky sunnuvabitch."

Mary looked at the judge, raising her eyebrow. The judge gave her a slight smile. She sat down. The prosecutor had no further questions for Norman.

In turn, all four of the male Twoshoes clan who were in the car with Norman told the same story. Bonny, now seventeen, was called last.

She hesitantly walked to the witness box, her eyes fixed straight ahead. She was sworn in. Finch smiled at her in a reassuring way, then asked her the preliminary questions to establish that she was present and armed with a rifle on the day of the incident.

"Ms. Twoshoes," he asked, "would you please tell the court what happened after the exchange of insults between your cousin Norman and the accused?"

"Norman," Bonny began in a soft, almost inaudible voice, "was real mad. When we pulled up in the truck, all the guys got out with their rifles. I stayed in the truck 'cause I was scared. I didn't want anyone to get hurt. I think the guys were going to take Jeremy somewhere and teach him a lesson. Then Clint shows up. After the tough talk, the guys moved forward with their guns. I was watching this and thinking that someone is going to get hurt."

Bonny paused. Finch checked his notes with a bit of a scowl.

"Is that when the accused shot Norman?"

"Objection, Your Honour," Mary jumped up, shouting. "The Crown knows better than that. It's a leading question."

"Yes, Mr. Finch. Perhaps you should rephrase the question."

"Fine, Your Honour. Tell us, Bonny, what happened after the tough talk?"

"Like I said," Bonny said hurriedly, "the guys moved a step closer. That's when Clint grabbed his .22 from his pick-up and fired into the ground."

The judge, who had been racing to keep up as he took notes in his bench book, looked at her.

"Please speak up, Ms. Twoshoes," he asked kindly. "And speak a little more slowly so I can write down what you say."

Finch, obviously taken aback by Bonny's testimony, looked at her statement in his hand and then looked back at her, shaking his head. After a moment's thought, he left well enough alone and sat down.

"I have no further questions," he advised the court.

Mary recognized Bonny as a gift witness for the defence. She stood, restraining a smile.

"Bonny," she asked, "do you think that Clint was aiming his gun at Norman when he fired?"

"No. If he was aiming it at him, he would have shot higher. He was shooting into the ground."

"Do you think that Clint firing into the ground with his .22 rifle made things better so that no one would get hurt?"

"Yes. The guys stopped and the RCMP came."

"Thank you. Those are all my questions."

Much relieved but still nervous, Bonny Twoshoes walked to the back of the room to face the none-too-pleasant stares of her kin who had already given testimony.

Finch called the RCMP officer who had arrested Clint. He testified that Clint had been questioned but had not given a statement on advice from counsel. Mary had no questions for the officer. The prosecutor rose with much satisfaction and looked at the clock, its hands reaching toward twelve.

"That's the case for the Crown, Your Honour," he announced.

"Ms. Kent, will you be calling evidence?"

"Yes, Your Honour. Clint Lalula and his half-brother Jeremy Hawthorn."

"The court will adjourn till two."

When court reconvened, Jeremy took the stand. He looked tough owing to his size but, when he was sworn in, had a soft voice and a gentle manner.

Mary established who Jeremy was and his relationship to Clint.

"Now, Jeremy, you were behind the Stampede ground stands on August first last year."

"Yes," he said hesitantly.

"You met Norman Twoshoes, whom you knew?"

"Yes," he answered more confidently.

"Please tell the court what happened behind the stands on that day."

"Norman came up to me. He said that I had roughed up his mother and fired a shotgun at his uncle's door."

"Did you do those things?"

"No, I didn't."

"Go on."

"I told Norman that it wasn't me. I guess he didn't believe me. I turned to go and he attacked me from behind. He put a chokehold on me."

"What did you do?"

"Well, I threw him over my shoulder and picked him up and hit him a few times."

"Did he hit back?"

"Yeah, then he backed off and said, 'You better watch your back because I'm coming after you.'"

"Did you see him again that day?"

"I did. I was in front of the hotel and I saw him drive up in a pick-up with four or five of his family. Guns were sticking out of all the windows. It looked like a fucking porcupine."

The judge raised his hand.

"Jeremy," he said disarmingly, "we don't use that language in court. I know it's confusing. If a swear word is used by someone during the event, then that is evidence and it is proper to quote it. But you should not use it in court to describe a porcupine."

"Sorry, sir," Jeremy said in a whisper.

"What did you do when you saw the Twoshoes arrive?" Mary continued.

"I stood there. They all piled out of the truck with their guns, except Bonny. And Norman said, 'I've got you now, you motherfucker.'" Jeremy looked up at the judge. "That's what he said."

Elizabeth restrained a giggle.

"What were you thinking?"

"That they were going to shoot me."

"Where was Clint?'

"Clint came out of the hotel and called Norman a pussy. Then Norman took a step forward with his gun and called Clint a sunnuvabitch. Clint grabbed his rifle from the back of his pick-up and shot at the ground to warn him off. Then the RCMP came."

"Thank you, Mr. Hawthorn."

The prosecutor rose slowly from his chair and looked at Jeremy with a withering glance.

"You are familiar with guns, are you, witness?"

"I know what a gun is."

"As a First Nations man, you have the right to hunt in all seasons and you hunt with a gun."

"Yeah."

"And all your friends and members of your band do the same."

"Yeah."

"It's not unusual to keep your guns in your trucks."

"Yeah."

"So when you saw the Twoshoes with guns, that was not unusual."

"I felt threatened."

"Then why didn't you go into the hotel?"

"I'm not a chicken."

"When your brother showed up and insulted Mr. Twoshoes, who then returned the insult, that was just normal talk between your families?"

"We are not on good terms."

"Neither you nor the Twoshoes have ever resorted to gunplay?"

"We haven't. They sure looked armed and ready to shoot."

"Come now, witness. No one threatened in words to shoot you."

"Yeah, but…"

"Thank you, witness. I have no further questions."

Mary rose from her seat.

"Mr. Hawthorn, were you going to add something to your answer?"

"Yeah. I felt threatened by the Twoshoes' actions. They were moving forward with raised guns."

Jeremy stepped down from the stand.

Clint was called forward and sworn in. He answered Mary's preliminary questions, which placed him at the scene.

"Please tell the court," Mary asked her nephew, "what happened in front of the hotel on that day."

Clint held himself before the judge proudly.

"I was in the hotel restaurant when I saw the Twoshoes family roll up in a pick-up bristling with guns. My brother Jeremy was standing outside the restaurant and they almost drove into him. Jeremy was in trouble, so I ran out and stood beside him as they piled out of the truck with their guns. I remember calling Norman Twoshoes a pussy."

"Why did you call him a pussy?"

"Because he had to come with an army to fight my brother."

"Then what happened?"

"He called me a motherfucker and moved towards us with his gun raised. I was standing by my pick-up and grabbed my gopher-shootin' .22 rifle from the box and fired at his feet to scare him off. Then the RCMP came along and I was arrested."

"Did you have any intention to harm Norman Twoshoes?"

"No. Just scare him off."

Finch was scribbling in his notebook and took some time to organize his notes. The judge waited patiently. Finally, the prosecutor rose.

"Mr. Lalula, how old are you?"

"Nineteen."

"Old enough to vote and drink?"

"Yeah."

"You were drinking on that afternoon?"

"I had a beer at lunch."

"I suggest you had more than one beer and your judgment was impaired."

"No to both questions."

The judge took his eyes off his notes and had a hard look at the witness. Then he scribbled something in his bench book.

"If you weren't impaired, why would a sober person fire off a gun in downtown Anahim Lake?"

"My brother's life was being threatened by five armed and angry people. I wanted to warn them off."

"And you did that by shooting Norman Twoshoes?"

"I didn't mean to shoot him, just scare him. All of them."

"You could have shot in the air?"

"Yeah. I guess."

"I have no more questions, Your Honour."

Mary looked back at the papers on the table. Clint, still at the witness stand, held up his hand as if he was trying to get a teacher's attention.

"I believe," said the judge, "your client wishes to say something, Ms. Kent."

Mary cocked her head and took in Clint's raised hand. She started to rise to prevent him from throwing away his defence, but thought better of it and settled back.

"Do you have anything to add, Clint?" she asked warily.

"Yes. I just want to apologize to Norman. I didn't mean to hurt him."

Sitting in the back of the courtroom with his father, Norman shook his head.

Before Clint could say anything more, Mary stood.

"That's the case for the defence, Your Honour," she said.

"Thank you, counsel. Argument?"

Mary remained standing and the judge nodded.

Elizabeth was proud of her boys and of her sister. She had seen a lot of lawyers over the years and could tell Mary was a good one. She didn't grandstand or put on a show. She talked to the judge like he was sitting across a kitchen table having a coffee. Just good normal talk about the facts and getting to the root of the dispute.

"Your Honour," Mary began, "all these young men allowed their emotions to get the better of them. Because of past slights and grievances and perceived wrongs to an elder, this led to a fight which later escalated to a show of force. We may say now that the Twoshoes family meant only to scare Jeremy Hawthorn, but to Jeremy and his older brother — who are very close — it was a real and present danger. The accused did what he thought was the best thing to do and that was to fire a warning shot in self-defence. It was not his intention to harm Mr. Twoshoes."

Mary paused for effect. Judge Savage, who was closely following Mary's argument, looked past her to see Norman Twoshoes slouching in a chair and making a wry face.

"Bonny Twoshoes," Mary continued, "testified Clint didn't aim at Norman. Unfortunately, Mr. Twoshoes was struck in the foot. Fortunately, the wound was not too serious and Mr. Twoshoes has been able to carry on without any disabilities. My client is sorry for the harm caused and has apologized to Mr. Twoshoes. I ask for an acquittal."

"Mr. Finch?" The judge raised his eyebrow.

"Yes, Your Honour. All the ingredients of the crime are there. This was a reckless use of a firearm and the victim was injured. The extent of the injury matters not."

"Thank you, counsel. The court will adjourn for fifteen minutes and I shall deliver my decision when we reconvene."

In the teachers' lounge, Judge Savage looked at his bench book, taking particular note of Clint's answer to the prosecutor: "No to both questions." He thought to himself, *Pretty rare a teenager gets the better of Finch like that. He knew what he was doing today and I think he knew what he was doing when he fired that gun. He intended it as a warning shot.*

The court reconvened.

"Thank you, counsel, for your assistance in this case. The facts are not in dispute. The issue is: did the accused, in that tension-filled moment in November, intend to shoot Norman Twoshoes? He says he did not. He says his intention was to warn off Mr. Twoshoes and his family. His counsel argues that the gun was fired in self-defence. He was cross-examined on that by Mr. Finch and I am persuaded that he was telling the truth. I have also considered the evidence of Bonny Twoshoes who was able to see what happened from the truck and confirmed his evidence. Before I give my verdict, please stand, Mr. Lalula. You are sorry for the harm caused Mr. Twoshoes?"

"Yes, Your Honour. I apologize."

"Did you hear that, Mr. Twoshoes?"

"Yeah," Norman said from the back.

"Mr. Lalula, I find you not guilty of the charge. I believe you fired into the ground and any injury was accidental. However, you could stand to handle firearms with more care."

"I will, Your Honour," Clint said solemnly.

The judge stood and the clerk's voice rang out as the judge left the room.

"Order in court!"

The not-guilty verdict took the air out of the Twoshoes family, who shuffled out of the courtroom and assembled outside, except for Bonny, who was nowhere to be seen. They had thought Clint would serve time. And Clint's apology was something different.

The others filed out of the building with less speed. Noah, who was in the courtroom for the whole trial, approached Ray Twoshoes and held out his hand.

"No hard feelings, Ray."

Ray reluctantly took Noah's hand and grunted. Noah hadn't finished.

"Did you hear that Big Momma was shot by Bald Eagle?"

Ray wasn't ready for that.

"What the hell are you talking about?"

"You know. Big Momma. The grizzly."

"Yeah, that was a shame," Ray said, moving away from Noah.

"Well, whoever did it —and I got a good idea who did — is going to pay for it."

Elizabeth and Mary intervened, leading Noah away.

"Come on, Dad," Elizabeth smiled. "This is a time to make up with the Twoshoes. Like your grandson did by apologizing in public."

She looked around for Clint without luck. She was just about to check back inside, when she saw him down the block, his arm around Bonny Twoshoes. She put one and one together and got one.

So much for the Hanlon-Twoshoes feud.

Dead Ends

Mary phoned Stone on Wednesday.

"Stone, I have your searches."

"Congratulations on the acquittal in your nephew's trial yesterday. I'd expected to cover it, but Muriel had other plans for me. I was reporting on the Stampede."

"Thanks, Stone. Clint's going to make something of his life and he doesn't need a criminal record." She quickly changed the subject. "I have the land registry searches on the numbered companies and the company searches. Northern Drilling and the numbered companies are owned by further numbered companies in the Grand Caymans with their registered office at a lawyer's address. The lawyer refuses to reveal who his client is. I'm afraid I've hit a dead end, other than that all the land titles can be traced to the original crown grants that include mineral and gas rights. I've left my searches and a covering letter at reception for you to pick up. Sorry I wasn't able to be of more help. Perhaps you know someone connected to these companies who can pry the information out."

"Thanks for your help, Mary. I'll come right over."

Harriet's connection to Northrop Oil was the only card Fred could think of which was left to play. Should he ask Harriet to make enquiries by lying, telling her he wanted the information for another story for his fictional novel? Or should he tell her the truth: that he believed the search would prove a secret deal between Bull and her father that would likely end her father's chances for the nomination?

He opened the door to Mary's front office. Janice was there, looking cute and disappointed.

"You've come to ask me out on a date," she said, her voice heavy with sarcasm.

"To tell the truth, Janice, I'm in love with another woman. If I wasn't, we'd be drinking at Ginty's right now." Then in a more serious tone, "I'm here for some documents."

She handed him a thick package.

"Here you are. You don't know what you're missing."

"Bye, Janice."

By the time he returned to his office at the *Tribune*, he had resolved the question about how he would approach Harriet. It was time to tell her the truth.

Dear Harriet,

Thank you for keeping my email address to yourself. I'm fine.

I have a confession to make. Since I left Copper Beech on Labour Day weekend, I've been on the run.

He read over the sentence. Something was wrong. Yes. 'Labour', the Canadian spelling. He'd adapted more than he'd realized. He corrected it to 'Labor'.

When I was in the Copper Beech library, I accidentally
overheard a conversation between your father and Bull that
has the potential, if proved to be true, to deny your father the
nomination. You're so caught up in your dad's campaign that,
although you had no knowledge of the deal, it could also
affect you.

It has to do with a secret illegal payoff to Bull for his services
as a political strategist and the offshoot is that it could
damage the ecology of the Chilcotin. I would have shared
what I heard with you at the time, but I was found out and
threatened by Bull. I thought I'd go away, collect myself
and then speak to you. I was in Wyoming when Bull had
someone threaten me again. I left for the Chilcotin, where
I have been working as a reporter under an assumed name,
Stone Clearwater, and following the leads. Bull has found me
again, but at this stage I don't care.

I now have a paper trail that shows a systematic control of
the mineral rights for large blocks of land including that of
First Nations (what we call Indians in the US). The owners
are numbered companies registered in the Grand Caymans.
This means nothing unless I can connect the companies to
Bull. If you could use your influence to get the company's
legal department to provide you with the names of the
owners of these companies, I've attached a list.

I realize that this is a tall order from a guy who loves you.
I know I haven't been upfront with you and I apologize. I
thought it best that I email you to give you a chance to think
about my request and your answer. I wouldn't blame you
if you refuse. In any event, it is my intention to make my
investigations public before the Republican convention.

Whatever your answer, my feelings for you would not change, if you'll still have me.

All My Love,
Fred.

Connections

J oel would be giving a talk on climate change at an environment conference in Atlanta. He'd prepared his presentation and packed his bags, then suddenly realized he hadn't made any arrangements to get to the airport. There was enough going on with the family, so he decided to call Fred for a ride. As a bonus, maybe he could offer some insight into the drilling on Potato Mountain.

They arranged to meet at the Rendezvous Café as it was easy enough for Joel to drive there with his bags. His truck could be parked on the street there while he was gone. Fred was waiting for him when he arrived.

Hazel, after taking their soup and sandwich orders, took on her usual inquisitorial role.

"Stone, I see you're interviewing another Hanlon. Shouldn't we be charging you for using the café as an office?"

"From the size of the tips I give you, I thought you were," Fred snappily replied.

"Just mention us in your next article."

She walked away with the last word and a smile.

"Did you find out who's behind the drilling company?" Joel asked Fred.

"Mary did a search. The company is registered in BC, but its shares are owned by a Cayman Islands company whose directors are lawyers. They won't reveal their client."

"Is there another way of finding out?"

"I have a contact in Atlanta. I've asked her to search it out for me. Until I find the legal link to O'Connor, I don't have a story."

"Who's your contact?"

"Harriet Applebaum."

Joel shook his head in wonder.

"You never cease to surprise me. She's the one who invited me to this conference. She's going to introduce me. How and where did you meet her?"

"She's my girlfriend."

Joel nodded. That explained a great deal about Stone Clearwater.

Fred drove Joel to the airport in Frederica. There was a climb to the airport hill from the highway which proved a chore for her aging engine. She slowed to a crawl.

"This old dog should be put down," Joel remarked.

"I courted Harriet in this car. It's my good luck charm."

He dropped Joel off at the terminal and said goodbye.

Full of loving thoughts about Harriet, Fred returned to Williams Lake with Frederica behaving beautifully on the downhill return trip.

Fred found himself tapping nervously on the steering wheel, anxious about his email to Harriet. After months of digging for proof, he had placed himself in the hands of his girlfriend.

Coded Message

Harriet's reply came within a day.

Dearest Fred and Stone,

The truth is that I have been too busy and preoccupied with Dad's campaign to question your story of writing your novel in the wilds of Wyoming. "Secrets." I now realize the title was a coded message.

I have been looking for ways to dump Bull as Dad's political strategist. I will speak to Northrop legal today and get back to you.

I want to see you ASAP! You know why.
Also, you must not keep secrets from me again.

Harriet xox

For the first time since Copper Beech, Fred felt that he could exhale and start to feel human. The two parts of his identity, Fred and Stone, were coming together. He could see an end to his ordeal. This feeling was not about to last, for Harriet sent another email the next day.

Dearest Fred,

What a day. I am in Atlanta at the Global Warming conference. About your search of the Cayman companies, Dad has placed all his shares in a blind trust and can't have anything to do with Northrop for fear of conflict, so I couldn't ask him. I met with Northrop's lawyer in the early morning. The lawyer assured me that Northrop is not associated with Northern Drilling or the numbered companies. I asked him to find out who did own these companies and to get back to me.

Meanwhile, I met Joel Hanlon. I am going to introduce him at the convention as the keynote speaker. He told me about his aboriginal roots in the Chilcotin, about his father, Noah Hanlon, the celebrated painter, and Potato Mountain. And he told me he knows you!

I was interrupted. The lawyer just got back to me: A Texas company, Bullivant Holdings, owns Northern Drilling and the numbered companies. Bullivant is owned by Bull. I'm going to confront him. The lawyer will provide me with the documentation. You have your proof! Speak to me before you use it.

Please come home.

Love,
Harriet xox

Fred tried to phone Harriet to tell her everything about Bull, but she wasn't picking up.

He had purposely kept his investigations from Harriet to keep her safe. He had now placed her, an innocent, in harm's way. He hadn't asked Harriet to go the next step if Northrop Oil didn't own Northern Drilling, but should have known she would use her initiative. Through her enquiries, she had connected Bull to the plot and Bull was not a man to be crossed. He would want to know why someone was checking into his company and would find out who that someone was. Fred had enough facts to take the story public — to expose Bull, and by extension Billy Joe who, contrary to all the pundits' earlier predictions, was still in contention for the Republican nomination.

Fred went online and booked a flight. He texted Joel Hanlon to tell him that he was flying to Georgia and would like to meet him in Atlanta for lunch the next day.

Fred had promised Muriel he would give her the story. She had proven to be his mentor and her careful editing of his writing was making him a better reporter, so he felt even more of an obligation. She was balancing the books in her office when he knocked on her door. With no time to prepare her, he just told her outright.

"Muriel, I've got the proof on that story I've been working on. It implicates Billy Joe Northrop III and it affects the Chilcotin. I'm flying to Atlanta tonight. I promised to give you the story too."

Muriel had seen many surprising events in her newspaper life. But the connection of the Chilcotin with a presidential race was enough to make her break her rule of not drinking before four. She reached for the bottle in the bottom drawer of her desk and poured two stiff ones.

"Well, spill the beans," she said.

It took him a half-hour to outline the facts.

"Who're you going to give the story to?" she asked.

"I thought I'd speak to the editor of the *Atlanta Herald*."

Muriel shook her head.

"You're on a tight deadline. The paper will take a week to do their own fact-checking and then run the story up the ladder for approval. Then they'll give it to a seasoned reporter and you'll just be part of the story."

"I hadn't thought of that," Fred admitted.

"I think you should go with a political website who will be able to publish quicker. I met Sarah Procter at last year's newspaper convention in Toronto. From Atlanta. She gave a balanced talk on online news. Her site has over half a million readers. If you can convince her you have the goods and she puts it on her site, your story will go viral within the day."

Fred held out his empty glass. Muriel refilled it. He hadn't expected that a small-town editor would have a connection to a blogger from his hometown.

"Of course I've heard of Sarah. She even gave a speech at our graduation." Fred wished now he'd paid more attention then, rather than being so dismissive. "Do you know her well enough to give me an introduction?"

Muriel had read his mind and picked up her cellphone.

"Fred, an editor doesn't just edit copy, she actually decides what goes into the paper from advertising to editorials. And she has connections. Just to be clear, this means you don't get the initial byline."

"Call her."

"You'll want to pump yourself a bit if you want to do a follow-up piece." Muriel kept scanning her contacts. "I'll pull together a file of your work with us. Your *Herald* articles are up to you, of course."

She found Procter's name and hit 'dial'.

"We're friends," she told Fred. "She likes Canadian Club."

Muriel took a swig from her glass as the phone rang.

"Sarah, Muriel Steeves. … That's right. How the hell are you? … Myself, I'm in top form. I've been following your coverage of the Republican race. You don't seem to appreciate Northrop's abrasive style."

Muriel held the phone away from her ear.

"That goddamn blowhard is bringing America down to his level," blared out of the speaker.

Fred grinned.

"Yeah, well, look, one of my reporters who hails from your beautiful Atlanta has a story that'll knock the socks off of Billy Joe and his political strategist."

They went over the details and Sarah agreed to take the story forward. Fred was beaming as Muriel hung up.

"So, I guess we should talk about a story with the local angle for the *Tribune*," he offered.

"You don't think you were going to be able to leave this office before that, do you?"

She refilled both their glasses.

The Shoe Drops

Bullivant S. O'Connor sat on the divan in his suite in a downtown Atlanta Hotel. Balance sheets and poll numbers littered his desk, while persuasion and threats filled his mind. To what end? In Bull's mind, it was to keep America for Americans, to stop the erosion of American power in the world, the power for good. Billy Joe had the background, the money and the ambition to be president. Bull was supplying the know-how. One of his master strokes was to have Billy Joe attack rich financiers. The irony wasn't lost on Bull. The rich didn't mind being attacked verbally by one of theirs as long as his policies, should he get elected, didn't affect their bottom line.

Bull wasn't interested in fiction. He read history and the biographies of great men. He admired the Prussian chancellor Otto von Bismarck and, from the same era, President Abraham Lincoln. Both were strategists of the highest order and models for O'Connor. Bismarck had gained the confidence of Kaiser Wilhelm I of Prussia, then built the Prussian army in the 1860s into a war machine that united Germany under Prussian rule.

In the same decade, Lincoln had successfully fought a civil war to maintain the union. These were Bull's heroes.

His private phone rang, interrupting his thoughts. The display showed it to be Coulson. He punched talk.

"Yeah?" he muttered.

"Bull, did you authorize Billy Joe's daughter to get the records from your Cayman holdings?"

"What the hell are you saying? Did you give them to her?"

"No."

"That's good."

"We gave them to Northrop Oil's lawyer who probably gave them to her."

"Coulson," Bull growled, "you should be taken out and shot or at least disbarred."

Bull meant it.

Coulson wasn't about to play Henry Whittington to Bull's Dick Cheney. He spoke clearly and coldly.

"Bull..." He paused for effect. "...let's just say we're even after that grizzly bear hunt."

He hung up the phone.

"Damn you, Coulson!" Bull shouted over the dial tone.

The half-interest in the Chilcotin gas play was his prize for delivering the nomination. He and his consortium would cash in big. All that would now be public.

His team of Texan millionaires and Wall Street financiers had put together the Informed Citizens Super PAC which was supposed to be independent of Billy Joe's campaign. If that got out, as he knew it would now, there would be all hell to pay.

He had had a nagging thought of a possible hitch in his strategy: Fred Scully. *Pity that Harriet's boyfriend breached my security wall*, Bull mused. All the money he'd spent on electronic security, firewalls and encryption couldn't prevent old-fashioned eavesdropping. This had been eating away at

Bull's confidence — with the convention in a few days' time and Fred Scully in the Chilcotin, he'd been expecting a shoe to drop. And it finally had.

Something had to be done to silence Scully and Harriet. His best hope was to turn Billy Joe against his daughter and ride out the bad publicity that was bound to come when the press got hold of the secret deal. Of course, finding out what 'Stone Clearwater' had been up to was no big deal.

Bull's thoughts returned to what he was going to get from Billy Joe's presidency. After all, the Northrop Republicans were prepared to forgive Billy Joe anything including crime based on his promise to keep America for Americans. He could make this work either way. What would Billy Joe give him for that? Bull was thinking that an appointment as Secretary of State would suit him, just as it had suited Seward after he'd lost the nomination to Lincoln. Bull would then use his influence on President Northrop to bind Canada even closer to the States. In his mind, in the minds of the American moneyed classes, Canada was already a vassal state and the only way to confront China would be for America to have its northern neighbour subject to even closer control. Of course, he would maintain the fiction of separate nations. There was too much socialism in the Canadian welfare state for the Republicans' liking, for a political link. To bring Canada into the American federation would taint American capitalism and wasn't necessary, as American companies already controlled most Canadian trade and commerce. If Canada didn't show signs of cooperating he, as Secretary of State, would threaten trade sanctions.

The first thing he'd get Billy Joe to do as president would be approving the Midcontinent Pipeline, moving oil from Canada to Texan refineries on the Gulf of Mexico. The Midcontinent would be a symbolical umbilical cord joining the two nations' economies.

He had sold Billy Joe on building a super-wall between Mexico and the US as part of the platform. There was no wall suggested between Canada and the US, only the strategy of forging closer ties with their northern neighbour: in other words, closer control. Of course, the next step would be the sharing of water. He would keep these thoughts to himself for now, although as the nomination convention came closer, this strategy kept rising to the forefront of Bull's consciousness.

There was a knock on the door to the suite's kitchen. The maid brought lunch, a cart piled with dishes of food. She placed a plate on the sideboard and began dishing out food: a porterhouse steak, roasted potatoes, squash and carrots, each item on separate plates.

Bull ignored the food and dialled Harriet's room number.

"Harriet, it's Bull. Would you drop in to see me now? The maid has brought lunch. I'll have her serve the usual for you."

Overhearing this, the maid quickly retrieved more food from the kitchen. She set down another small plate and placed some lettuce down as a bed. She sliced a tomato on top and drizzled some oil and vinegar over it, finishing it off with some Ryvita on the side. She knew from experience a light snack was all Harriet would be able to get through before she was sick of Bull.

It wasn't long before Harriet knocked.

"Come," Bull's voice rang out.

She entered.

"Sit down," he said.

The maid placed the salad in front of Harriet before opening a diet soda for her. She opened a second Pepsi for Bull who was already attacking his almost-raw steak. The blood trickled from the corner of his mouth, but he didn't use a napkin — he rolled his tongue and licked it off his face. He waved the maid away and she retreated to the safety of the kitchen.

244

"I'm glad you're supporting your daddy on the hustings. You know that…" He waved his hand to indicate a blank. "…that global warming conference tomorrow? Hanlon is speaking and you're introducing him. I'd like you to get to know this Joel Hanlon."

"How do you mean?" Harriet replied, her tone guarded.

"You know. Find out a little about him. Is he married? Family? Is he more than a scientist? Is he a socialist? What are his politics?"

"Why do you want this?"

"I have my reasons," Bull said, smiling and chewing. He took a swallow of Pepsi before adding, "We might hire him for Green Trust. You know, fund some of his research."

She didn't reply.

"Have you heard from your boyfriend?" he asked.

He sensed that she was immediately on her guard.

"No," she said angrily.

"Do you know where he is?"

Harriet toyed with her salad, took a small bite and broke off some Ryvita.

"Why this sudden interest in Fred?"

"I shook his hand. Nice guy. Maybe we could use him on our team once your daddy is officially nominated. Give me his phone number or email and I'll get in touch."

"He doesn't have a phone or internet connection. He calls me from a payphone. I'll let him know you're interested in speaking with him when I hear from him."

Bull finished his steak and fixings. He buzzed the maid back in. She cleared his plate and set out his dessert: an entire lemon meringue pie.

After the maid left, he took a bite of pie, then dropped his bombshell.

"I was in the Chilcotin last month. I saw your boyfriend in Williams Lake. He was with a woman."

Bull looked for the hurt on Harriet's face. Instead, she smiled.

"I know," she said convincingly, recognizing that Bull was lying.

Bull felt the shift of power from himself to Harriet and found that suddenly he was on the defensive.

"If that's all, Mr. O'Connor..."

"Not quite."

He took a forkful of pie.

"I think," he said, his mouth full of pie, "you and I should go up to Williams Lake. Pay a visit to Fred. He's working as a reporter by the way. Calls himself Stone Clearwater."

"No thank you, Mr. O'Connor. But you go ahead. I know your real interest in the Chilcotin and it isn't environmental protection."

"You Southerners are so damn polite. I answer to 'Bull', not to 'sir' or 'mister'. You've been snooping around my affairs and I don't take kindly to that."

Bull was starting to lose his temper. Harriet just nodded and stood as if to leave. She was calm, ready to bait this man with the short fuse. Bull got up from the divan. She paused, thinking about what he had said about being polite and deciding he was right. *Now's the time*, she thought.

"If you don't answer to 'Mr. O'Connor'," she said contemptuously, "do you answer to 'Asshole', you miserable piece of shit?"

Bull had seldom been called an asshole to his face by anyone, let alone a piece of shit by a woman. And this from what he believed to be a genteel Southern belle. His normally controlled and passive face betrayed shock. Had Harriet been a man, he would have lunged at her in the wild fury building inside him.

"It's not politeness," Harriet continued, "that stops me from uttering your obscene name, it's contempt. I've followed your vile, vicious campaign style because of my dad — not my 'daddy' — who I admire and who wants to become president. I think he'd make a good president. You've corrupted his path to the presidency and I'm going to spend the rest of this campaign fighting your strategy and your Chilcotin takeover. You think you can get to me by saying Fred betrayed me. Well, think again. He is a loyal, decent man and he's on to you. We both are."

She didn't wait for a reply. She turned for the door. She wasn't fast enough.

Bull showed some all-American speed. He cut off her exit, grabbing her from behind and holding her in a bear hug. With his paw over her mouth, he whispered in her ear.

"Show a little respect for the man who placed the crown on your daddy's head. I know you came into my room for a little action. I'm going to give it to you and you won't tell anyone 'cause that would ruin your daddy's show."

He relaxed his grip. She turned and pulled away suddenly, his hand still on her shoulder. Her blouse ripped. He was upright, towering above her, but exposed. She drew back her hard leather walking shoe and kicked him in the crotch. He doubled over. She dove for the door and freedom.

Bull smiled to himself despite his pain. *That bitch will go to her daddy. But her daddy has an appetite for the presidency and he knows I can deliver. Now he has to choose and I'm the only choice he can make.*

Once out the door, Harriet adjusted her clothing and smiled to herself as she hurried to her next appointment. *I'll tell Dad tomorrow over breakfast. He needs a new political strategist.*

Dear Fred,

I was assaulted by Bull today. He asked me to see him in his 'war room'. He is a vile nasty man who may get Dad nominated, but the American public would never elect him based on the campaign Bull has masterminded.

Bull knows you're Stone Clearwater. He wanted me to get
to know tomorrow's guest speaker, Joel Hanlon, to find out
about his family and his political leanings. I refused. Bull's
used me to balance his rhetoric about making America
for Americans with a touch of green. I've done everything
that's been asked of me, including accompanying Dad on the
hustings and putting up with this pig of a man.

As I was leaving, I told Bull what I thought of him. I won't
repeat it here. He lost his temper and lunged at me, ripping
my blouse. I was able to kick him in the crotch and got away.
I have him where I want him.

Love,
Harriet

Fred read the email carefully. Twice. He realized that his
Harriet had learned on the campaign trail what academics could
only speculate about. She had learned how to win in a man's
world of raw politics.

Moderation

Joel was five minutes late for his lunch with Harriet. A huge bald man was sitting with her at the table and the conversation didn't seem friendly. He recognized the man, having met him with Ray Twoshoes last year in Williams Lake. After he approached, the man stood. He towered over Joel, who realized this was an act of intimidation rather than a courtesy. The man held out his hand as Harriet introduced him.

"Dr. Hanlon, my father's political strategist insists on meeting you. I believe you've met Mr. O'Connor."

Meat hooks, Joel thought as he winced in pain, his hand buried in Bull's paw.

"We met in Williams Lake," Joel mumbled.

"I don't remember."

Harriet's mouth dropped. She shrugged with her hands out.

"Call me 'Bull'," he replied curtly. "I played nose guard for the Texas Longhorns. These hands came in handy then." He assessed Joel with a glance as if he was looking at modern art that was beyond him. "I hear you're Canadian."

"That's right."

"It's said that a Canadian is an American with manners."

"Well, Mr. O'Connor, when manners were handed out, the South got its fair share."

"Dr. Hanlon," Harriet interrupted, "is a leading expert on climate change."

"In Texas, we don't believe in man-made climate change. The weather is a card that God dealt us and we have to live with it."

"Dr. Hanlon," Harriet continued, "gave a talk this morning at the conference that showed *scientifically* that the US is emitting too many greenhouse gases into the atmosphere. He suggested ways that we can clean up our environment. Ecology is much like politics, don't you think, Mr. O'Connor?"

Joel had to cover his mouth to restrain his smile.

"So you want to shut down the oil industry," Bull spluttered. "What are you, a... a socialist?"

He looked at Harriet while he said it. She met his stare. Joel's smile faded.

"Moderation in all things, Bull," Joel said quietly, as if admonishing a child.

"Your daddy," Bull told Harriet in a venomous tone, "wants you to go with him on a campaign swing to Florida tomorrow. He'll be leaving from the airport on his private jet at ten. Be there."

He rose from the table and walked away, fuming.

"Charming," Joel said.

"He's the leading political strategist in the world. Dad swears by him. I can't stand him. I think if Dad wins the nomination, Bull's campaign strategy will ruin his chances for election. Actually, Joel, I'm afraid of him. I think he's mad."

"As in crazy?"

"Yes."

"Have you told your father?"

"Yes. And I'll tell him again tomorrow."

Bull waited in the foyer of the restaurant. He could see his car pull up at the entrance with his two-man bodyguard. He wasn't thinking of his next appointment, only of that goddamn Canadian talking about moderation, sitting there smug as a boll weevil in a cotton field, sucking the vital juices out of America. He twirled around on his tiny feet and headed back to the table.

Harriet and Joel were drinking coffee when her phone went off. She excused herself.

"Hello?"

"Harriet, darling! Are you all right?"

"Fred, it's you," she said with relief. "I'm fine."

"I'm coming to Atlanta tomorrow."

She hadn't heard Fred's voice for ages. It was stronger, more resolute then she remembered.

"Oh, Fred. It's so good to hear you. I'm with Joel Hanlon. Bull just left. I've got him where I want him."

"You kicked him in the balls?"

"Yeah," she laughed.

Fred joined in her laughter with relief and pride.

"I have so much to tell you," she said. "Dad wants me to go with him to Florida tomorrow. I'll be back tomorrow evening about eight. I need to see you. Come to my mom's house for dinner at nine."

"I'll give you a call when I get in. Don't tell anyone."

"Bye, sweet."

"Bye."

There was no Harriet to divert attention when Bull came back to unload on Joel. Bull opened his mouth and started his rant before he reached the table.

"Have you any idea," he spat, "what would happen to Canada if we put up a tariff wall? Your economy would collapse in a year. You're desperate to sell your tar sand oil to us and would have to make a buffalo park out of Alberta if you can't. The only way your country can work is if you cooperate with us. Try that on for size as a piece of moderation."

With that broadside, Bull turned and left just as Harriet returned.

"What was that all about?" she asked.

"Bull, who doesn't like moderates or socialists, wanted to apologize to me for being so rude earlier and to give me a sneak preview of your dad's speech on diplomacy tomorrow in Florida," Joel explained.

He didn't have to let her in on the sarcasm. She saw his raised eyebrow and nodded.

The next day, Fred bused in from the airport to Joel's hotel. They met for lunch in the hotel restaurant. After they ordered, Joel looked carefully at the young man opposite. He could have been one of his graduate students.

"Was it Harriet or Georgia on your mind when you decided to come to Atlanta?"

"Harriet, I guess. Look, Joel, I'm in trouble. I've gotten Harriet in trouble."

"*Pregnant* trouble?"

"No, no. I've crossed one of the most powerful men in America. That's why I came to the Chilcotin, to hide and to prove what he's up to. You saw the seismic work being conducted on Potato Mountain in April. We knew that Northrop Oil and O'Connor were behind it, but I had to prove it. I asked Harriet to check it out. She didn't find a connection through Northrop Oil, so she used her legal contacts at Northrop to see who was behind the exploration."

"Who was it?"
"Bull O'Connor."
Joel nodded.
"Is he the trouble?"
"Yeah."
"I met him yesterday. He interrupted my lunch with Harriet."
"Sorry to hear that. I'm sure that was an ordeal."
"Yes. He was an asshole."
Fred nodded. *Strong words for a scientist*, he thought.

Crushed Roses

When Fred arrived at Harriet's mother's house, it was twilight and the streetlights were on. He was early so he walked up and down Maple Street, trying to calm his racing heart. At nine, he stood on the front porch with his briefcase, a bottle of Malbec and a dozen pink roses clutched to his chest. He set the briefcase and wine down on the porch and knocked hesitantly. He hadn't seen Harriet for over eight months. It was as if he was a soldier coming back from the war to his sweetheart, hoping that they could carry on as if it was yesterday — but it wasn't yesterday. He could understand, considering what she had gone through in his absence, that she might question his loyalty and love.

She opened the door wide. He didn't get a chance to even look at her before she rushed into his arms and crushed the roses between them. He extracted his arms from her hug and embraced her. He found her lips and kissed them through the thorns, petals and leaves. The pain of the thorns only added to their passion. After a long minute, she stood back and looked at him.

"I've wanted to do that for so long now."

254

"Me too."

They picked up the crushed roses and Fred's briefcase, then headed in. Harriet arranged the roses in a vase while talking a blue streak about everything except what was on her mind. She placed the vase on a side table near the door in the den.

"When did you start wearing glasses?" she asked.

"Oh," Fred replied, realizing she had never seen him wearing them. "I always had them, but usually wore my contacts. Guess they just kind of grew on me while I was gone."

They went to the kitchen where Harriet opened the fridge door and pulled out a bowl of cooked macaroni. She freshened and tossed it with olive oil and herbs.

"I'm afraid we have to dine on leftovers," she announced while putting the macaroni in the microwave. "It's better than the frozen food I've been eating. The campaign and all."

They both nodded, but left the subject untouched.

With the salad and paired with the Malbec, the macaroni was more than passable — with ketchup. They avoided talking about what was in the briefcase, instead toasting each other and eating mostly in silence. Fred poured the last of the bottle and they went into the den.

Fred took some papers out of his briefcase.

"I owe you an explanation," Fred said. "I need to tell you everything."

"You did treat me badly. You declared your love one day and then disappeared for eight months. And you didn't take me into your confidence."

"I know. The reasons I gave and the updates were all lies."

"This has something to do with Bull."

"It has everything to do with O'Connor."

Fred took a deep breath. He looked at his sweetheart sitting next to him on the sofa.

"When I left, I was in shock. You remember at the reception, after the speeches, I came up to you and said I had something important to tell you? I understood the importance of what I'd overheard. I wanted to share it with you so we could talk it over. You introduced me to your dad and I met him. He loves you. I could see it."

"I know. And I love him and am doing everything I can to help him get elected. So, what was the important thing you were you going to tell me?"

"As I mentioned in my email, I accidentally overheard a conversation between your dad and Bull."

"Where was that?"

"At Copper Beech. I was in the library reading and they walked in, arguing. They didn't see me." As an afterthought, he added, "Joseph Conrad's *The Secret Agent*."

"Oh, that's where you got the idea for the title for your novel."

"I never intended to write a novel. I should have told you the title of my fake novel was *Lies* rather than *Secrets*. In the library, they agreed that Bull would act as your dad's campaign strategist and be paid millions of dollars by Northrop Oil by way of a half-interest in a huge natural gas discovery. That's a campaign expense contrary to the Elections Act. They also talked about using the Informed Citizens Super PAC as a cover. The gas extraction would be by way of fracking on a scale that would ruin the balance of nature in the Chilcotin for generations."

"That's terrible. Why didn't you tell me?"

"Like I said, I intended to. Your name was mentioned. Bull was using the Green Trust as a stalking horse to buy up lands for conservation and then transferring them to Northrop for drilling. Your dad said you wouldn't agree to that and Bull said he didn't give a damn whether you agreed or not."

"Bull is deranged," Harriet hissed. "You told me you left Copper Beech without saying goodbye because your dad was ill."

256

"I'm not proud of that. I'll tell you why."

Fred got up from the sofa. He paced around the small den, gathering his courage to say what he'd never admitted before, even to himself.

"I intended to go to my room. First, I had to go to the library. I'd left the book on a chair and had to put it back in its place. I approached the library, the door opened, and there was Bull, standing there with a sneer on his face. He called me by name."

He took a deep breath.

"'Fred,'" Fred mimicked Bull's voice, "'step in here a moment? I have something to show you.'"

"I can picture his face. That ugly leer," Harriet said with a shudder.

"I told him I had to use the bathroom and would be right back. I was looking for an exit. Bull smiled a toothless smile at me. His eyes narrowed to a stony glint.

"'Oh, I'll come along, tell you what I found,' he said. I knew what he had found. He'd found *The Secret Agent*. We went to the bathroom together. He was followed by two large men in suits who waited outside. We were in a crowded house. I didn't think I was in any danger."

Fred was wringing his hands, his voice becoming strained.

"You must know the room — small, two urinals and a stall. Bull went into the stall, leaving the door open. In order to carry through the charade, I stood in front of the urinal and unzipped my fly. 'You know what I found in the library?' Bull asked from the stall. 'Lots of books,' I said flippantly."

Fred's voice was getting shriller. Harriet reached out to him and stroked his shoulder in a reassuring gesture.

"It was the wrong thing to say… the wrong thing to say… Why did I say it?" Fred shouted.

"Fred. Fred, listen to me." Harriet shook him. "Nothing you said made any difference to Bull."

"Yes, okay." Fred took a deep breath and continued. "Bull said, '*The Secret Agent* caught my eye.' Then he moved in behind me and smashed my face into the wall. He grabbed my arm and twisted it behind my back. The sheer bulk of the man... the surprise of the attack... I was overwhelmed."

"Fred," Harriet said in a soothing voice, "no wonder you were afraid for your life."

"There's more, Harriet. Bull shouted in my ear, 'I know you were in that fucking room, I saw you come out. You heard me and Billy Joe talk.' I could hardly speak. I told him I'd heard nothing. He laughed. With his free hand, Bull unbuckled my belt and pulled down my pants."

Fred's rush of words ended in a sigh of anguish. Harriet took his hands in hers.

"Go on, dear. Get it off your chest. Tell me everything. It's all right."

Fred choked up a bit, but continued.

"My pants were down," he said. "Even now, I remember feeling Bull's fat body pressed against my bare ass. His probing erection and heavy breathing."

Fred gagged.

"Harriet, the man is insane," he cried out.

"I know. He ripped my blouse." She placed her hand on his shoulder. "It's all right," she said reassuringly. "Go on. Tell me *everything*."

"I heard the crowd come out of the ballroom. There was somebody starting to open the door. 'It's occupied,' Bull shouted. He kicked the door shut. I heard Bull's suits manhandle a number of people at the door. I tried to shout. Bull let go of my arm and placed his hand over my mouth, then yanked me from the urinal and threw me into the stall. I could hear him pulling up his pants, then running the water. I heard him calmly dry his hands and throw the paper towel into the bin."

258

Fred caught his breath.

"'If I hear or see you again,' he growled, 'if you mention anything that you heard in the library, I'll finish the job and finish you.' The door opened and shut. I was left gasping for air. I had to pick myself up and wash my bloodied nose. I collected my things from my room and headed back to Atlanta. I couldn't get you involved. Bull had no quarrel with you."

Fred sat down, deflated, his head bowed.

"What was your plan, dear?" Harriet asked gently.

"My plan was simple enough: just get the hell out of town. But where would I go? And how could I explain it to you, Harriet? That was the hardest part. If I told you then and there, you would want to know the facts, see proof of the things I'd overheard about your dad. It would be my word against Bull's about what happened. I had to get away and, yes, I admit it, I was scared. I didn't come to my senses until October when Bull sent a reminder to keep my mouth shut by way of an attempt on my life."

"What happened?"

"One of his men tried to drown me while I was taking him on a trail ride in Wyoming. But the attempt had the opposite effect on me. It shook me out of my depression, my indecision. I decided to go to the Chilcotin to get the facts. I landed in Williams Lake in late November. I had no money, just Frederica and a few dollars I earned from wrangling at the guest ranch. I got a job as a reporter at the *Williams Lake Tribune* and started my research."

"What did you find?" Harriet was more than curious.

"I'll tell you. I spoke to Sarah Procter today and told her I have something that could affect the results of the convention. I'm going to see her tomorrow and I want you to see everything I intend to show her."

"I've read her work. She's very astute. She's the one who gave the address at our graduation."

Fred nodded and laid out his case before Harriet. The secret contract that could be worth billions. The contraventions of the Elections Act. Bull's lining up Super PAC money. The titles to land bought by numbered companies that were traced to Bull's consortium. The pictures of the seismic drilling activity. The papers left in the garbage that showed that the work was done by Northern Drilling. Then there was the deal with Ray Twoshoes.

It was about midnight when Fred finished his exposé.

"That's the whole story. I'm sorry, it will probably mean your dad's campaign for president won't survive when this becomes public, but in this election, you never know. Oh, I almost forgot. Did you get the documents from Northrop's lawyer on Bull's connection to the numbered companies and Northern Drilling?"

"Yes. I'll print it out for you."

He realized what that meant for her and simply nodded. There was nothing he could say.

Harriet went to her desk computer, brought up the file and pressed print. Her printer began spitting out paper. She gathered it together and handed it to Fred. It wasn't just Bull's company named as owner of the Grand Caymans company — there were others. Fred recognized some of the names as prominent Republicans and recalled the name of the Informed Citizens Super PAC. He Googled the PAC and compared the donors' names to the names of the owners of the Grand Caymans companies. A number of them were the same. They had uncovered another of Bull's scams. They were too tired to congratulate themselves.

"One thing is certain," Fred told Harriet, "your dad can't keep Bull on as his political strategist."

Harriet had spent the last year of her young life completely caught up in her father's ambition. She intensely disliked Bull and his strategy, yet it had worked. Billy Joe was the frontrunner going into the convention. To this point, she hadn't been able to convince her father to get rid of Bull.

"My dad's not the person who's running for the nomination. O'Connor, the puppeteer, believes it's him. Dad's just his surrogate. O'Connor believes that only he can fix America and that he can do so by using Dad."

"I'm sorry I'm the one who has to expose your dad."

"Fred, darling, don't be sorry. I couldn't convince my father to disown Bull. He refused to get rid of his Svengali, his evil side, even for his own good. Now he will. When I tell him what you've just told me, he'll get rid of him, even before I tell him about Bull's attack on me. I can turn your evidence into an advantage."

They went to bed exhausted by the events of the day and the thoughts of what lay ahead. It didn't occur to them to consider the forces that didn't want that information published.

At two a.m., a car pulled to a stop on Maple Street. There was no other movement or sound in the leafy suburb. The two men in the car sat there for five minutes, making sure there was no one about. They exited the car, being careful to close the doors silently.

They walked to Harriet's mother's house boldly, as if they lived there. The short one took the lead, inserting a key in the lock and opening the door. They walked in, closing the door silently behind them. The taller man nearly tripped over Fred's shoes, earning him a glare from the short one. They went directly to the den. The tall one flicked on his flashlight and quickly spied a thick file of papers and Fred's laptop on the writing desk. He grabbed everything then handed it to the short man. The other, seeing they had what they came for, went to a light fixture and took out a listening device, putting it in his pocket. They turned to go and doused the flashlight. As they passed the side table by the den door, the tall one brushed up against the glass vase of crushed roses. It crashed to the floor.

Fred heard the sound of breaking glass and leapt out of bed. Naked, he ran downstairs as the two shadows gained the front door. The short one ran toward the car. The other stopped and faced Fred. Fred tackled him and they both landed on the porch. The short man started the car and drove away while Fred and the other man wrestled on the porch. Fred was at a weight disadvantage and struggling. The thief was able to get a hand free and punch Fred. Fred recoiled and the thief gained his feet and fled. Fred got up to run after him as Harriet came to the door.

"Let him go," she screamed.

He turned his bloodied face to her.

"They've stolen my file and my computer," he said through swollen lips.

Harriet hung her head and patted him on the arm.

"Oh, Fred, what are we going to do?"

"We're going to call the police."

"But your files…"

"Don't worry about the files. I have most of it backed up on a flash drive."

Fred brought the flash drive to his appointment with Sarah Procter. They spent the better part of the day going over the facts. The story needed further fact-checking because of the stolen files. This would take another day while the convention date loomed ever closer.

Predicting a Win

It was a warm summer morning and Billy Joe was in good humour. Why shouldn't he be? With his own innate leadership abilities and Bull's political strategy, he was on the cusp of pulling off one of the most unlikely campaigns since Lincoln beat Seward for the Republican nomination in 1860. And he would be starting the day off with breakfast with his daughter.

Harriet sat sipping orange juice at a small table, freshly laid with monogrammed china and silverware, on the acacia-shaded terrace overlooking the river, when her father arrived looking dapper and smelling of Brut, newspaper in hand. He placed it in front of his daughter, with its bold letters on the front page: "NORTHROP FAVORED TO WIN REPUBLICAN PRIMARY".

"Look at that headline, will you, Happy? The *Herald* is predicting my win at the convention."

Harriet smiled, watching her dad as he sat opposite her. *This may be the last time I'll see him in such a buoyant mood,* she thought, pouring him a juice from the pitcher on the table.

Billy Joe took a sip of his juice as the butler arrived with bacon, eggs and fritters.

"What's so urgent that you have to call a special meeting to talk to your dad?"

She decided on beginning with Fred. She had to start somewhere.

"Dad, you know my boyfriend, Fred? The one who was writing a novel in Wyoming?"

"Yeah. I met him once here at the start of my campaign. Don't tell me he's proposed."

"No," she said, her voice modulated and monosyllabic. "He was in the library that day when you and Bull went over your deal. When you signed away half of Northrop's Chilcotin gas rights to Bull's consortium for his campaign services."

Billy Joe, about to take a bite of scrambled eggs, paused instead, putting down his fork and staring in disbelief at his daughter. His first instinct was to deny it, but he couldn't lie to Harriet.

"I see," he finally responded. "What does he intend to do with this?"

"He's going public. A well-known blogger is putting the story online this afternoon."

She could see the colour rising in her father's face as he slowly took in the implications of what she was saying.

"When did you hear about this?"

"Fred told me late the day before yesterday. The same time your political strategist heard about it."

"Bull? He never told *me*." His voice raised to a shout.

"No wonder. Bull had to have had Mom's house bugged. After Fred told me and we had gone to bed, two men with a passkey — the police found no signs of forced entry — entered the house and stole Fred's papers and computer. The only items stolen were Fred's stuff in the den. Fortunately, he had a backup."

"What?" He was incensed. "Are you okay?"

"I'm fine, Dad. We both are."

Billy Joe sighed, nodding.

"Why didn't Fred come forward sooner — like at the time?" Billy Joe asked, his annoyance showing.

"Good question, Dad. He was going to tell me that night in September, but Bull intervened. He assaulted Fred and threatened worse if he said a word. Fred was afraid for his life and for good reason. Bull followed up on his threat with an attempt on Fred's life in Wyoming. After that, Fred went to the Chilcotin to find proof of what he had overheard. He has that proof, Dad. You have to get rid of Bull. He's a liability."

Billy Joe looked lovingly at his daughter, his constant supporter since he'd declared his candidacy. She had been as helpful in getting him to within reach of the nomination as Bull had. He didn't want to have to make that choice. Surely the team could hold together until the convention.

Harriet understood the hard choices that her father had to make. She broke the silence that lay heavy between them.

"Two days ago," she said quietly, "Bull assaulted me when I faced him with the truth. He tore my blouse and I had to run from his room."

"Damn!" He rose from his chair. "Are you all right? Were you injured?"

"I'm okay, Dad. I was able to fend him off."

"That's it! I can't let a man like that loose in my house, let alone on the nation."

After his outburst, Billy Joe quieted. He put his left elbow on the table, placed his chin in his open hand and stared across the expanse of lawn where, ten months ago, he had stood and introduced Bull O'Connor to his campaign team. He was four days away from being the nominee representing the working people of America, protecting their jobs, guaranteeing their security. *America for Americans.*

"It's okay, Dad. I personally know each one of your campaign team. They believe in you. They'll support your firing Bull."

Billy Joe didn't head a Fortune 500 company because he was weak-willed or couldn't make hard decisions. He stood up, carefully placed his napkin on the table and smiled at his daughter.

"Thank you, Harriet. Please stay while I make a call."

He took out his cellphone and dialled.

"Bull," he said into the phone. "Harriet has told me everything. You're fired."

He listened for a moment on the phone as Bull tried to make his case. He cut him off.

"I know the working man deserves a leader in the White House, but I don't need you. When you messed with Harriet, that was it. I want you gone before the news breaks about our arrangement. I'll be issuing a press release within the hour."

Bull hadn't finished. Billy Joe, ever the gentleman, heard him out a bit more.

"Who's going to be my strategist in these last crucial days?" He looked at Harriet. "Why, that's obvious. She just out-strategized you."

He put down the phone. He walked around the table and put his arm around his daughter.

"What does my new political strategist say we do next?"

Harriet had been expecting the question.

"Inform our campaign team before the story breaks," she said, without a moment's pause. "I'll send a letter to Bull confirming his dismissal and send people to his office to take over all his files. You'll issue this press release." She handed him a sheet of paper. "It says that Bull has been relieved of his duties, that he's no longer a member of your election team and that I've replaced him as your political strategist. Then we'll assess the damage after the story breaks and take remedial action."

She paused to let him take it all in. He nodded slowly.

"We're going to turn this negative into a positive. You'll be the lead story on the news right up until the convention. You'll be the next Lincoln. You'll represent the majority of Republicans that believe in your message."

She tapped at her phone as her father watched with a mixture of pride and awe.

That morning, Harriet's team went through the papers in Bull's war room. Before noon, she got back word that they'd uncovered proof of the agreement between Ray Twoshoes and Bullivant Holdings.

Bullgate

Four days before the Republican convention, Sarah Procter posted the story on her site. What gave it a sense of immediacy and relevance was that there was a Watergate-style break-in at Harriet's mother's house. The final touch was that Billy Joe Northrop's daughter Harriet was his new political strategist.

As Muriel had predicted, the story went viral. The major news broadcasters aired it in primetime. The political talk shows spoke of nothing else and newspapers such as the *Washington Post* and *New York Times* gave it front-page coverage. The *Herald* dubbed it 'Bullgate'. In short, the remaining days until the Republican convention were filled with Billy Joe Northrop. The spin that Harriet put on it was that Bull had concocted the illegal payments and Super PAC scheme on his own for his own personal reasons and gain. By getting rid of Bull, the campaign had cut out the disease.

In normal times, Billy Joe's campaign for the nomination would have been dealt a crippling blow, but these weren't normal times and his poll numbers increased. All the bad publicity fell on Bull O'Connor. Gone was the cynicism and nastiness, replaced by fresh young political strategist Harriet Applebaum.

The Start of the Deal

On July 18th at the convention in Cleveland, the Republican establishment put up Senator Adam Rockwell from California to oppose Billy Joe in a brokered convention. The other candidates had all dropped out, but the backroom brass decided they could put in their own man to garner all the anti-Billy Joe votes.

The streets around the convention centre were cordoned off for blocks. Outside the cordon were camps of Northrop supporters, angry that the political establishment was denying their saviour and spokesman his rightful opportunity to represent them in the White House. The delegates witnessed the anger of the crowds as they were bused into the arena. The shouts of protest and music could even be heard in the hall itself. Bedlam and chaos reigned in the streets while delegates jostled and argued in the Quicken Loans Arena. Both camps had rooms in the arena, as it wouldn't be wise to transport the leading figures from their hotels through the crowds.

This was Harriet's chance to prove herself in the pressure cooker of a convention. Fred, meanwhile, was negotiating with the *New Yorker* to write an article on the Tŝilhqot'in vote on the contract with Northern Drilling.

The establishment coalition, consisting of candidates that had fallen by the wayside in the primaries, the large corporate lobby groups and a high percentage of Republican congressmen and senators favoured the senator from California. Rockwell was considered to be an astute politician from a populist state and willing to do the party's bidding. If the party pushed the convention to a countdown, each of the fifty states and two territories would rise in turn on the convention floor and declare for either Northrop or Rockwell, only adding to the explosive mix. No matter who won, the Republicans would be split asunder.

The numbers separating the two candidates were so tight that no one had any idea who was in the lead. Even if they did, the delegates could change their vote at the last moment and the floor managers in each camp were twisting arms until the end.

Harriet believed in her father's campaign, for it had given voice to many Americans that had felt silenced up until then. She had campaigned with her father every step of the way. In these last days, Billy Joe had turned to her for advice. She had prepared herself for the opportunity and was going to make the most of it.

On the morning of the 20ᵗʰ, Harriet took her father aside.

"Dad, Rockwell is a decent man. I think you and he should talk about what will happen to the party after the vote."

"What do you mean, Harriet?" Billy Joe asked, genuinely perplexed. His mind had been on winning. "*After* I win the nomination, I'll decide who will be my vice president. I have a few people in mind."

"Dad, your victory is not assured. Our people on the floor can't tell us who'll win. I think Mr. Rockwell, for the good of the party, may consider withdrawing as a candidate on certain conditions."

"I don't know, Harriet."

Billy Joe shook his head, yet Harriet could tell it was not a rejection.

"At least speak to him," she added, "Just you and me, Rockwell and his campaign manager."

The day before the vote, Billy Joe walked from his suite to an elevator that had been kept private by an aide. Harriet had entered two floors above. It descended with father and daughter to the basement and the Cleveland Cavaliers' dressing room. Senator Rockwell and his campaign manager were making the same journey from another part of the building.

They met, just the four of them. It had come down to this after a year of campaigning involving millions of people and millions of dollars: Harriet and her father, Rockwell and his campaign manager, Maria Santos — two men and two women deciding the future of their party and their country in front of Lebron James' locker. No one outside the room knew the two contenders were meeting. Both their teams believed they were in their private suites with their political strategists, working on their speeches.

Adam Rockwell entered and extended his hand to Billy Joe. Billy Joe took it and placed his free hand on Adam's shoulder.

"Thank you for meeting with me, Adam. We owe this to our managers. We have a volatile mix amongst our supporters in the arena and outside on the streets of Cleveland. I believe we have it in our power to negotiate a way of resolving this schism without destroying the party."

Adam Rockwell was, on the surface, an easygoing fifty-year-old man. Small in stature, nattily dressed and with closely-combed blond hair, he had a sunny disposition and was well-liked in the party. One columnist said he was "like a Ronald Reagan with brains."

"The reason I'm here, Billy Joe, is because whatever happens after the vote, in order to keep the party together, we'll have to come to an understanding. If we take it to the floor for a vote, no matter who wins, there will be riots. Maria and Harriet have boiled it down to this: we believe that for the good of, and the unity of, the party, we're going to have to run on the same ticket."

"I agree, Adam. I couldn't have said that a week ago, when I heard that you were going to run against me without having faced the primaries. My daughter has given good counsel."

"All right, Billy Joe. We don't have much time. I want to look you in the eye when I tell you my conditions if I withdraw in your favour."

Billy Joe nodded his head and waited.

"First, obviously, I'll be your running mate."

"Agreed."

"Second, there will be no ten-foot wall between the United States and Mexico."

Billy Joe raised an eyebrow.

"In the end, I'll give way somewhat, but I want it as a bargaining chip for negotiations." Billy Joe was adamant.

"Running the United States of America isn't the same as running a corporation, Billy Joe," Adam said, his tone raised.

"I'm fighting for Americans."

Billy Joe was digging in his heels. Harriet and Maria exchanged glances.

"The wall," Harriet said, "is a metaphor for more security on our border with Mexico. Isn't that what it comes down to, Dad?"

"Yeah," Billy Joe nodded. "I think we can work out the wording of our message without alienating the Latino vote."

"I'm glad to hear it, Billy Joe," Adam replied with a reassuring smile. "My third condition is that you name Jonathan Baker as your Secretary of State."

Billy Joe threw a questioning look at Harriet.

"I vetted him, Dad, and he is the best," she said. "From Princeton. He is *the* foremost Republican foreign affairs critic."

"Okay. I've met the man and liked what I saw. Is that it?"

"My last condition is that you act presidential during the campaign and in the White House."

"Adam, I'll not only act presidential, I'll *be* presidential."

The two men shook hands.

The floor vote was to be held the next day and the crowds were getting restless.

Harriet met with Fred at her father's suite after negotiating the specifics of the deal. She took a minute off to munch on a burrito and explain to Fred how she had manoeuvred her father into the deal.

"When will he announce his vice-presidential choice?" Fred asked.

"The delegate vote by states is set for tomorrow. There'll be a press conference tonight. Senator Rockwell will announce his withdrawal from the race and throw his support to Dad, in effect making him the candidate. Dad will then name Rockwell his running mate and explain that the party is united behind his leadership. The establishment is satisfied that they have some control over Dad's policies and Dad's base will be pleased that he, as president, will be their voice in the White House. I wish I could give you the scoop."

She smiled. He leaned over and gave her a hug.

"Well done. I've got news too. The *New Yorker* agreed to a story on Tŝilhqot'in democracy in action. I'm afraid I fly out tonight."

Waiting for the Sign

On July 21st, it seemed like a whole platoon was riding out of the Bar 5 Ranch towards Tatlayoko Lake. The kids were the scouts, racing their horses in front, then came the women, riding their horses in a group and talking amongst themselves. They were followed by the men, mostly in single file. Bringing up the rear of the column, Joel and Will flanked Noah, who was riding Rocinante. Brent followed behind them, watching his father diligently. Fred rode at his side.

The winds coming off the lake were calm and all was serene as they began climbing Potato Mountain. They rested every half-hour to allow Noah the chance to take in the mountain air and look down on the deceptively placid lake below.

He lingered a long time at one clearing — he and Justine had arranged to meet there before they married and a police patrol had, unknown to her, followed her and interrupted their rendezvous. Noah had sadly watched from his hiding place as she turned and retraced her steps, thinking he had failed her. He had kept that image in his mind during their life together so he wouldn't disappoint her again. He did, of course — once — and she had forgiven him. Joel had to shake him out of his reverie so the group could move on.

The family kept pace with Noah so they would all arrive together at the crest. On the steep parts of the climb, Joel rode ahead and Will dropped back behind Noah in case old Rocinante slipped. It took them longer than it should have, but they made it. At the crest, the scene below was as familiar to Noah as the palm of his hand, having painted it in many of his landscapes, along with the people, camps, tents and fires of the Tŝilhqot'in Nation.

The grandchildren, previously held back by the slow ascent, broke free of the elders and galloped their horses to meet the others already there with whoops and war cries. The family set up canvas tents around a central campfire and cooked their evening meal of salmon with wild potatoes and onions. Noah was tired, but at the same time elated he had made it to the top. Each sound, each sight and taste, was experienced and amplified, then compared to his past.

Noah walked to Ta Chi's grave. The marker had been restored and someone had placed a bouquet of wild potato blooms by it. He took off his hat, remembering seeing his mother digging up the tubers in years gone by.

"It won't be long," he said aloud to Ta Chi, "before we meet again. We will roam the Chilcotin mountains and valleys together. I wait for the Creator to give me a sign that will make my last act significant to our nation."

The assembled members of the nation ate together, then filled the night with drums and song until finally, as if some secret signal had been given, the party hushed and everyone moved about quietly, as if the silence were fragile.

While most of the family settled into tents, Noah opted to sleep outside, brushing aside Elizabeth's concern.

His night camped under the stars with his family around him should have quieted him, yet he was uneasy. He thought about Justine and the years they rode together through the ancestral lands that fed and sheltered them and their children. All this was being threatened by Bald Eagle, who had shot Big Momma. He looked up. There were the three brothers, stars in the night sky banished by their grandmother, as told him by Ta Chi a long time ago. The stars were circling about the Earth, or so it seemed.

He heard some shuffling sounds as a figure moved into the family's camp.

"Who's there?" Noah asked.

"It's me, Grandad. Clint."

"Oh. Clint. Out tomcatting, I see."

"What do you mean, Grandad?"

"Have you thought about how you are going to navigate through life?"

"Why do you ask, Grandad?"

"Well, you're a man now. You've just graduated from high school. What do you want to do with your life?"

"I'd like to be an astrophysicist."

"That's a good goal, but you're not going to get there by shooting Norman Twoshoes."

Clint chuckled.

"What about you, Grandad? What are your goals now that you finished Granma's portrait?"

"I'm Raven after Eagle."

Clint was aware of his grandfather's obsession.

"I don't know, Grandad. Maybe you should let Uncle Joel look after Eagle."

"I painted a picture of Bald Eagle late yesterday. Would you like to see it?"

"Yeah."

From his pack, Noah pulled out the print of the raven with its head cocked, looking downwards. Clint stared at it in the moonlight. Then, as a cloud moved overhead and the light shifted, he saw ruby and scarlet splashes of thick paint beneath the raven — fire and blood fresh on a yellow background — enveloping an indistinguishable figure. It was unlike anything Noah had ever painted.

"I don't see an eagle there, Grandad."

"It's there, Clint. It's there."

"Goodnight, Grandad."

"Goodnight, Grandson."

Noah had the sign. His grandson's future, his nation's future and the spirit of Justine all pointed to what had to be done.

In the Creeping Light of Dawn

Noah rose before the sun, wandering amongst the sleeping tent village. Angus caught up to him as he walked toward Echo Lake to see for himself the remains of the survey camp. In the creeping light of dawn, he sat on a rock overlooking the desecration left by the survey crew. After a few minutes, he thought he heard some rustling in the low bushes surrounding the small lake. He motioned to Angus to stay. He watched.

Ray Twoshoes stepped out of the bush and walked toward the helicopter pad, checking it over. He then set up a disc antenna, took out a satellite phone and dialled, having an animated conversation with whomever was on the other end.

Noah got up from his rock and walked softly toward him. Ray was so engrossed on the phone he didn't notice.

"No, *no!*" Ray yelled. "Don't come now. We're in the middle of our annual party. ... We're voting on our partnership today. ... Wait until the nation leaves in a few days. ... Yes, the vote will be in your favour."

Noah tapped Ray on the shoulder.

"Who you talking to Ray? Bald Eagle?"

"What the fuck!" Ray leapt into the air and came down yelling. "Noah, you old bastard, get out of here!"

Noah signalled Angus to corral Ray as he would a maverick cow. Distracted by the barking, darting dog, Ray stumbled and Noah grabbed the cellphone.

"This is Raven," he said into the phone. "I know who you are. You're Bald Eagle. I'm ready for you. I'm ready to go."

He flung the phone into the lake. Ray threw up his hands in disgust.

"Old man," he spat, "our nation is not going to survive unless we embrace progress. Sure, you can throw my phone into the lake, but think, man, that phone connects us to the world and the world wants — hell, the world *needs* — what we got."

"You're going to give them our land, Ray? We've defended our land from time immemorial against other tribes, against the Hudson's Bay Company and roadbuilders like Waddington. We stopped the hydro project on the Homathko and we won the *Roger William* case, declaring this land ours. Now you want to give it up. The whites call that irony."

"Call it what you want. I want my kids to sleep in a nice house, not a shack, go to a decent school, to all have clean running water and indoor plumbing. It's not a dream. This gas play will make that happen."

"Enough. Today, the tribal council of the six bands meets. Make your case to them."

Noah walked away.

"Come, Angus."

The dog stopped circling Ray and took off after Noah.

The sun was peeking over the rim of the mountain and the mist lifting from the little lakes. The people who had partied hard with drums and song the night before were starting to stir as

Noah and Angus returned. Noah's heart was pounding after the confrontation with Ray Twoshoes. On his deathbed, old Antoine had charged him with a duty to guard their land. He couldn't have done it alone — Justine had been there beside him in the past. In grieving the loss of Justine, he had let down his guard.

A distant figure detached from the camp and walked towards him. It was Joel, a good sign. Joel would know what to do. Noah sat on a rock and Joel sat beside him.

"Joel," Noah said in a quavering voice, "I won't speak at the council. I leave that to you and Elizabeth. Your mother and I have decided that you are the next *deyen* of the Stoney. We know you will protect our land and we will be with you."

"Dad, calm yourself," Joel smiled. "It's an honour to be named a future *deyen* and, after many more years, when you join Mother, I will take up those responsibilities."

"Thank you, son." Noah seemed calmed. "We will see what the day brings us."

There was coffee and bannock when they returned to the fire. Parents had roused their children who, while on the mountain, were getting used to not checking their cellphones or playing online games. Instead, they sat next to their grandfathers, looking bored.

Of Noah's ten grandchildren, the two girls, Elizabeth's Alice and Joel's Rebecca had always been close, but of late, Alice's few more years had transitioned her from big sister to babysitter. They were into horses like their mothers and grandmother and were practicing barrel racing, riding around rocks instead of barrels. The boys were getting up their courage to ride a mountain race in the afternoon. Of course, they were boasting. Clint and Jeremy were tending their horses when Norman came up to them.

"Hey Clint. I'll bet you a hundred bucks I beat you down the mountain."

"Where you getting a hundred bucks?"

"I do odd jobs for Ray. He says after the tribal council votes this afternoon, we're all going to be rich."

"Okay, man, you're on. I'll take your hundred bucks."

In the cool morning, wild potato pickers combed the mountain for their food staple. Elizabeth couldn't say why she had the need to grub for these potatoes or pick saskatoon berries or forage for wild onions. Joel told her it was in her DNA. To her, it wasn't biological but cultural, something that was passed down from Justine, Ta Chi and their ancestors.

Alice went with her mother, grumbling about doing forced labour, but became excited when her basket began to fill with the small tubers. She was almost as excited as when, later, she watched Clint race past Norman Twoshoes to win the mountain race.

Treat All Creation Equally

T he council of elders met in the afternoon in the outdoor
amphitheatre where the speakers would address the people
and their Creator under open skies.

The debate would be over the nation's response to Northern
Drilling's extraction of gas and minerals on their lands. The
company was planning to pipe gas through the Homathko
River Valley to tidewater at Bute Inlet where there were plans
for a liquid natural gas plant. Ray Twoshoes had the contracts
prepared for signing, believing he had majority support in the
Tŝilhqot'in Tribal Council.

Noah had asked for, and the council had granted him, time to
unveil his portrait of Justine. He'd framed her portrait in birch
wood. He held the frame in his hands as he made his way into
the circle of the governing body of elders, elected chiefs and
councillors representing all six Tŝilhqot'in bands. Noah would
normally be having a nap at this time of day, but today his heart
was racing and he had the energy of a young man. An easel had
been set up and he carefully, almost reverentially, placed the

282

covered painting there. Everyone settled a bit as the old man, still a bit stooped from his bout with pneumonia, looked about him. He straightened and held his shoulders back while waiting for their attention.

"Our chiefs and councillors, my people," he began, "bear with me. I have stood here and spoken to you each year at harvest time. Here on this spot in the centre of our lands fifty-five years ago, I told you what happened between Bordy and me on the day that he died and you believed me. It was here that the Creator gave me the words to talk about the threat of encroachment on our lands. And in every year from the beginning, my wife Justine stood by my side, until this year. Now, I am left to address you alone. Justine remains in my thoughts and continues to give me counsel."

Noah had the full attention of the assembly, for they all revered Justine.

"I was able to survive with the help of our children so that I could paint her portrait. I have tried to show Justine the way she appeared to me in the springtime of our youth. In doing this, I realize that it is just one man's perspective. Yet, I have another purpose, to give our nation a lasting legacy of one of our greatest elders. I had tried many times to paint my mother, Ta Chi. I could not paint a likeness, for my eye directed my hand to paint the setting — the Chilcotin, the land itself. That is Ta Chi. And the sparrow in the left-hand bottom corner of all my paintings is but a symbol of her presence. I am humbled and overwhelmed that you have given me this chance to unveil Justine in this sacred place where Ta Chi is buried and which is the origin of all my dreams and of all our people's dreams and aspirations. There is a balance in this portrait between Justine and our land, which in the end is what I believe is important. We must treat all of creation equally."

Joel smiled. This was his father's way of *not* speaking at the council.

Noah removed the covering from his Justine. The covering stuck a little and he fussed with it.

"You are still stubborn, my shy love," he exclaimed, only half to himself.

Then the portrait was unveiled and Justine gazed on the Tŝilhqot'in. Each of them felt Justine's gaze as if it was meant for him or her alone. It was a look that those who had known her, which they all had, experienced when she was flesh and bone. She was sitting straight-backed on a stone, her left arm resting on her knee, creating a distance between her and the viewer. The background landscape was of Potato Mountain looking south to T'sil?os in the distance, where Lendix'tcux and his sons had been turned into stone.

The assembly applauded the artist who, overcome by his exertions, sank into a chair next to his wife's portrait. His family surrounded him. A few applauded only out of courtesy, the Twoshoes family among them.

It was a tableau Fred Scully would remember.

On Our Way

Bull wasn't about to give up his claim on the Chilcotin. He had a signed contract with Billy Joe, after all. Nor would he forgive Fred for humiliating him. As soon as he had been fired by Billy Joe, he'd begun making arrangements to secure Northern Drilling's contract with the Tŝilhqot'in Nation. Ray Twoshoes had to win the vote.

"This is Bull. We're on our way."

He listened for a moment, then stared at his phone.

"Ray? What's going on? Who is this?"

After a moment, he shrugged and pocketed his cellphone. He watched the three Northern Drilling helicopters at the Williams Lake airport, two troop-carrying Sikorskys and one small Bell, which were being loaded with mining and camp equipment by a swarm of surveyors and workers. Bull's conversation with Twoshoes was interrupted by a strange man who called himself Raven and talked about Bald Eagles.

Bull had arranged with Twoshoes that Northern Drilling would finish the seismic survey on Potato Mountain with the blessing of the Tŝilhqot'in Tribal Council, a blessing he'd been assured would come that afternoon. Bull had given Twoshoes hundreds of thousands of dollars to spread around the nation to ensure that it did happen. Before the stranger interrupted their call, Twoshoes had said to wait, but Bull was not about to wait for a chance to secure one of the biggest gas plays in North America. He urged his men on. He would lead them in the two-seater Bell. He had been denied taking his place beside Billy Joe by that white trash, Fred Scully, and by Billy Joe's daughter. He would not be denied the realization of his share of the spoils of Billy Joe's success.

The drilling would begin as soon as possible.

Raven's Basket

F red had his notebook open, ready to record the debate between
the two factions on this historic occasion.

Willy Henryboy, the elected chief of the six bands which made
up the Tŝilhqot'in Nation, had earned a reputation as a mediator
between the factions. He had been on the legal team in the *Roger
William* case. He brought the assembly to order.

"This council," Willy began, "will decide whether and where
our lands will be mined and drilled and farmed, ranched and
logged. We are divided. There are those who are convinced that,
to maintain our way of life, we have to find work for our youth
to keep them off the streets of Williams Lake, that we must
use their talents by training them to participate in the mining
and drilling of our lands while still keeping to the old ways, the
ways of sustaining our life and the culture of hunting, fishing
and gathering which we have practiced from time immemorial.
Others say, no, our food gathering is part of our culture and the
land on which we harvest our food is sacred. We can't disturb or
scar our land. We must respect our land as we respect each other

and it will respect us. Listen to what the speakers have to say. You will be asked to vote on Ray Twoshoes' proposal to partner with Northrop Oil and Northern Drilling to extract natural gas from our lands."

With that, he took an eagle feather from his hat and gave it to Ray Twoshoes.

Ray Twoshoes stood in his cowboy boots, denims, checked shirt and white Stetson. Two hundred eyes watched his stout frame stretch to his full height and his hat added six more inches. He felt confident the 'yes' side would win. He looked at his audience and smiled.

"Tŝilhqot'in, river people, today I see you grubbing for little bulbs in the ground, then eating the haunch of a white-tailed deer. Maybe have some cheap whiskey and live off a little money from the government. You deserve more. Our land has great riches and we owners will get our share. We will go into partnership with a large company that has tested and proven the riches locked in our land, and each Tŝilhqot'in will prosper from the development of our lands. Each family will have a quad in the yard, a new house, clean drinking water and indoor plumbing. We will educate our sons and daughters in the new ways and the old. There will be work for our youth in the big corporation. They will learn to run machinery, work in the office, and will remain on our land for generations. How is this possible, you ask? Northrop Oil and Northern Drilling, two of the biggest corporations in the world, want to enter into a joint venture with our nation to realize our resources: mineral, gas and timber. They will supply the money and the know-how. This is an opportunity that will benefit all of us equally."

A voice from the crowd yelled, "How much money are you promising us, Ray?"

"I'm glad you asked. Our share of the profits will give our nation the money to build a model reserve for each of our six bands and each member of our nation will receive five hundred dollars per month in addition to your government money. When we sign this letter of intent, our nation will receive…" He paused for effect. "…*ten million dollars.*"

Ray sat down smiling, believing that with all the advantages and money he'd distributed and promised to distribute, he had delivered the trump card. Those sitting next to him seemed to think so, too. They patted him on the back and called out "Vote! Vote!"

There was no order of speakers. Willy took the eagle feather from Ray and handed it to Elizabeth Hanlon. The crowd quieted.

"Our Creator, our ancestors who breathed the air we breathe, elders, our unborn children," she began. "Tŝilhqot'in, we the living are not owners of our land, we are trustees for our children and our children's children. I am a social worker in Williams Lake. I am in the front lines of a battle with the white institutions to save our children. Many are on the streets of Williams Lake and in the jails. They keep the white establishment in jobs: policing, judging and jailing. The government and our tribal council should be spending money on providing our youth with challenges and employment. Our youth have little to do except form into gangs, do drugs and fight with the Carrier and Shuswap youth. We don't have the resources to keep them on the land. Of course we need to develop our resources, but not with any of the largest Wall Street companies. And certainly not with Bull O'Connor, the man who killed Big Momma."

There was a rumble in the assembly of many voices voicing their displeasure. Elizabeth waited for silence.

"If we let it be known," she continued, "that we need capital and expertise, there are companies in Canada we can partner with, not for the whole of our lands, but for some of our lands which are not used for our way of life and our culture. Ray paints a picture of a turkey in every oven and a quad in every yard. I say bring your children home to the Tŝilhqot'in and make them part of the solution. It's been done by other nations."

"Like which nation?" Ray interrupted.

"You know of the run of the river hydroelectric plant at Kanaka in the Fraser Canyon that is half-owned by their nation. With the money from that resource, their chief and council and elders are training their youth."

Elizabeth sat down. She didn't make empty promises of future wealth, but she didn't give up the feather either.

"If we walk in small steps, building on our win in the *Roger William* case, we will continue to enjoy the respect of other nations, including BC and Canada. Not to mention our own self-respect."

She then returned the feather to Willy. He walked around the circle to Frank Lalula. He was an elder, stooped with age, his face weathered by the elements. He took the feather as if he didn't know what it symbolized, absentmindedly looking at it. After scanning it thoroughly, he stood and looked carefully at the hundred Tŝilhqot'in around the circle all waiting on his words. They knew him well. He was a storyteller.

"This happen long before my time, this story I tell here on Potato Mountain." He spoke with the voice of a man half his age, deep and strong and slow. "Raven, he was one time entertained by a powerful host in another land. They went out together on the host's land to pick saskatoon berries. Raven, he picks berries and places them one by one into his basket. The host, by use of magic, she fills her basket without having to pick. Raven sees this, he imitates his host, but uses wrong magic formula and Raven's basket becomes full of dung."

There was much nodding of heads.

"Later, Raven tries to imitate host who has obtained salmon eggs by tapping foot with a stone, but Raven only succeeds in bruising himself."

The audience chuckled at the thought.

290

Frank handed the feather to Willy and sat down.

Willy took the feather and looked around. He spotted Joel outside the inner circle and went to him. Joel took the feather from Willy and stood.

"My mother and grandmother were Stoney, people of the Western Chilcotin mountains. I was raised in the Chilcotin and learned the Tŝilhqot'in ways from Noah and Justine. I now live in the city, but am conducting experiments on our grasslands. I have travelled our lands with my father and mother for all of my years. I have studied our trees, shrubs and grasses and have experimented in how best to preserve them. The non-aboriginals' footprint on our lands from the time of their arrival has been ranching and forestry. It has been at times abusive, but we have worked with the ranchers and some of us have ranches. Times are changing. Resource industries have helped build this province. Carefully managed resource industries can help build our Tŝilhqot'in Nation. We can manage our resources. Not by magic but by scientific knowledge. Yes, it is within our knowledge to fix our mistakes, but we should avoid mistakes in the first place. Let's go slowly. Let us control our own destiny. Let us not act like Raven and end up with a basketful of dung. Bull O'Connor and Northrop Oil will abuse our land. We can find better partners."

Joel gave back the feather to Willy.

There was a feeling among the assembly that they had heard enough. Willy sensed it. It had to do with the movement of the sun, the shift and strengthening of the wind whipping the tents, the smell of the salt air wafting from the coast up Bute Inlet and the Homathko River Valley across Tatlayoko and onto the flat ridges of Potato Mountain. When it comes to discussing their rights, Tŝilhqot'in are not at a loss for words, but they know when they have heard all sides and listened to the land speak.

"We will vote on whether we should enter into a partnership with Northern Drilling," Willy announced. "There are ninety-nine eligible voters. Each has been given two cards: one green, a vote in favour, and one red, a vote against. All those in favour raise your hands holding the green card and then move to the south side of the circle where you will be counted."

Hands were raised. It appeared to be a sea of green cards that moved to the south. Were they enough to ratify the agreement? Two trusted elders picked by the chair each conducted a count. The two finished the count and consulted, the more senior announced the vote.

"Forty-nine in favour of the agreement."

A great cheer went up from the Twoshoes camp. Chief Henryboy brought them to order.

"Settle down, people. Now all those against the Northern Drilling deal raise the red card and move north of the circle."

Everyone would have to vote, there could be no abstentions, in order to defeat the deal. Again, hands were raised, this time with red cards, and there was a shuffle of people moving to the north, accompanied by the rising wind. The count was taken and the two again consulted. The only sound heard when the senior counter stood in the middle ground between the yeas and nays was the wind.

"Fifty votes against the agreement," she shouted. "Our Nation has spoken. There is no deal!"

The cheer doubled as the throng of onlookers joined in.

Over the noise and bedlam came the baritone roar of Ray Twoshoes.

"You have said no to the largest corporation in America and to ten million dollars," he bellowed. "Don't be surprised if Northern Drilling doesn't accept your vote."

Raven and Eagle

During the talks, no one had noticed that Noah had risen from his chair and made his way to the outer fringe of the circle, where Rocinante was tethered. He had witnessed the vote and was pleased with the result. When the faint noise of the helicopters was heard above the rising wind, he was ready to meet the evil spirit.

He saw the three whirlybirds crest the lip of the ridge. He knew what he had to do for Justine, for the nation. The helicopters were proof that their nation's vote was but a goose-down feather in a high wind to the large corporations like the Northern Drilling Nation that was built, not on respect for land, but on excessive greed for money and power. With the two Sikorskys hovering in the background, their blades beating the air and frightening children, the Bell darted over the crowd. The crowd looked up into the face of the passenger, leaning out of the open door, a gross man with a bald head who appeared to be sneering at them.

Noah mounted Rocinante bareback. A searing pain stabbed him and he clutched his chest. He had decided not to speak to the question of Northrop Oil. After his encounter with Ray Twoshoes at Echo Lake, he knew what he had to do. He knew he would encounter Bald Eagle, the slayer of Big Momma. Noah had done his speaking when he unveiled Justine's portrait. His children had spoken for him and for Justine far better than he could. His speaking days were over. Antoine and Ta Chi and Justine had prepared him for action.

The small helicopter found a landing spot on the open meadow a good half-mile from the council. Noah brought Rocinante's head around. He controlled his horse with rein and bit, walking him towards the machine, almost in a trance. He thought back to his early formative days with Belle, the beatings from Bordy and, slowly, Bordy's authority meeting his resistance. Then Antoine took hold of Noah's dreams and aspirations and Ta Chi taught him that he was the land and the land was him. His marriage to Justine on Potato Mountain was an affirmation, a confirmation of what he had been taught and what he had been teaching his whole life through his paintings.

He moved Rocinante to a canter by just thinking it. Joel, who had been caught up in the vote, suddenly sensed his father was not sitting in the chair beside Justine's portrait. He looked about him and saw Noah riding toward the smaller machine that had settled some distance from the tribal circle. Joel sprinted to his own horse, Sugar, and jumped on its back. He spurred the horse forward as the wind increased to a gale.

Noah's thoughts raced in time with Rocinante's hooves.

Klatsassin was our war chief in the time of Tŝilhqot'in wars. Antoine was the storyteller, the deyen, *who told me about the Tŝilhqot'in War, the first sightings by Simon Fraser, the smallpox inflicted on our nation by traders. We Tŝilhqot'in were never dislodged. Why? Why didn't we just die as the non-aboriginals wanted us to do?*

He was a quarter of a mile from the machine, its blades whirl-ing windmills before him.

Ray Twoshoes had told Bull that Northern Drilling would win the vote. It appeared to Bull that this lone bareback old horseman, barely able to keep himself on a horse as old as the rider, was riding towards the helicopter to welcome Bull to the Chilcotin, to tell him the vote was in his favour. He saw a younger man riding at full gallop some distance behind. The younger one looked familiar, but he couldn't say why.

"Will you look at that old coot?" he said to the pilot. "I'll bet he falls off his horse. Shut her down. I'll get out and see him."

The pilot shut down the engine, but the rotors continued to turn. The big Sikorskys were landing behind his machine, one with the drilling rig, the other with the survey crew.

Noah felt no pain now. His blood was up, his heart beating in time with Rocinante's galloping hooves and wheezing gasps for air. He felt Ta Chi's strong wind at his back urging him on.

Justine is my inspiration. I challenged Bordy for her. I cheated on her once. She demanded the best from me and I gave it. I know why the Tŝilhqot'in as a people didn't die — individual Tŝilhqot'in have suffered, are suffering and will suffer and die, die for their land so that their people will live.

He closed on the whirlybird.

My grandfather, Dean Hanlon, the tough white rancher, rode Tornado at the Anahim Lake Stampede to the bell, beating his own son, my father Bordy. Dean died in his saddle that day.

On their horses, Clint and Bonny looked down on the tribal council from a distant knoll. Without warning, three helicop-ters popped up over the crest and hovered menacingly over the nation's leaders. The smaller helicopter, the one with what appeared to be a bald man in the cockpit, landed some distance from the council. A man on the fringe mounted an old grey and rode toward the helicopter.

"It's Grandad," Clint exclaimed.

He saw Noah start the horse at a walk, then a canter. He was about to turn away when he suddenly realized the significance of his grandad's painting of the bald eagle. He stood up in his stirrups and shouted into the strengthening wind.

"No, Grandad. No!"

"That Indian ain't gonna stop," the pilot yelled at Bull.

It was too late to power up. He opened the door of the cockpit.

"Jump," he yelled.

The pilot jumped himself, while the whirling blades continued to turn.

Bull didn't jump. He knew now the old man on the ancient horse was not riding to greet him, he was riding as a warrior to kill him. He had been ousted from Billy Joe's campaign in disgrace and now there was no doubt he had lost the Tŝilhqot'in vote. Bull unholstered his six-shooter and looked at the chambers. They were loaded with fat greased cartridges. He then looked at the old man whose horse, now at full gallop, was fifty yards away. He looked down the barrel of his six-gun at the horse and rider.

"Hot damn," he grinned. "I always wanted to do this."

The rider was almost on top of him. He squeezed off three rounds. A wind blew fiercer, as if in response.

"What's happening?" Bonny screamed at Clint.

Bonny's horse shied at the sound of gunfire. She brought it under control.

"Grandad is charging the helicopter."

The wind struck the helicopter with hurricane force. The copter

296

began to sway before Noah and Rocinante, a half-ton of galloping flesh, crashed into the machine.

Chasing after his father, Joel heard Noah's last triumphant yell. "JUSTINE!"

With the force of the wind and the impact of the horse and rider, the copter slowly tipped onto its side, the still-rotating blades flaying the ground. Bull fired the last three rounds of his gun wildly. Joel reined up. He flung himself to the ground.

The copter exploded in a ball of orange and red fire.

Clint and Bonny's horses reared. They brought them under control and watched, transfixed.

"Grandad," Clint sobbed. "He's dead, Bonny. Last night, he showed me his last painting, a vision he had. He called it 'Bald Eagle'. To me, it looked like a ball of fire."

Bonny put her hand on Clint's arm.

"Yeah," Clint nodded. "His vision came true."

Epilogue

On July 22nd at the Quicken Loans Arena in Cleveland, the future came to pass as agreed between the two Republican presidential nominee hopefuls. The pact engineered by Harriet calmed the riotous waters surrounding the nomination process and, strangely enough, after all the rancour and bad faith, the Grand Old Party that Lincoln forged held together.

Harriet phoned Fred with the news. He heard her out and then told her of the tragedy on Potato Mountain.

When Fred filed his story with the *New Yorker* on the Tŝilhqot'in vote, he was asked by the editor to do a follow-up assignment. He immediately phoned Harriet in Atlanta.

"Harriet, the *New Yorker* accepted my article."

"Darling, that's wonderful."

"The editor wants me to do an article on Noah Hanlon and the events leading up to his tragic death. I said I'd let him know."

"You're going to accept, aren't you?"

"I don't know. That's why I phoned you. Noah's life was so complicated and rich, so intertwined with the Chilcotin, I can't do it justice in an article. I think it needs a book."

"That sounds terrific, dear. Especially since it'll be a *real* book this time. But couldn't you do both?"

There was pause on the other end of the line.

"You know, in all the excitement I hadn't thought of that. Would you like to be my agent?"

"I'll think about that after Dad's inauguration."

At Noah's funeral, his life was eulogized, his family proud, and his nation respectful of his accomplishments.

"In the short time I knew Noah," Fred told the crowd, "I found that he led a meaningful life, for he gave more of himself than he got from others, except his family and the land, the Chilcotin."

Noah was buried to Justine's right in the family graveyard on the shores of Tatlayoko Lake.

At the gravesite, Joel stepped forward. The family fell silent.

"My father," he said, "your *deyen*, had asked, 'What are we Tŝilhqot'in going to do with our freedom now that we have some of it?'"

He let silence take the moment.

"The answer," he continued, "may come from the west wind that blows across Tatlayoko Lake and over Potato Mountain, stirs the spirits of our ancestors and moves the present generation to action and interaction."

A Chilcotin Saga
Bruce Fraser

chilcotin.threeoceanpress.com

> ❝ He saw the Creator's amphitheatre: the wild white potato flowers appeared as snow on the hills surrounding the stage, a bare grass-covered area with two small lakes glistening side by side in the afternoon sun. In Noah's mind, they were the eyes of the mountain — a connection to the spirits of their ancestors. ❞

The Hanlon family has many problems facing them, but drawing strength from the land beneath them, they take on challenges from rodeo grudges to a small-town sheriff with a chip on his shoulder, from betrayals to loss, from cancer to a presidential candidate with a secret that crosses borders.

A CHILCOTIN SAGA explores the mysteries of the vast canvas of the rugged Chilcotin region of British Columbia through the lens of a family whose roots, lives and hopes are embedded in its soil.

ON POTATO MOUNTAIN

The unforgiving winter of the Chilcotin envelops young Noah Hanlon, on the run after being charged with murder. Moving across the endless terrain, he reconnects with his Indigenous heritage while hoping to find the real killer.

THE JADE FROG

Secrets start changing lives until a mysterious death causes deeper upheavals. Questions haunt the people of the Chilcotin, with the divinations of an artist-shaman and the studies of an English teacher the best chance to find truth.

NOAH'S RAVEN

A billionaire presidential hopeful's route to the White House weaves a twisted path to the vast Chilcotin. History and the region will change forever if an Indigenous elder can't overcome personal tragedy to fight for the land he loves.

threeoceanpress.com